Thank you for buying *Payback*. Enjoy it!!!
We would truly appreciate you giving us a review of the book
on Amazon. Here's how:

- Go to www.johnwendelladams.com
- From the home page, click on the Amazon icon
- Scroll down to "Customer Reviews"
- Move your cursor over the "5 stars"
- Choose and click on the one you want
- Here is where you can write your review

Thank you so much – John Wendell Adams

Mary –
Thank you for your excellent advice and counsel. Every writer should have an editor with your skills.

PAYBACK

A NOVEL

You absolutely made my book better. Whatever success I achieve would not be possible without your help & investment.

Sincerely

John

5/2018

JOHN WENDELL ADAMS

AMS Strategic Solutions Corporation
7548 North Crawford Avenue, Unit D
Skokie, IL 60076
Copyright © 2018 by John Wendell Adams

Cover Design by Monika Suteski
Interior design and typesetting by Clark Kenyon

This book is a work of fiction. Names, characters, places, and incidents
either are products of the author's imagination or are used fictitiously. Any
resemblance to actual persons, living or dead, events, or locales is entirely
coincidental.

Visit our website at www.johnwendelladams.com
Published in Skokie, IL. AMS Strategic Solutions Corporation

Printed in the United States

First Edition, February 2018

ISBN: 978-0-9903650-3-7 (Paperback)
ISBN: 978-0-9903650-4-4 (eBook)

10 9 8 7 6 5 4 3 2 1

Books may be purchased by contacting the publisher and author at the above
address or by visiting www.johnwendelladams.com. Quantity sales: special
discounts are available on quantity purchases by corporations, associations,
libraries, and others. For details, contact the publisher at the address above.
Orders by U.S. trade bookstores and wholesalers. Please contact the publisher
at the above address or visit www.johnwendelladams.com

To the memory of my mother, Hazel Vivian Halliburton, who always believed in me, never gave up on me, encouraged me to strive to be the best, and most importantly, gave me life.

I am doing a great work and I cannot come down.
—Nehemiah 6:3 *New American Standard Bible NASB*

PROLOGUE
MID-SUMMER 2001

"**WILL THE DEFENDANT PLEASE RISE?**" The bailiff said.

Jack Alexander watched from the back of the courtroom. Catherine and her attorney both stood. Catherine wore a dark blue suit, a white blouse, and gold earrings. She kept perfectly still and looked in the judge's direction.

"Has the jury reached a verdict?" Judge Thompson turned and looked at the ten men and two women.

"Yes, your honor, we have," replied the foreman.

"What say you in the case of the United States versus Catherine Frazier?"

"We find the defendant, Catherine Frazier, guilty on all counts," the foreman read.

The press hurriedly left the courtroom so they could tell the rest of the world what had happened. There was such a big commotion going on that Judge Thompson pounded his gavel three or four times while screaming, "Order, order in my courtroom." Initially, no one obeyed his directive. Finally, people sat down and looked in the judge's direction.

Judge Thompson turned his attention back to the jury and said,

"I'm going to ask each of you if the final verdict the foreman read is your verdict."

One by one, Judge Thompson asked each juror. The verdict was unanimous.

Then the judge said,

"Catherine Frazier, you have been found guilty of knowingly executing schemes with the intent to defraud the United States federal government, you will be sentenced two weeks from today."

Jack watched as Catherine's husband, Frank, slowly lowered his head and didn't look up for several minutes. He kept shaking it. Those close to him could hear him saying over and over,

"this can't be happening…this can't be happening."Having met Catherine's parents years ago, Jack spotted them a few rows from where he sat. He'd been told they had come to court every day for two weeks. Her father held her mother while she cried softly. Jack was close enough to see the tears in his eyes and he made no effort to conceal them. Jack focused on the lead prosecutor, Harry Wright, the judge, and jury.

The foreman stood still, not exactly sure what to do. Jack noticed him alternate holding both hands in front of himself and then putting them behind his back. The judge then said,

"Thank you foreman. Thank you members of the jury." Jack had never been to a jury trial before. So he tried to target all the little details. He turned his attention to the jurors. Two or three of them nodded their heads and squinted their eyes, as if to say, "She got what she deserved." One of the older jurors looked down at the floor and she didn't look up. Another woman juror sat there with her arms folded and stared at Catherine with a harsh look on her face.

All of a sudden, Catherine yelled,

"Your honor, this isn't right. I shouldn't be guilty of anything. I was simply following orders. This isn't right!"The judge used his gavel again. He said to Catherine's attorney,

"Mr. Harris, you will instruct your client to refrain from any further outbursts." The attorney whispered something in Catherine's ear and she nodded slowly. The judge went on,

"Since you're on bail, I expect to see you here in my courtroom on April 22 for sentencing. Is that understood?" Her attorney looked at Catherine, then turned in the direction of the judge and replied,

"Yes, your honor." With that, the judge turned to the jury and said,

"Thank you again, members of the jury. This court is adjourned."

The bailiff said,

"All rise," and with that, the judge disappeared from the courtroom.

Other than during his testimony, this was the first time he had been able to be there. The defense had filed a Motion for Sequestration before the trial began. So, Jack couldn't be in the courtroom since he was a witness for the prosecution. Also, the defense didn't want Jack influenced by other testimony during the trial. Now he sat riveted to his seat. He kept looking at all the people, the jury as they filed out of the courtroom, the court reporter as she got up and packed away her device, and the defense attorney as he talked to his client. Jack especially focused on Catherine's mother and father who had walked over to Catherine's husband. The three of them hugged each other in the row behind the defense attorney's table. Nonetheless, Catherine's husband still had his head down. Jack felt truly sorry for Catherine's family. He could only imagine the pain and suffering they were now going through, and all they would face in the future. He did feel some remorse for being the "whistleblower." He was the one responsible for getting Catherine and others arrested. As he stood up to leave, Catherine saw him. She turned, looked at him, and pointed her finger in his direction.

"This is all your fault! I'm going to get you. I don't care how long it takes. You wait and see. Count on it!"

CHAPTER

ONE

EARLY SPRING 2001 (BEFORE CATHERINE'S TRIAL)

GLORIA AND JACK GOT HOME early Saturday morning from their Friday date night. They had a great time. They went to dinner and then Latin dancing at a brand new club that had recently opened in Chicago's West Loop. By the time they got home, it was after two a.m. They were still feeling the pulsating beat. Before they turned off the lights, Gloria made Jack promise that Saturday would be a lazy, hazy day; no cell phones, no computers, and no nothing. About ten the next morning, Jack dragged himself out of bed. He looked over at Gloria and she was still fast asleep. He tiptoed out of the bedroom, closed the door, and headed to one of the bathrooms down the hall.

He looked at his bleary eyes and smiled. He thought, *we did have a terrific time but I'm not built for 2:00 a.m. partying anymore.*

When he came out, he decided to head for the kitchen and make Gloria her morning drink. It basically amounted to a concoction of natural juices, aloe vera, honey, and flaxseed. *Ugh!* She claimed that it kept her healthy and youthful looking. He certainly couldn't disagree with the results. She was an amazingly beautiful woman. After all their years together, she looked like she hadn't aged a day.

He pattered back up to their bedroom and put her drink on the nightstand. She was still fast asleep. Jack quietly retreated to his home office, turned on his cell phone, and hit the Enter key on his computer. As soon as the screen refreshed, the very first image he saw was a picture of Catherine Frazier. The caption below it read, "An unconfirmed report indicates that Catherine Frazier, Senior Vice President of DTA, a Chicago-based company, who was arrested a few weeks ago in conjunction with the defrauding scheme of the Department of Defense, will be prosecuted as the mastermind of the scheme." As Jack clicked on the link that said "Read More", his cell phone buzzed. Jack read the screen, Lenard Shapiro.

"Hey, Boss, how are you?"

"Great. Did you hear in the news about Catherine Frazier? I've been trying to reach you all morning."

"Yeah, I was reading about it when you called. Gloria and I had a late night out and decided to sleep in."

"Oh, sorry, my friend, I thought you'd want to know."

"Hey, no worries, I'm up now. What else have you heard?"

"Just what you read. I did get a call from a lawyer friend of mine who told me that one of the firms where she worked is deciding whether to press charges against her for similar stuff she did."

"Sounds like a real hot mess. I feel sorry for her family."

"Jack, I'm thankful that you blew the whistle on that whole thing before we acquired DTA. Universal Systems' stockholders and all of us would have suffered greatly. Their problems would have become ours."

"I was just doing my job, as they say. When I worked for Catherine at DTA, she was extremely difficult to work for but I never thought she would do illegal stuff for her own personal gain."

"Oh, that reminds me...it looks like you and Harvey Johnston are going to be called to testify at Catherine's trial. Our general counsel told me late Friday. In any case, I'll let you get back to enjoying your weekend. See you on Monday."

"Yeah...thanks for the call. See you soon."

As Jack disconnected, he thought, *Catherine's trial... I'm surely not looking forward to that. I wish there was some other way I could get out of the whole thing. Looking back, if Len had assigned someone else to the DTA acquisition, I won't have been a part of any of this and it would have been someone else's headache. Why couldn't Harvey Johnston have called somebody else? Boy, I remember it all like it was yesterday.*

CHAPTER
TWO
JACK THE WHISTLEBLOWER—EARLY FALL 2000

WHEN THE PHONE RANG, JACK was finishing the last paragraph of an important pre-acquisition document. He glanced to see if Beth, his assistant, would pick it up. She wasn't at her desk. "This is Jack Alexander, how can I help you?" Jack could hear someone on the other end of the phone muttering. He could barely make out a voice, but couldn't figure out what was being said.

"Hello, this is Jack Alexander, who am I speaking to?" The muttering didn't stop. Only now it was a bit louder.

"I knew something didn't look right. I'd seen it before but not like this. They tried to tell me things were fine. But I knew different."

"Who is this? Who's calling?"

Then he spoke up, like he finally realized that he was on the phone.

"Oh, is this Jack Alexander? I was told to call you and show you this. It's a real mess and I know some heads are going to roll over this. I want to make sure my head isn't one of them. This isn't pretty. In fact, it's downright ugly." This guy was on a roll. He hadn't stopped talking, and Jack still didn't know who he was or what he was talking about. "Hold on. Stop for a second. Who is this?" It seemed to Jack that this guy wasn't used to normal conversations. But he stopped ever so briefly and then started up again.

"My name's Harvey Johnston. I'm one of the team leaders on the Finance Discovery Transition Team. I was instructed to call you and tell you about this mess I uncovered."

"Wait, wait. Hold on. What did you uncover?"

But he never stopped.

"I found a similar mess twelve years ago but this one is even worse. It's the worst I've ever seen. Somebody's got to do something. I was told to call you and tell you about it." The guy was starting to repeat himself and he was picking up speed. Jack had to slow him down or he could do some serious damage to himself. Plus, Jack still had no idea what he was talking about.

"Okay," Jack said. "Let's just slow way down. What seems to be the problem here? And whose head is going to roll?" It seemed that now Harvey was getting paranoid. "I can't talk about this over the phone. I was instructed to talk to you. But I can't discuss this on the phone." He was starting up again.

Jack looked at his electronic calendar.

"Look, Harv. Can I call you Harv? Let's determine a time to meet. How about 7:30 tomorrow morning? Can this keep until then?" Jack could sense he was thinking about the question, he could hear him muttering something about times and schedules.

Finally, he spoke up.

"7:30, 7:30, okay. But I can't come to your office. I don't want anyone to know that I've talked to you about this."

Jack thought about the comment for a moment, *why all the secrecy?*

"No problem. I'll reserve the Lion conference room on the ninth floor. See the receptionist and she'll direct you to the room. I'll already be there so there should be no issue for you. Okay?" Harvey said nothing as if he was again calculating everything twice over in his mind. "Okay, Mr. Alexander. I'll be there at 7:30 tomorrow morning in the Lion conference room. I'll have the ninth floor receptionist show me to the room. And, yes, you can call me Harv, everyone else here calls me by that name" This guy was like a human computer. He repeated everything Jack said."Great, Harv, see you then." As Jack hung up he kept thinking…*Weird guy*!

Jack's afternoon and evening were jam-packed. He went from one meeting to the next, with no breaks.

***

So, Jack, tell me, is this merger going to be the blockbuster deal that everyone is saying it will be?" You couldn't tell large institutional investment firms to go pound sand when they tried to get morsels of information regarding merger and acquisition activities. To Jack, these discussions were a lot of talking while saying nothing. Len had schooled Jack well. He told him,

"Make sure you only say what you know has already been communicated to the press. If you get asked a question that is out of bounds, simply say, 'I'd love to answer that but you know I can't.' Or, 'Great question, but you know as well as I do that I'd be shot at dawn if I responded to that'."

It seemed to Jack that this was all worthless dialogue. *But I have to go through this dance so investors will feel more comfortable with their position regarding this new merger,* Jack thought, *I would have loved to have told this guy, and the rest of the world, "Yes, we're buying DTA and their brand will be nonexistent in less than a year."* But of course he couldn't say that. So, Jack spent the rest of the evening doing small talk with this guy."Hey, Marty, thanks for the dinner discussion. I hope it was helpful. Call me if there's anything else I can do for you." Translation: *"You thought you might be successful at getting a scoop from me. But, sorry Charlie, you'll have to go with what you've already gotten."* As Jack drove home, he went through the laundry list of items associated with the merger. Jack noticed the Chicago Skyline as he drove home up Lake Shore Drive. The sky was filled with a deep red-orange sunset that gave way to the evening, but not before it sent streaks through the clouds like God's pronouncement. Jack stared at the sun's laser-like bursts minutes before it fell below the horizon. It was a momentary diversion from his many thoughts after a full day.

CHAPTER
THREE

JACK HAD SOME THINGS TO attend to before his meeting with Harvey. While he took care of those, he determined that Harv was going to be a real handful, especially with his endless muttering. But Jack sensed there was something ominous about it all. There was something eating away in the back of Jack's mind. Jack got to the conference room at 7:15. Harvey hadn't arrived yet. Jack got the sense from their conversation that Harvey was one for following instructions. Jack thought, *"If he was told, be here at 7:30 a.m., he'll be here right on schedule.* Jack called Beth and verified his morning meeting following the Harvey discussion. Jack checked his watch as he hung up. It was 7:28.

The receptionist stuck her head in.

"I've got Harvey Johnston here for your 7:30."

Jack mused, *Wow, two minutes early! I'll have to speak to him about following instructions.*

"Yes, Helen, thank you." Jack got up from the conference table.

"You must be Harvey Johnston."

The guy who stood in front of Jack was an odd-looking man in his 50s. Five foot eight and probably one hundred sixty-five pounds soaking wet. He wore eyeglasses that must have been four inches thick. He had on a blue short-sleeve shirt with four pens in his breast pocket protector and black khaki pants. This guy looked like an accountant right out of the 1960s.

"Yes, yes…I'm Harvey Johnston.""Did you have any problem finding the room? Would you like something to drink?"

It was clear that he was uncomfortable. Jack got the distinct impression that he'd never been in an executive conference area."No, no sir, I'm fine, just fine. I'm ready to get right to work."

"Ok, Harv, have a seat right here." Jack pointed him to a chair.

As he moved to the

table, Jack couldn't help but notice both his laptop and an armful of papers.

After they sat down, Jack asked,

"So, what was so important that you wanted to show me?"

He went right to work, turning on his computer and lining up the various reports he'd brought.

"Well, sir," he started, "I needed to talk to you because I've checked these spreadsheets over a dozen times, maybe more. I was told there was no problem and I should ignore it. But there are definitely irregularities."

"Okay, what are they, Harv?"

"Well, Mr. Alexander, I've been with Universal for fourteen years. I've been in the finance area for the last nine. Over the last five and a half years, whenever there has been any M&A activity, I've been put on the Finance Discovery Transition team."

Jack stopped him before he got wound up and started another full locomotive engine train ride.

"Thanks, Harv, for your employment history. But what are the irregularities?"

Harvey looked at Jack as if he was trying to decide if he should continue.

"Sir, here's the situation. I was given the responsibility to look at DTA's revenue streams from their existing customers over the last three years. My task was to determine if there had been any significant spikes by customers in the current year as compared to prior years. Once the list was created, I was expected to ask the DTA finance people to explain the reasons for any variances."

"Okay, that makes sense." So far, based on his explanation, Jack didn't see the reason for his hints of a four-alarm fire. What he described was one of the standard operating procedures in M&A discovery. It was typical to explain significant year over year sales variances, especially in the year of acquisition. No one wanted to take over a company only to discover that the revenues were grossly overstated. If it was determined that this was the case, the instances would be recorded and a settlement would be made to reconcile the overstatement."Harv, nothing you've told me thus far is as earth-shattering as you portrayed it over the phone. What you were asked to do was pretty standard."

Harv shifted uncomfortably in his chair before he spoke.

"Yes, Mr. Alexander, but look at this list. This is represents all of the customer revenue variances. What do you notice?" Jack took the report and reviewed it. It detailed the variances high to low and gave a percentage difference year over year. The very first customer account was the U.S. Department of Defense, DOD as it's referred to. Jack knew this was a large account for DTA. It was well known throughout the industry they did several million in business with the DOD. In fact, they had a staggering number of contractors on assignment to the DOD. This account alone represented more than 25% of DTA's revenues. Then it hit Jack, *how is it that in the current year, there would be a difference of eight or nine times the revenues of the prior year and twelve times higher than two years prior?* The explanation in the report simply read, "New Business Development." This was very strange; there was no other increase like it on the page, and every other variance had a fairly detailed explanation.

As Jack looked up from the report, Harvey said,

"See, this is what I have been trying to say. This doesn't make sense and it's a huge irregularity. In my five and a half years on the team, I have only ever seen this once before. But never this large."

Jack looked at the report, reviewing the other entries. There were no other customer entries even remotely close to the DOD financials.***

"What did the finance people in DTA say to you about this? How did they explain it?"

Harvey shifted uncomfortably in his chair a second time.

"When I asked their finance guy, he told me it was due to more consulting services sold at a much higher price."

"Okay. Did you check to determine what was sold and did you compare it to the prior years?" "That's the thing. When I looked, the consulting services resources sold were essentially the same, at a much higher rate. For example, in the prior years a contractor was sold at a billing rate of about $150 an hour. But in the current year, the same type of resource was sold at $1,250 per hour." "Did you ask why the big difference?" Harvey started to answer.

Then he hesitated and looked down at his notes. When he spoke next, Jack couldn't hear him.

"I don't want to get anyone in trouble. I'm just here to do my job. There may be a logical explanation for these irregularities, but I couldn't find any."

Jack looked Harvey straight in the eye and repeated his question.

"Did you ask why the big differences? If you did, what were you told?"

Jack's voice and tone let Harv know he wanted answers.

"Yes, I asked. They told me the variance was due to a huge cost of sales." Harvey looked down at his reports and waited for Jack's next question. "Harv, did you check to determine if what you'd been told was correct?"

His reply was a whisper.

"Yes."

"What did you find, Harv?"

The air conditioner kicked on; the single sound resonating in the conference room. Jack decided he wouldn't say anything for a while and let Harv squirm around until he answered. After what seemed like forever, Jack lost his patience.

"Harvey, I need answers and I need them now!" Jack's voice boomed and Harvey jumped.

Jack remembered Harv wanted to help. He'd been the one to bring this to management's attention. Jack decided to back off.

"Harv, I'm sorry I yelled at you. I shouldn't have. Forgive me. Let's start over." Jack stopped and took a deep breath.

"Okay, Harv, when you checked out the story you got from DTA's finance guy, what did you find out?"

Now Harvey found his voice and spoke up.

"I found out the cost of sales was essentially the same for the current year as it had been in previous years. Essentially the DOD was being gouged by DTA."

"I see. Who gave the approvals for this?"

"Sir, there were only four people involved: the finance guy, the salesperson, his manager, and one of the vice-presidents."

Jack thought for a moment about this newly conveyed information.

"Who approved these irregularities?

the vice-president who signed off on this report every quarter?"

"Harv, who was the Vice President that approved these irregularities?"

"Her name is Catherine Frazier."

FOUR

T HE REST OF THE WEEKEND turned out to be great. Jack spent a few minutes explaining to Gloria the conversation with Len and the things he had read online about Catherine Frazier. They talked about it, but decided not to allow it to get in the way of the rest of their time together. After they finally got up and started their day, they agreed to go to the local farmer's market. Each Saturday, farmers from Illinois, Michigan, and Wisconsin would find their way to Chicago's North Shore to sell their wares. All kinds of fruits, vegetables, flowers, and cheeses would be on display. Gloria loved to wander through the aisles, talk to the farmers, pick up tips, and buy lots of fresh goods. While Jack wasn't a big fan of the excursion, he was glad to be spending time with her, doing something she enjoyed.Once they had loaded all their newly acquired purchases in the car, they decided to take a drive along the lake. They headed north on Sheridan road. They didn't have a specific destination. They simply wanted to drive and appreciate the day. It was a warm summer day, so they opened the sunroof and let the windows down. A gentle breeze moved through the car and whisked past their faces. As they rode through the communities along the North Shore, Kenilworth, Glencoe, and Winnetka, they caught glimpses of the lake in between the homes and the trees. The afternoon sun reflected on the waters. There were lighter blue waters close to the shore and then three other shades, each slightly darker, moving east toward the middle of Lake Michigan. It was beautiful to see the sky meet the waters at the horizon. The drive was both pleasant and enjoyable. While they didn't say much, it was clear that their hearts and minds were aligned as they held hands. It was as if they could read each other's thoughts. They'd brought a picnic basket filled with food Gloria had selected. So, after more than an hour of driving, they found a quiet, secluded spot on the beach, took a blanket from the car, and started walking south along the shoreline for a while. Gloria took off her shoes and Jack followed suit. The sand was hot so they allowed the lake water to rush over their feet. As they held hands, they absorbed the radiance of the sun, the sounds of the water, as well as the majestic Chicago skyline off in the distance. They'd had some great moments together during their marriage. Jack felt that this was certainly one of them.

Finally they found an ideal spot to spread out their blanket and have a quiet picnic. They hadn't said much to each other as they walked. But as they reclined on the oversized blanket, Gloria was the first to speak.

"Jack, this is great. Thanks for suggesting that we come out today, take the long ride, and have a picnic."

"Yeah, Babe...this is terrific."

"This is a perfect capstone to our Latin dance night. We should do this every weekend."

"Hey...sign me up!"

"Will you be able to find this spot again?" She asked without looking at him.

"Babe, of course, I could find it in my sleep."

She rolled over on her side, took out her salad specialty, hummus, pita, a bit of cooked salmon, and fruits. She filled two bowls. She passed one to Jack. She looked at Jack for what seemed like a long time. Then she spoke.

"Honey, I don't want to break the mood but I need to talk to you about a couple of things."

Sensing that they were about to have a somewhat serious conversation, Jack sat up, put his bowl down, and turned toward her.

"Okay, what's up?"

***

Before she said anything, she intently studied his face. Then she spoke.

"There has been so much drama with Catherine and all that FBI stuff. I'm hoping that's all behind us and our lives will go back to normal. My question is, when will the nightmare be over?"

Jack had to think about her comments. *Yes, things have been horrific. I, too, want things to settle down but there're still some obstacles that need to be dealt with.*

"Babe, I know all this has been hard on you. You've been extremely supportive, but you need to know we'll be living in the 'New Normal' for a while longer. The difficulty is I can't tell you how long it will be."

"What do you mean, the 'New Normal'?"

"The truth is there are a few things that I haven't told you."

"A few things...like what?"

Jack hesitated, not wanting to overwhelm her.

"In addition to the stuff I told you this morning, Len said that I would have to testify at Catherine Frazier's upcoming trial."

"Why do you have to? I think you've done enough already." Gloria put down her bowl and stared off at the lake.

Jack couldn't tell if she was upset with him or just disappointed with the entire set of circumstances. He moved closer to her on the blanket. He didn't say anything for a while. Then he softly said,

"Look, I know you want this to be done with. I do too...and it soon will be. But remember, I was the whistleblower. I was the one who took the whole thing to the FBI." She turned and looked at Jack. There was harshness to her voice as she spoke.

"I know, I know…I want all this to be over…done…finished! Courtrooms and testifying…I don't want you to go through any of that."

"I don't either but it has got to be done."

She stood up and walked out to the edge of the water. Jack's initial feeling was to let her go and be alone with her thoughts. He watched her. He knew she was in his corner and wanted what was best for him. She wanted him to be protected and not have to deal with a bunch of unnecessary issues. Jack got up and went to her. He hugged her from behind and whispered,

"I love you, Mrs. Alexander. You are a marvelous lady. You're the best thing that's ever happened to me." She turned to face him and said,

"I love you too. For weeks I have been praying to God for His help to get through this. I just want this all to be over."

"And it soon will be."

"My question is when?" She said pleading with him.

"The simple answer is…right after I testify. I just don't know when that will be."

"What happens in the meantime?" Jack stopped short of giving her a glib answer. He could tell, like the tire commercial, there was a lot riding on his next answer.

"Honey, I've already talked extensively to Len. He wants to turn the page and move on as much as we do."

"So?"

"So, he wants me to get significantly involved in the next acquisition that Universal is planning."

"What is it?"

"I don't know all the details since we're still in the initial stages but it will be an important one."

Jack appreciated that Gloria always left him to his business unless he asked. With everything going on in his world, he could tell Gloria wanted to know more. Jack looked over at her.

"What's bugging you? Is there something you want to know?"

"So how do you feel about it right now?"

"Great...I feel great about it. I don't know much right now but it has some elements that I've already found intriguing."

"Like what?"

"Well, first of all it's the acquisition of an international company. The company is a consulting firm. Those two factors alone get my juices flowing."

"Honey, that's great. At least you are returning to business as usual. I never liked you coming home every night freaked out about fraud, government issues, and the FBI."

"You've got that right! But what I want is for us to get back to our perfect Saturday afternoon picnic, deal?"

"Deal!"

FIVE

"I WANT TO CALL MY LAWYER."

"Catherine, we already gave you one phone call. You should have called your attorney then,"

"I didn't reach him. Please, I need to make another call."

"Are you sure you don't want to give us your statement? All of your cohorts have already told us that you approved the inflated billing of consulting services to the Department of Defense."

Catherine sat back in her chair. She took a minute to observe her surroundings. She was in a ten by twelve room. She determined there were other agents looking into the room and observing her. In front of her sat Agent Clarence Harper, one of the arresting agents who had taken her from Jack Alexander's office. She later found out he was the FBI agent in charge.

Agent Clarence Harper was a big, imposing guy who spoke in a very matter-of-fact fashion.

"So, what do you want to do? Are you going to give us a statement?"

"What kind of statement?"

"We want to know everything."

"Everything…what does that mean?"

"Everything. When it all started, who was involved, what you did, how much you overcharged the D.O.D…everything."

"If I tell you then what happens to me?"

"I can't answer your question until you give us your complete statement. Now if there's someone else involved who was ultimately responsible for all this, the government will likely show you some leniency. But I can't promise you anything at this point."

Catherine thought, surveying her surroundings, which gave her more time to ponder his offer, *if I decide to talk; things could go better for me. I could tell him what he wants to know, how high in DTA this crime against the government goes. If I answer all of his questions, I would have to implicate Priscilla. There would be no getting around that reality. Plus, she literally threw me under the bus when I called to tell her that I'd been arrested. I need to spill my guts. What do I have to lose?*

She took a deep breath.

"Okay, I'm prepared to give you my statement. She could tell he didn't react. He simply took him pen and started writing something on his notepad. Catherine couldn't see what it was.Finally, she waited for him to speak as his piercing brown eyes watched her every move.

"Fine, are you agreeable to us recording your statement?"Catherine thought about his question for a minute. Then she said,

"What the heck, it doesn't matter at this point."

She saw Agent Harper produce a small recorder from a drawer under the table and turned it on.

"This is FBI special agent Clarence Harper. Catherine Frazier, Vice President of DTA, has agreed of her own free will to give a statement regarding her involvement with the alleged scheme to defraud the DOD, and her statement has not been coerced."

She knew what his next words would be.

"Now it's your turn. Please state your name for the record."

"My name is Catherine Frazier."

"And you are providing the FBI with your statement of your own free will?"

"Yes I am."

"Okay, from the beginning, tell us how this whole thing started."

Catherine thought she would spend only a few minutes. Several hours later, she was still responding to questions. She described in detail how the elaborate scheme was created to bilk the DOD for DTA's consulting services. She explained how one of the procurement managers of the DOD was recruited to join the scheme. Catherine told them how her team was able to overcharge the government eight to ten times the correct amount for consulting services. She detailed how they started small and how the operation had grown. She laid out how all of the accomplices received their payoffs, either in cash or in a paid bonus. Hour after hour, question after endless question, Catherine gave answers. Finally, it seemed that the end was in sight. She had answered every question and told the FBI exactly what they wanted to know. Then Agent Harper asked her the question she had been waiting for.

"So whose original idea was this whole scheme and from whom did you take your directions?" Catherine knew the question was coming, but it still surprised her. She didn't say anything for a long time. She realized that if she implicated Priscilla Edwards, DTA's corporate CEO, Catherine would have to somehow prove it. Catherine thought, *it might be her word against mine but I'm not going to go down for this by myself. Plus, she rejected me when I called her for help. She was my first and only phone call. It was crystal clear that she had no intention of throwing me a lifeline.* She took a deep breath and answered,

"Priscilla Edwards."

***

Catherine watched the surprised look on Agent Harper's face.

"Priscilla Edwards, the CEO of DTA?

"Yes, the same."

She felt Agent Harper's stare.

"And you can prove that she was involved?

"Well, I don't have any documents or emails from her, if that's what you mean."

Still staring at her, he asked,

"Did she ever talk to anyone else or give directions on this whole scheme to someone else other than you?"

"I don't know."

"Did she ever tell you that she had spoken to anyone else at any time?

"No."

"So, other than your word that she was the brains behind all this, you have no proof?"

"No, I don't."

Catherine noticed that Agent Harper never took his eyes off her. It seemed he was processing what she'd told him, trying to figure an angle other than the obvious one.

Then he spoke. "You could be simply trying to drag somebody else down with you so you don't take the fall by yourself."

"Is there a question in there?" Catherine asked. The smirk on his face told her he hadn't missed the humor in her question. His next remark frightened Catherine. She simply wasn't ready for it.

"I have to be frank with you. If you can't link the CEO to this, you'll take the fall all by yourself."

Catherine felt like someone had opened up a blast furnace on her. She could feel the heat and the sting of his words... *"You will take the fall all by yourself."* She racked her brain. She had to think of something that would lessen the blow.

"I've told you everything. You now know all the details. If you arrested her or simply brought her in for questioning, with all you know, I'm sure she'll crack and confess."

"What if she doesn't?"

Catherine looked him straight in the eye. "Look, she orchestrated this whole thing. You get her in here and she'll crumble like a chocolate chip cookie." She appreciated it when Agent Harper took his eyes off her for just the second time in what felt like hours. She sensed he was weighing everything, trying to make a decision. Decisively, he spoke.

"Alright, we'll try bringing her in for questioning. But if we can't find a way to get her to corroborate your story, we'll have to cut her loose."

Breathing a deep sigh of relief, she offered,

"If you press her with some of the same questions you asked me, I'm sure she'll crack and confess. She knows exactly how the billing was structured. She is the one who told me what to do."

"I hope for your sake you're right."

SIX

"JACK, I'M NOT AT LIBERTY to tell you a lot since this is an active investigation. But we have Catherine and the others in custody."

"Okay, have you found out about what had been going on? Did you get Catherine to confess?"

"Again, Jack, you know that I can't comment on any of the details except to say we are progressing with our investigation."

Clarence was a good friend. Jack had known him and his wife since college. He also knew, given Clarence's elevated position in the FBI, he took seriously his role and responsibilities. Jack had reached out to him when he found out that Catherine and others were defrauding the DOD. out of millions of dollars in felonious consulting fees. Since the initial call to Clarence, so much had happened.

"Okay, Clarence, if you can't tell me anymore about your investigation, how can I help you?"

Looking down at his notes,

"Did you ever hear anything about Priscilla Edwards being involved with all this?"

Jack was taken completely by surprise.

"No, I haven't. Why do you ask?"

"So, no one has ever said anything or even hinted about her in the DOD. scheme?"

Jack sat back and thought about his question for a minute. *While no one had implicated Priscilla, we had uncovered the amazing similarities in financial irregularities that had occurred in the three previous firms where she had been CEO. Clarence needs to know what we know.*"Well, as a part of our due diligence during any acquisition, we conduct a thorough investigation of the senior management team at the firm we are acquiring."

"Okay, that's pretty standard. What does that have to do with Priscilla and this investigation?

"I don't know. I only know our investigators determined there had been financial irregularities in three of the past firms where she had been CEO."

Jack had known Clarence a long time. When he cocked his head, he knew it was a sign of renewed interest."What did you do with the information you found?"

"Our CEO and I presented it to the Board of Directors at DTA. There was a 'gentleman's agreement' not to disclose the information we found."

Jack noticed that Clarence started taking copious notes.

Clarence stopped and asked, "Did any of the irregularities involve the federal government?"

"No"

"What else did you do with the information?"

"Nothing, she never worked for our firm, there wasn't anything further for us to do."

Jack observed Clarence sit back in his chair, look over his notes as he pondered the information he'd received. Finally he said, "Interesting, why didn't you decide to tell me about this before today?"

"Clarence, as I said, we agreed to not disclose what we found. I felt that if there was some action to be taken, it should be done by DTA."

"Come on, man, don't you think that this information would have some bearing on this investigation? Don't you think that you owed it to tell me about this?"Jack thought about it for a minute. He stared at his desk and then looked at his friend and said,

"Clarence, you're right. Regardless of what I agreed to, I should have found a way to tell you. I'm sorry."

There was an uncomfortable silence in the room. Neither of them said anything as they both looked at each other.Finally, Clarence broke the silence.

"Jack, for all it's worth, I understand the dilemma you were in. You gave your word and you felt an obligation to it. But why did you decide to tell me now?"

Jack thought over the question and then said,

"Well, you asked some pretty direct questions. If I didn't give you honest answers, I would have been lying to you. I wasn't going to lie to you. Aside from our friendship, I came to you with this whole thing. I needed to be honest."

Jack saw the frown on Clarence's face relaxed a bit.

"Thanks, man, I appreciate it." Jack then saw Clarence's manner abruptly changed.

"So, how's the family? What's Gloria doing with herself since she left the marketplace?"

"Hey, man, the family's fine. Everything is going well. Gloria's never been happier. It was absolutely the best decision we've ever made, well, except for getting married."

"That's great. We still need to figure out a time for the four of us to get together. The little woman has been asking me about it every time I mention your name."

"Okay, let's make it happen. I can tell you that Gloria will make herself available for any date."

Clarence gave Jack his big smile and replied,

"Terrific, I'll get back to you. Oh wow, the time sure has flown." Clarence abruptly got up from his chair.

"I've got to go!"

Jack stood up as well.

"Clarence, please keep me posted with whatever you can tell me about the case.

" Jack looked away in order to collect his thoughts. Then he said, "Clarence, again, I'm sorry, my friend."

"No worries; don't spend any more time thinking about it. You told me now and that's more than enough. I'll share with you what I can." He gave Jack a hug and then he was gone.

Jack sat back down and looked out of his office window at Lake Michigan. Summer was in full bloom. The sun was bright and high in the sky. He could see lots of boats moving across the water. In spite of the fact that his office was on a high floor, he saw people smiling and enjoying the warm weather. He saw people riding bikes, walking around, and sitting on park benches. Jack thought about Catherine, who was probably sitting in a cell or some other confined space. He thought, *she likely doesn't have a window to look out of. She essentially has no access to the outside world.* He felt bad for her, her husband, and family. He realized that while she brought it down on herself, he had compassion for her. Jack was also struck by Clarence's questions about Priscilla. He thought if anyone could uncover the ringleader of this scheme, Clarence could.

SEVEN

"**M**R. HARPER...MS. EDWARDS WILL SEE you now." The executive assistant led him back to the CEO's office. "Mr. Harper, you can have a seat here. Can I get you anything to drink?"

"No, I'm fine."

The windows in Priscilla Edward's office were ceiling to floor. They offered both an eastern and a southern exposure. On a clear, sunny day seeing across Lake Michigan would be attainable. Looking south, the Shedd Aquarium, Soldier Field, and the Field Museum were highly visible. Clarence's first thought was, *what a terrific view.* He looked around her office. It was massive. At the FBI, he could fit twenty people into the same space. She had some interesting art on the walls. As he walked up to a couple of them, he realized they weren't prints but originals. He could also see that she had some authentic artifacts that looked like they came from someplace in South America. Clarence strolled over to her desk and among the photographs she had on her credenza, were photos of her taken with the current and past presidents of the United States.

"That one was taken on the White House lawn. I wanted the first lady to be in the photo but he wanted just the two of us."

Clarence turned as Priscilla walked in through a side door. She extended her hand to Clarence. He realized what a firm grip she had. She was five foot four but seemed taller. He'd read that she was in her early fifties which seemed about right. She had a bit of a hawk nose, with dyed jet black hair, deep set eyes, and the sunken cheeks of a seasoned executive. It was clear to Clarence she was trying to be relational."Agent Harper, I'm so sorry to keep you waiting. Did my assistant ask if you wanted something to drink?"

"Yes, she did. No problem, I haven't been waiting long."

"Well, do sit down." Clarence watched as Priscilla made a point of sitting next to him instead of behind her huge desk. He saw the big smile appear but there was definitely a strong business side to her. He waited and then she asked,

"Agent Harper, how can I help you? On the phone, you said it had something to do with the case against Catherine and the others."

Harper started slowly, not wanting to rush into this interview."Yes, tell me what you know about what's happened, Ms. Edwards."

"Oh, please call me Priscilla. And I don't know much more than what you told our general counsel and me shortly before all the arrests were made."

"I see...nothing else?"

"No, not really. There have been things written in the papers and on the news but that's all I know."

Harper decided to try a slightly different approach.

"Priscilla, did you have any idea about any aspect of the crime going on against the DOD?"

"Why, no? Did someone tell you I did?""Right now I'm asking the questions. If you had known anything about it going on, who would you have told?"

"Agent Harper, again, I knew nothing about it. But if anything had come to my attention, I would have gotten our general counsel and HR involved."

Harper decided he would get right to the point.

"Priscilla, I would like you to come down to our offices for questioning." He watched Priscilla's body language as she reacted with surprise. "Am I under arrest?"

"No...not at this point. We only want to ask you a few questions and we'd like to do it in our offices." Clarence studied her as she said nothing, looked away, and obviously thought about what was being asked of her.

"How long will it take? I have a company to run."

"Oh...it won't take very long."

"If it's okay with you, I'd like to have my attorney present."

"You can if you like but it won't be necessary."

"Right, but if you're asking me to come down to the FBI offices, I feel like I need to have my lawyer present during any questions you might have."

Harper remained casual and his tone was even.

"That's fine. We'd like you to be there at 9:00 a.m. tomorrow."

"I actually have a very urgent meeting tomorrow morning."

Harper looked at the calendar on his smartphone.

"Okay, then come at 9:00 a.m. the day after tomorrow."

"Fine, I'm happy to accommodate your request. But I would like to know what's driving this."

"Priscilla, it's pretty simple. We have an ongoing investigation, you are the CEO of DTA, and we need you to answer some questions."

"Am I being charged with something? I need to know."

Again, Harper was casual in his comments.

"Nope...you're not being charged with anything at this time."

"Not at this time...what does that mean?"

Agent Harper stood up and extended his hand to her.

"Priscilla, it means exactly that. You are not being charged with anything at this time. Thank you for meeting and talking with me. I look forward to seeing you as we agreed. Have a good day."

***

He turned and walked out, leaving Priscilla still sitting in her chair. She sat there reflecting on all of the elements of their conversation. She thought, *what does he know and is not telling me? If he did know something, who would have told him? Now I've got to get in touch with my attorney. I'm not going to see the FBI alone.*

EIGHT

GENT HARPER WALKED INTO THE interrogation room and immediately sat down. Priscilla Edwards was already there. She was sitting at the table along with someone he had never met.

Harper felt some tension coming from Priscilla. The three of them sat in an investigation room in downtown Chicago at the FBI offices. Harper sat on one side of the table and Priscilla sat on the opposite side. There were two other agents in the room. Neither said anything. They were simply sitting in chairs along the wall, closest to the door, observing and taking notes. The room had no windows and the conference table could have comfortably sat twelve people. The FBI agents' body language indicated that no one was leaving until they said so. "First off, Ms. Edwards, it's good to see you this morning. Thanks for coming in as I requested. Can I get you anything to drink?

Clarence saw the scowl on Pricilla's face. She replied,

"No, I'm fine. You said you had some questions for me. I'm ready to get on with whatever you need."

"Great, I realize—"

The person sitting next to her interrupted him.

"Agent Harper, I'm Ms. Edwards' attorney." He pushed his business card across the table and then extended his hand. Agent

Harper shook his hand, picked up the card, read it, and then looked him straight in the eye.

"Mr. Lewis...Gene Lewis, thanks for your card. It's good to meet you."

"Yes, well, I'm here representing my client. I'd like to know why you've asked her to show up here instead of allowing her to be in her office running DTA as the company's CEO. Is she being charged with some kind of crime?" Gene Lewis was dressed in classic white-collar corporate litigation attire. He spoke with a high degree of confidence.Harper didn't miss a beat in responding."I appreciate your concern. Nonetheless, I need to know, are you representing Ms. Edwards personally or have you been retained by her firm, DTA?"

"I'm representing her personally."

"Were you recently retained or have you been her attorney for a long time?"

"Agent Harper, that's privileged information. I'm not required to answer."

Now Harper pounced on him.

"Mr. Lewis, you can do whatever you want but know you're dealing with the FBI and this is an ongoing investigation. So, you should consider how cooperative you want to be."

"Sir, is that a veiled threat?"

"There's nothing veiled here and I certainly don't need to threaten you."Harper chuckled to himself as the attorney leaned back in his chair, looked at Priscilla, whispered something in her ear, and then answered.

"I was retained by my client more than five years ago. We have a longstanding relationship."

"Well, now, we're getting someplace."

"Priscilla, we have a few questions we'd like to ask you about what happened with the overbilling to the DOD and what you know about it."

He could tell that she was not happy with this repeated line of questioning.

She replied,

"As I told you in my office the other day, I don't know any more than what I read in the papers and what you told my general counsel and me before you made the arrests."

"Well, we have Catherine Frazier next door and she tells us you know a lot more than you're telling us." Clarence waited as Priscilla looked at her attorney who again whispered something in her ear. She looked down at her binder on the table, whispered something back, and then spoke.

"I don't know what Catherine could have possibly told you. If she defrauded the DOD, she did it on her own and with her accomplices."

Harper looked down at his notes simply for affect. He looked up and said, "That's interesting, because she told us that you were the ringleader, the mastermind. She told us you were the one who approached her and told her what to do."

"That's simply not true."Agent Harper opened his binder again, took a long look at his notes, turned a couple of pages, and then asked,

"Did you arrange a meeting with Catherine shortly before and after she was hire at DTA?"

"Yes I did."

"Okay, what did the two of you discuss during those meetings?"

Harper watched as Priscilla looked at her attorney, whispered something, and he nodded his head.

"We discussed company business. I asked her about her background during our first meeting and I congratulated her on being hired during the second meeting. It was pretty standard stuff."

"I see...did Catherine report to you during that time?"

"No, she didn't."

"Who was she reporting to?"

"She reported to a divisional president."

"What was his name?"

"Art…Art Carter was his name."

"What happened to him?"

"He left the company."

"He left on his own free will?" Harper observed her carefully as she hesitated again, whispered something to her attorney, he nodded, and whispered back to her. She then answered,

"That's confidential company information. I'm not at liberty to convey the details of his departure."

"Priscilla, I want to be clear. We can go subpoena your company records and then start this all over again. Or you can tell us now."Her attorney interjected,

"Ms. Edwards is not required to answer that question. You might want to move along so we can get through this."

"Gene, I'll say this only once. We can do this the easy way or the hard way. Right now Ms. Edwards is here to simply answer a few questions. We can get an arrest warrant, show up at DTA with a bunch of agents, and make life very uncomfortable. The choice is yours, or should I say hers'. Let me know."The two of them huddled and whispered back and forth for a couple minutes.

Finally Priscilla said,

"Mr. Carter was released from DTA."

"Well, thank you. Now what was he released for? Did he steal something, lie, or worse?"

"No, none of those things, he was released due to a reduction in force."

Harper comfortably leaned back in his chair and then asked,

"What does that mean exactly?"

"DTA was being consolidated into a smaller, tighter organization. Mr. Carter's division was being eliminated. So, his services were no longer needed."

"I see. How many other divisions were there at that time?"

"There were three others."

"How many of those division presidents were released?" Harper smiled as he watched her huddle again with her attorney before answering. Then she said.

"None of the others were released."

"Why?"

"It was decided that Art Carter's division would be the easiest to assimilate into the new company we were building."

"Okay...so, Art Carter was let go?"

"Yes."

"My understanding is that he was called into a meeting with you and released the very same day. Is it true he had to clear out his office and leave immediately?" Harper took note of the fact that Priscilla's face got beet red as she convened with her attorney once again.Her attorney spoke up.

"Ms. Edwards isn't required to answer that question."

"Okay, let's end right here. Know that I'll be at DTA's corporate offices bright and early tomorrow morning with an arrest warrant." With that, he stood up and waved the other two agents to do the same thing.As he turned to leave, Priscilla said,

"Yes, it's true, Art was required to leave the same day."Agent Harper turned around, looked at her,

"Okay, thank you."

He could tell that Priscilla was not happy. With a scowl on her face, she asked,

"Are we finished here?"

"A few more questions for you. Why was Art Carter given the bum's rush, literally pushed out the door?"

"We simply needed to get on with implementing our plans."

"I see. How long had Art been working there?

"More than four years."

"And in those four years, how had his division performed?"

Harper saw from the frown on her face as she spat out,

"I'm sorry, Agent Harper, that's confidential information."

Harper laughed out loud and then said,

"Really, the details are in your annual report."

"So if you know, why are you asking me?"

"Priscilla, it might come as a surprise to you but I'm asking the questions here. So answer what I'm asking"Harper noted that she was contemplating his comment. Then she calmly said,

"His division performed well."

"Isn't it true that for three plus years his division exceeded all of its financial numbers and outperformed every one of the other divisions?"

"Yes." She answered in such a soft tone. If Harper hadn't been so close, he would have asked her to repeat her answer.

"Then why would a strong senior leader get unceremoniously dumped after such a stellar performance?"

"As I said before, we were building a new, slimmer company and his division was being consolidated."

"Is that what your company does...fire outstanding performers?" There was silence for an extended period. Harper didn't react to the angry look on Priscilla's face. She said nothing and looked as him.

"Priscilla, you should know Catherine Frazier told us all about your elaborate scheme which included dumping Art Carter so that you could implement the rest of the plan to start overcharging customers, including the DOD. Do you deny that?"

"Yes I do," she shouted.

"I've done nothing wrong."

"We now have a sworn statement detailing every aspect including dates, times, and conversations associated with your executed plan."This time she didn't confer with her attorney. She lashed out,

"We make decisions all the time that might seem strange to people on the outside."

"Whose decision was it for Catherine Frazier to make untrue statements about Art Carter to DTA's board? And who arranged for her to be at the board meeting to tell her tale?"Harper paid close attention to Pricilla as she attempted to avoid eye contact with him. She brushed off her attorney's attempt to talk. She said,

"I'm not at liberty to discuss the details of DTA's board meetings."

Harper pressed the point.

"Again, Priscilla, we have sworn statements from Catherine Frazier telling us details of how you used her to taint Art Carter's image and reputation." He watched her as her anger continued to build. There was a grimace on her

face; the twisted expression was one of disgust and loath for Agent Harper.

This time she didn't even turn in the direction of her attorney."I never did any of the things you are alleging. Whatever Catherine had told you, she's making it up!"Priscilla, it will likely surprise you that we subpoenaed the records of the other companies where you worked previously. We wanted to know if there had been any financial irregularities like the ones at DTA. Would you like to know what we found?" Harper let the question hang in the air.

Harper saw she exhibited a cool air about her. She tented her hands in front of her and leaned back in her chair.

Agent Harper repeated his question.

"Would you like to know what we found? There were financial irregularities at each of the last three firms where you were CEO. In addition, when we hinted about the DTA situation, each company was more than mildly interested. So, what would you like to do?"There was no whispering, no huddling, only silence. The three agents looked at Priscilla, her attorney started doodling in his notebook, and she looked down at the table. There was no coughing, no throat-clearing, nor any other sounds. It was as if Priscilla had taken a deep breath and everyone else was waiting for her to exhale. Her next words were telling. She asked softly,

"Agent Harper, exactly what do you mean by your question?" All of the venom and anger were gone from her voice and her manner. She looked like the walls around her were closing in.

Harper waited with his reply. He knew that he had her on the ropes. He wasn't interested in letting her off them yet. Finally, he said in a low but very direct tone,

"You can either tell us everything we want to know about your creation of this scheme of yours or you can continue to carry on with your little charade. The choice is yours."

Harper observed her as she looked at her attorney for a lifeline but he kept on with his doodling. She looked away and then down at her hands, all the classic signs of capitulation. Agent Harper knew the telltale signs from interrogating so many other suspects.

Then she took another deep breath and asked,

"So what do you want to know?"

CHAPTER
NINE
CATHERINE'S TRIAL

SEVERAL WEEKS HAD PASSED SINCE she'd agreed to implicate Priscilla Edwards. Catherine's lawyer was now telling her that she would still have to stand trial. The fact that she had helped the prosecution and the FBI was a positive factor. But it didn't change the fact she would be prosecuted. Catherine's husband, Frank, had managed to get her out on bail. They had used all of their savings and had borrowed money from both sets of parents for her bond. She had to meet regularly with her attorney to build her defense. But he made it clear that she would end up serving time in prison. The only question was how much. Catherine's legal defense team was sucking up money at an incredibly fast rate. With all of their savings exhausted, they had to take out a second mortgage on their home. Before long, they would have to sell their home in order to keep up with the legal bills. She was surprised their money went so quickly. But she was told by three different sources that federal litigation was extremely expensive. As the trial date got closer, Catherine was given an opportunity to see the list of people the prosecution would be calling to testify. She was angered and yet not surprised by two names on the list, Harvey Johnston and Jack Alexander. She felt like she was destined to have Jack continually plaguing her life. She thought, *it isn't bad enough he's the one who blew the whistle on us; he is now* *going to try to put the final nails in my coffin at my trial. I hate him and everything he represents. I can only imagine him gloating over his final revenge. While he alleged he didn't hold any animosity toward me for dumping him, I never believed him for a second. My life is wrecked because of this guy. Somehow, some day, I will have my revenge.*

***

The first day of the trial was chaotic. When the car stopped, Frank got out of the car with Catherine, her attorney, and her parents in front of the Dirksen Federal Building. The press was everywhere and made it difficult for them to walk. Aside from the movies, Frank had never seen anything like this. The media were riddling his wife and attorney with so many questions all at the same time and sticking microphones in their faces. Frank wanted to tell them all, "Back off, can't you show some class?" Then he realized, this was what reporters do. His wife's attorney had already instructed her not to speak to anyone and to make no eye contact. Nobody said anything to the press. Frank was the last one to walk inside the building. As he took everything out of his pockets in order to go through security, he realized how much he would rather be any place else than in a federal building on the way to a courtroom. This entire experience took on a surreal feeling. The jury and the foreman had already been selected. The attorney told them the judge was allowing the press in the courtroom. As Frank looked around, he realized virtually every seat was filled with spectators. Earlier, Frank had listened to Catherine tell her attorney she would only plead "not guilty." This was the reason for the trial. She was adamant about the fact that she was only following the directions of Priscilla Edwards, the CEO of DTA. Her attorney had advised her to change her plea. His contention was she would likely get off with the lightest sentence possible and it would save her lots of legal fees and humiliation for her family. Catherine made it know that if she hadn't followed along, she would have lost her job and Priscilla would have wrecked any chance of her working at another company. Frank didn't understand the finer points of the trial but he agreed with the assessment of the attorney. He was all for saving the family's money and not putting them through anymore of this circus.

During the first two days of the trial, the prosecution called only three people: Harvey Johnston, Priscilla Edwards, and Jack Alexander. By the end of day two, Frank could tell his wife had little chance for an acquittal. Harvey Johnston, the guy who worked for Universal Systems, recounted all of the billing discrepancies he found during the discovery phase of the merger/acquisition of DTA. Frank stared at the prosecuting attorney when he asked Harvey Johnston,

"Whose name was on all of the approvals for the inflated charges billed to the DOD?"

Frank noticed Harvey hesitate, and then move forward in his seat so he was closer to the microphone. He cleared his throat and said,

"The name that appeared on all of the approval documents was Catherine Frazier."Based on Priscilla Edwards' confession to the FBI and her agreement to testify against Catherine, the prosecution decided to put her on the stand. It was a weird situation; Catherine had turned on Priscilla and now she was turning on Catherine. Frank had never met Catherine's boss. When she walked into the courtroom, Frank saw a woman who was filled with subdued anger. She looked over at his wife as she took the stand. She was sneering at Catherine and then smiled as if to say,

*So you decided to turn on me, now I'm going to bury you.*When Priscilla testified, she told how Catherine had asked to be intimately involved in the scheme to bilk the DOD so she could earn more money. She detailed how Catherine had come and requested an even deeper part in the scheme so she could secure a high position in the new organization with Universal Systems. Frank sat listening to Priscilla and thought, *this doesn't sound like my wife. I know she worked hard and has always been ambitious but I've never* *known her to lie, cheat, or steal. This is not the woman I married and she can't be the mother of my kids.*Finally, Jack Alexander's testimony was the most devastating. He told how she had shown patterns of deception when he worked for her at DTA and those same patterns were evident during the discussion he had with her in his office about the irregularities associated with the billings to the DOD and other customers. Frank watched Catherine's face during the testimony of Jack Alexander and the others. Her face was like stone. He was seeing a side of his wife he had never witnessed before.There was little her defense team could do to offset the damning testimony. During the cross-examination, her attorney tried but couldn't poke holes in anything said by the witnesses. Prior to the trial and after the first day of testimony, Catherine and her attorney sat and discussed the trial and their next steps. Frank listened to everything they discussed.***

Frank called to check on their children who were being kept by a babysitter. He hung up, walked into the holding area where Catherine and her attorney were already in discussion. Neither Catherine nor her attorney looked up when Frank entered the room. Lawyers scheduled these rooms for the purposes of conferring with their clients. It was not a pleasant meeting since the prosecution's witnesses had had some damning testimony.She had a frown on her face. She spat out,

"Priscilla said so many things that weren't true. We can't let them go down. What are we going to do about it?"

Catherine listened as her attorney said,

"During my cross-examination, I tried to discredit her; nonetheless the testimony was definitely damaging to your defense."

"You didn't do nearly enough. She described me as someone who was conniving and devious. You should have done more."

Catherine watched as her lawyer sat straight up in his chair, put his elbows on the table, and opened his hands up in front of him."Basically, it's your word against hers. You don't have any documents or recordings that support your position. No one was ever there with you when you met with her. You're not in a very good spot."

"Okay, then put me on the stand. I need to tell my side of the story."

"We can put you on the stand but the prosecution will bury you during his cross-examination. He'll bring up things you can't refute. In the end, the jury will see you as guilty. He will trap you into either saying you were intimately involved or you'll perjure yourself on the stand. Neither are great alternatives."

Catherine leaned back in her chair in frustration,

"Come on, there's got to be something we could do!"

She wasn't prepared for what she heard next.

"Yes…we can change our plea to guilty, as I suggested much earlier. You can avoid all that is probably going to happen over the rest of this trial. I can go to the prosecuting attorney and try to plea bargain for a lighter sentence. If he accepts, I know it will be better than what you'll receive when this is over."Catherine started yelling.

"Okay, okay…how many more times are you going to stick this in my face? I am not going to plead guilty. We are where we are. The question is…what do we do now? You're the lawyer, start lawyering!"

"If we are to get through this, you need to calm down."

***

Frank listened to the exchange between them. He thought, *I don't feel comfortable with inserting myself so I think I'll sit here and be silent. I'm seeing a side of my wife I've never seen. Has she been keeping this side of her personally hidden from me?*

The rest of the trial was a complete blur to Frank. The next thing he knew, the jury was filing back into the courtroom with their verdict. He studied as many of the faces of the jurors as possible. Some of them walked in with confident looks on their faces, staring over at Catherine smugly. Others sauntered in, and sat down. Frank saw the foreman fidgeting with the paper he had in his hands and he was perspiring heavily. After the jury sat down, Frank heard the judge ask,

"Has the jury reached a verdict?"

Frank noticed the foreman took a long time to rise to his feet. He looked at the paper in his hands and then said softly,

"Yes, your Honor, we have." "What is your verdict?" the judge asked. Frank was drawing on all the hope he had as he strained to hear the foreman softly say,

"In the case against Catherine Frazier and the federal government, we find the defendant guilty of all charges."

Frank couldn't believe what he heard. He thought his wife might be guilty of one or two charges. But he was shocked that she was guilty of all charges. He saw Catherine slump back into her chair. His heart went out to his wife. He heard her shout,

"This isn't right, this isn't right. I was simply following orders!" Frank wanted to hold her when she started crying and couldn't stop. Then he got emotionally caught up himself. He never heard the rest of what the judge said. He put his head down and he started crying. He felt a hand on his shoulder. He briefly looked up to see Catherine leaning over the railing that separated them, trying to console him. He saw her turn abruptly and looked at someone in the back of the courtroom. He saw her pointing her finger. When Frank turned, he saw Jack Alexander. His wife was screaming and lashed out at Jack.

"This is your fault. I'm going to make you and your family suffers like mine has, only worse. I don't care if it takes the rest of my life. You wait and see. Count on it."

CHAPTER
TEN

CATHERINE WAS STILL FREE ON bail so she didn't have to report to prison until after the sentence hearing. She didn't remember the drive home. The judge's words were still ringing in her ears. *"Catherine Frazier, you have been convicted of knowingly executing crimes with the intent to defraud both the United States and the federal government."* There was murmuring in the car among Catherine's family and the attorney. They were trying to talk softly so she couldn't hear them. It won't have mattered because she was overwhelmed with the reality of what had happened and what was still to come. Prison? Regardless of the multiple times her attorney had told her this would likely happen, there was no way she was ready for this. Leave her home, transfer to a federal institution, change all of her designer clothing for an orange jumpsuit, and be introduced to new living quarters smaller than the smallest room in her home; this was soon to be her new reality. The only saving grace was that she probably wouldn't have a roommate to share the tiny space. She also wasn't prepared to eat and shower with total strangers, people with whom she had nothing in common. The only common denominator was being charged with a federal offense. As the days went by, there had not been much communication between Catherine and her husband. They modeled the role of casual acquaintances; dormitory roommates would have had more interaction. Catherine realized Frank was avoiding her. She only heard from him when it was absolutely necessary. Catherine could feel his quelled hostility. She tried a few times to initiate a conversation but it went nowhere. In fact, they didn't eat meals together or sit in the same room together. She observed him going to bed early so he could turn toward the wall and give the impression that he was asleep. In some ways, Catherine felt her prison sentence had already begun. She returned to the same courtroom and before the same judge. Her attorney had explained to her the appearance was a simple formality. She would be officially charged and she would be told when she had to turn herself in to begin her sentence.

The judge was very detached. He announced he had reviewed all of the facts of the case and decided on her sentencing. To her, this was irrelevant because one year or a hundred years in prison meant her life would be forever altered. At this point, Catherine simply wanted to know when she would have to turn herself in.

The judge announced,

"Catherine Frazier, you will turn yourself into federal authorities sixty days from today. At that time, you will be taken to the Hazelton Federal Prison in Bruceton, West Virginia. You will be incarcerated until you fulfill your sentence of ten years."

The words hit her like bricks falling from a building ten stories up. She could barely stand as she covered her face with her hands. Catherine realized that in two short months she would be separated from her husband, her daughters, and the outside world. While there would be scheduled visits, it would be a real challenge and very costly since they lived in Atlanta. After the shock wore off a bit, she determined that she needed to get her relational house in order. Catherine felt her family needed her undivided attention. They would now become her primary focus.

CHAPTER

ELEVEN

FRANK AND CATHERINE DID NOT drive to the courthouse with her attorney. As a result, after they debriefed with her lawyer at the end of the hearing , they walked to their car and drove away. For some reason, the media had disappeared. Apparently, the sentencing did not hold the same interest as the original trial. Frank was quiet and very somber. He helped Catherine into the car, walked to the driver's side, started the car, and maneuvered his way on to the expressway. He did not utter a single word and looked straight ahead. He knew Catherine would eventually break the silence."Frank, I'm so sorry for putting you and the kids through this, especially since you had nothing to do with any of it. I wish none of this had happened." Her words seemed to hang in the air for a long time. Frank kept staring at the windshield, out at the traffic. Based on her prior comment, it was clear to Frank, Catherine wanted to have a longer conversation with him before they got back to the temporary apartment they considered home during the trial.

She finally said,

"I've got two months to get things in order with you and our daughters. I need your help. I'm not sure where to start but"Frank interrupted her.

"Catherine, you could have started by not getting yourself involved in this dumb, stupid, idiotic embarrassment."

"I'm sorry, I'm sorry any of this happened. I put you and our girls in real jeopardy and I wish I could turn back the hands of time."

Frank came to a stop light. He turned to Catherine with an angry look on his face.

"You have no idea the bad place you've put us in. I can't go outside of the house or to the grocery store without seeing or bumping into one of our neighbors."

"I know it must be hard."

"You only think you know how awful it's been. Trust me…it has been worse than anything you can imagine! Our kids don't know how to act and I don't know what to say. It's dreadful."

Frank listened as Catherine lowered her voice. Through a veil of tears she said,

"Frank, if I've said it once, I've said it a hundred times, I'm sorry. I want to try to get as reconciled as possible with you and our girls before I start my sentence. Maybe I could start driving them to school or taking walks with them in the park."

There was no sympathy from Frank. He ranted,

"Catherine, they don't want you to drive them anywhere. They get enough grief at school already. It would only worsen if they're seen with you."

"Well, there's got to be something I can do to bond with them. I don't want to get shut out of their lives."

"You should have thought about that before you got involved with your little scheme."

Frank looked at her as she quietly responded."I deserve that comment. It was irresponsible of me and I'll be paying for my error in judgment for a very long time. What can I do to mend fences between us and our kids?"

There was silence for a very long time. Frank was struggling with the question she asked. He had heard it all before and his heart was hardened. His first response was to lash out at her. Nonetheless, he came up with a civil reply as he cleared his throat, looked over at her, and said,

"We have so many things to try to get through right now. I'm not sure I can focus on that at this point. But I will say we've been together for a long time. We've had hard times in the past, but never anything like this."

"That's true."

As Frank said the words, he realized some of his anger had diminished. But when she interrupted him, he yelled.

"Let me finish! I've thought about your question many, many times. Maybe all of this started when I agreed to let you work in the marketplace while I stayed at home raising our daughters. If I hadn't agreed to it, maybe none of this would have happened. But we can't undo the past. So, I'm not sure how we mend our fences. Maybe we need to talk about what happens now and how we get through the next two months."

"That's what I want too."

Frank's irritation rose again. "Stop interrupting me! It's hard enough to talk about this. I cannot begin to think about life with you in prison but it's soon to be a reality. So, let's take things one day at a time and see where that leads us." Frank could tell that Catherine was looking in his direction, trying to be sure he was finished before she spoke and got accused of interrupting him again.He nodded at her and said,

"Now I'm finished."

"Great…I hear you. I agree with your assessment and I think your approach is the one we should follow. I want to find a way to get reconciled with you."

"Okay, but once we get back home I have to be the one to continue taking them to school. It will be better that way. Since you'll be at home every day now, we can figure out the best time each day to spend talking about the future.""I'm fine with that."

CHAPTER
TWELVE

AS CATHERINE SAT ALONG IN her home office, she was unhappy about both going to prison and Jack Alexander. She thought , *I've got to figure out something to make that guy suffer. His life can't go on scot-free. He needs to feel some discomfort. What can I do to cause him some annoyance and hardship? There has to be something. Oh, my goodness, I think I have it!*

***

Hello…

Hello, who is this?

"Listen to my voice. You know exactly who this is. This is Catherine. How are you?"

"I'm doing fine. The question is…how are you?"

"I'm okay, all things considered." Catherine paused before saying,

"I have a very important favor to ask of you. I wouldn't be calling you if I had any other way to make this happen. If you say no, I will understand."

"Catherine, you have done so much for me. You know I would do anything you asked of me. What is it you need?"

"Great. I am going to send you an anonymous package. There will be specific instructions inside. I will need you to follow them to the letter; everything according to the details I give you. Can you do it?"

"Well, it depends on what it is but I will try to comply."

"I need you to tell me now if you can do it."

"Can you tell me anything about your details?"

"No! But I thought of all the people I could ask, you were the only person who came to mind." Long pause...

"Catherine, I own my life to you. Whatever you're asking me must be important. So, yes, I will commit to doing whatever it is." Another long pause...

"Catherine, are you there?"

"Yes. Thank you for your help. I knew I could count on you. Now I've got to go. Oh, one last thing. I will send you my prison mailing address once I get there. So, every time you send me a note or a post card, include the number ten in the top left corner of your envelop or postcard. It will let me know you did what I asked."

"Okay...but I'm still not sure what I'm agreeing to."

"You will soon enough. Thanks again for helping me."

"No problem. You know I'm happy to help you. Do you need anything else?"

"Nope, this is more than enough. Goodbye for now."

THIRTEEN

SIX YEARS LATER

J ACK GOT TO WORK EARLY Monday morning and started reviewing his calendar to get a sense of the day's agenda. Beth, his assistant, showed up thirty minutes later and came in with the documents he'd need. She was the best assistant Jack had ever had. As a single mother of two teenagers, she worked hard to provide the best possible life for them. He had tried to be extremely generous with giving her bonuses at her evaluation time. But in reality, she more than earned every dollar.

The day was going to be a hectic one. Jack realized he had back-to-back meetings and conference calls all day long. The big meeting of the day was the senior management discussion regarding the new, potential acquisition. He was scheduled to meet with Len two hours before to go over the pros and cons. Len typically wanted to hash out everything and determine what might come up during the senior management roundup. It was early in the process, yet Len made it a practice to assign various individuals different elements of a potential purchase once Universal had zeroed in on a likely acquisition candidate. They addressed items such as cultural fit, economic viability, potential compatibility with the company's vision, cost to acquire, management challenges, public versus private entity issues, ROI, and market reaction.

But in the end, it would be a gut-level decision. Len would often pose the question to Jack,

"After all the facts and data are in, what does your gut tell you?" Ultimately, it was Len's decision. Yet, he heavily relied on Jack's input. As a result, Jack made sure he considered all the different aspects well in advance of their discussion. That way, he could give Len the benefit of his best thinking.Their relationship had grown over the years. Jack appreciated him as a leader, a confidante, and a friend. He did not always take Jack's advice but he listened to it, asked insightful, thoughtful questions, and sometimes he suggested further investigation. But it was clear after the DTA debacle, Jack's value proposition in Len's mind had greatly increased.As the CEO, Len was definitely engaged. There was no such thing as a cookie cutter acquisition, each one had to be viewed on its own merits.JSL Consulting was the firm they were strongly considering. It was an international company with offices in the Americas, EMEA, and Pan Asia. They had been in business since the early 80s. It was originally started by three people, two had worked for Janes Consulting and one had been a longtime employee of the IBM Corporation. They decided to take their skills, along with their contacts and start a consulting practice. After establishing their roots in the US market, they leveraged their prior success with clients into international locations around the globe. Originally, they used partners and hired contractors to fulfill consulting engagements. Little by little, they hired employees and market leaders. Overtime, they created the concept of country leaders, individuals who would be responsible for the P&L, Profit and Loss, for each country they managed. The JSL model was to hire people indigenous to the country markets they led. Clients and the local government liked this concept. It was as if JSL had little versions of itself all over the world. Clients liked the fact that they were dealing with people who understood their language, their culture, and their approach to business dealings. The governments appreciated the fact the JSL hired local people who paid taxes and reduced unemployment. The consulting model was consistent. JSL had a series of phases, steps, and milestones they had perfected. While there might be some variations, the basic model was a company asset. Clients came to appreciate the "JSL model." In order to insure the model was adhered to, the corporate headquarters brought newly-hired country leaders in for training and infused in them the "JSL model."

The marketplace recognized JSL Consulting as a leader. Their strength was in IT consulting. Preliminarily, the leadership team in Jack's firm, Universal Systems, saw the value proposition of JSL in multiple ways. JSL's consulting practice was the last important piece for Universal's brand image. Also, two of the founders had decided to leave and pursue other interests. The remaining partner wasn't viewed as a strong leader. So, it was a great time to strike.

***

When Len and Jack met, Jack knew that Len would have already reviewed the acquisition data Jack had sent him. He was a few minutes early for their meeting. He walked by Len's assistant who gave Jack the high sign indicating that he could go on in. Len simply said,

"Hey, you, come on in and take a seat. We'll get going in a second." Jack didn't say anything. He nodded out of habit and sat down at Len's side conference table. He opened up his laptop, spread out a few papers, and waited. A couple minutes passed as he looked out of Len's floor-to-ceiling windows. It was mid-morning and the view of Lake Michigan was magnificent. Summers in Chicago were generally a thing of beauty and today was no exception. There were a few boats on the lake. What Jack noticed were the tour boats, some tied to the dock at Navy Pier and others out on the lake. There was one in particular, *the Odyssey*. It was very sleek and could be identified a long way off. Jack sat there remembering the skillful way he had gotten Len and JSL's CEO to sit next to each other during a fund-raising luncheon on *the Odyssey*. Jack had been considering JSL as a possible acquisition. He needed Len to meet JSL's CEO, Jeremy Lane, in a seemingly impromptu fashion. This way Len would be able to form his own opinion about JSL's leader.

***

"Pass the sugar, please." Len was about to repeat himself when Jeremy slowly turned and looked at him.

Len pointed to the sugar on the table.

"The sugar, the sugar…could you pass me the sugar, please?"

Len smiled as he spoke. Len watched as Jeremy looked at the small sugar bowl, looked back at Len for a second, then picked up the bowl and handed it to him all without speaking.

Len seized the opportunity to introduce himself.

"I don't believe we've ever met. I'm Lenard Shapiro."

Len observed Jeremy staring at his napkin; his head not moving. He was trying to decide if he'd reply. After a few seconds he whispered,

"I'm Jeremy Lane."

Len extended his hand and said,

"It's good to meet you. I learned from the luncheon's program agenda that you're the CEO of JSL. Is that right?" "Yes, I am."

They spent the next several minutes talking until the actual program began. Granted, Len did the majority of the talking. Nonetheless, they each found out things about the other person and their respective companies. By the end of the event, Len told Jack that he believed JSL should be their next acquisition.

"I told Jeremy that I'd like to have breakfast or dinner with him."

Jack raised an eyebrow.

"What did he say?"

"The guy is an odd duck…he asked me why I wanted to meet with him because he had nothing else to say to me."

"Unbelievable…how did you convince him to meet?"

"I told him that I wanted to discuss buying his company."

"Well, Len that was a bold move. Did he shut you down?"

"Nope…he gave me the strangest look and then he simple agreed to meet."

Jack laughed. "So what's next?"

Len leaned back in his chair, tented his fingers, and said,

"He told me any day would be fine. He's either hot to sell or he's the weirdest guy on the planet." Len slid an envelope across the table to Jack and said,

"In there is his business card. It has his assistant's name and number on it. Get on the phone in the morning and set up a meeting. Let's do this."***

Jack called Jeremy Lane's assistant and set up the meeting. It was between Len and Jeremy. Nonetheless, Len brought Jack with him and Jeremy had his corporate counsel. Only the two CEOs spoke during the meeting.

As soon as they all sat down, Jack heard Jeremy blurted out,

"So we've established that you're interested in buying our company." Jack had come to realize that Jeremy was a man of few words. After observing Jeremy during the charity event, it was clear that he only spoke when it was essential. Len had led the conversation, asking questions and offering his insights. Jeremy provided one-word or one-sentence answers. Jack didn't expect the exchange now to be much different. Jack watched Len who responded,

"Jeremy, I'll be honest; your consulting firm is of interest to us." Jack had sat in numerous meeting with Len. He had seen him do this before; make a bold statement and let it hang in the air for a few seconds. It was clear to Jack that Len wanted to determine if Jeremy would take the bait. Jack listened as Jeremy looked straight at Len, put his head in his right hand, rested his elbow on the table and said one of the longest sentences Jack had ever heard from him,

"I have three questions...one, why are you interested in our firm? Two, what will happen to my employees? And three, have you got a price in mind?"

Jack saw Len made one quick note. Then he replied,

"Those are all great questions. I'll answer each one if you'll simply tell me...do you have an interest in selling JSL?"

Touche'. Jack closely observed Jeremy rub his forehead and briefly close his eyes. When he opened them he looked at Len and answered in something just above a whisper,

"For the right price and positive answers to my questions... yes, I might be interested in selling."

Jack knew that Len wouldn't hesitate with a comeback."So, here are the answers to your questions. Number one, JSL fits in with our business model. There are a number of things we find intriguing about your firm's consulting approach. Number two, some of your employees would be let go. That's the typical strategy associated with acquisitions. I'm certain you're aware of this practice. Nonetheless, there are many of JSL's employees we'd keep in order to seamlessly continue to deliver consulting services. How many would leave versus how many would stay, I can't answer that question." It was clear Jeremy was fine with the answers to the first two questions. Len continued,

"Finally, number three, the Universal System's price is a function of many things. Our preliminary due diligence is needed before we'd have a definitive offer for JSL."

Neither man spoke for an extended period. Both were content to stare at each other. Expert poker players typically watch the "tell", body language of the players as much as they watch the cards. In the case of Len and Jeremy, each was looking for any telltale signs that might indicate how far the other CEO would go to sell or buy.

Jack and Len discussed the fact that there could be a potential stalemate. So, they arranged for Jack to interrupt. When he realized that the two of them were at an impasse, Jack cleared his throat and interjected,

"Len, I hate to bring this up but you asked me to inform you when we needed to leave for your other meeting across town." Right on cue.

He looked over at Jack,

"Thanks for the reminder." He then looked back at Jeremy. He simply smiled, saying, "I wish I could stay longer but I've got to go. It seemed that we were warming up to each other."

Jack wasn't surprised as Jeremy looked down at his hands but said nothing.

Len went on,

"I'll have my folks respond to any additional comments or questions that you or your people might have."

Jack and Len stood up. Jack guessed Len's next move. He walked over to Jeremy and extended his hand,

"It was great seeing you again. I'm sure we can do some business together." Jack wasn't surprised when Jeremy tried not to notice the outstretched hand in front of him. Slowly, he got up and shook Len's hand. He said in something just above a whisper,

"Thank you, too.

Like that, the meeting was over.

CHAPTER

FOURTEEN

JEREMY STOOD THERE FOR SEVERAL seconds watching Len and Jack leave. He fell back into his chair. Allan Ford, the general counsel, finally spoke after watching Jeremy's actions during the meeting.

"Are you all right?"

Jeremy had almost forgotten that Allan was in the room. He turned his head quickly.

"Yes…yes, I'm fine. I need to spend some time processing what happened. I'll catch up with you later. That was Jeremy's way of dismissing him from the room.

As Allan got up to leave, Jeremy heard him say,

"Fine, let me know if you need anything from me.

"Jeremy thought to himself, *I realize I need to let this company go. I don't have the stomach for this business, this company, or anything else associated with JSL. I need to get out.*

He let out a big sigh. I remember a time when I couldn't wait to get here. With all that has gone on, I wish I had my partners here or my Uncle Harold. I need their advice. They would know what to do.

CHAPTER

FIFTEEN

ACK EXPECTED TO DE-BRIEF THE Jeremy meeting with Len. However, Len had an important phone call in the taxi ride back to the office. The call lasted until they got out in front of the building. Jack wasn't sure what to anticipate as they approach the elevators. Jack pressed the elevator button as he heard Len say,

"Jack, come over to my office. I have a few things to discuss regarding Jeremy and JSL."

"Okay."

Jack watched as Len said hello to a few people as they walked through the office.

"Sandy, I need to meet with Jack. Make sure I'm not interrupted for the next twenty minutes."

"No Problem."

Once Len and Jack were seated, Jack heard,

"So, what were your thoughts regarding the meeting with Jeremy?"

Jack didn't hesitate.

"I think you handled yourself in the manner we discussed prior to the meeting. Jeremy is clearly interested but he is hesitant to move forward. I think he needs some persuasion."

He watched Len's expression.

"We need to move quickly if we want this deal to happen."

60

Jack observed Len as he got up from his chair, came around his desk, and sat down next to Jack.

"I agree with you on all counts. So, I want you to go back and push him over the edge, get him to commit to the sale."

Jack watched him look off into space for a few seconds.

"We have to apply some muscle, some pressure. This guy needs it."

Jack was shocked. He had never heard Len talk like this. He always said "If the leader of the to-be-acquired firm wasn't willing to sell, move on to the next company."

"Len, what's so different about JSL?"

"We need this firm. It will give us exactly what we lack. So, go take care of it."

***

"That's right. I work for Universal Systems. I report directly to our CEO, Lenard Shapiro."

Jack waited for Jeremy Lane's assistant to respond.

"Yes, Mr. Alexander, I do remember talking to you. I'll have to check to determine when Mr. Lane is available."

"Fine, I can hold."

After an extended time period, the assistant came back on the line.

"Mr. Lane asked me to set up a time for the two of you to meet. When would be a good time for you?"

After they established a meeting date and time, Jack hung up.

***

Jack arrived at JSL's headquarters. The receptionist called up, confirmed his appointment, and pointed Jack to the elevators leading to Jeremy's office on the top floor. Jeremy's assistant met him as the elevator door opened. She led him to a conference room with a big table and twenty chairs.

"Would you like anything to drink?"

Two minutes later, Jeremy walked into the room. Jack noticed the look on his face. It was similar to the one he had when he saw him last; eyes cast down, almost looking at the floor. He looked at his watch as if he didn't want to be late for his appointment. Jack thought, *What an odd little man.*

"Jeremy, how are you? Len sends his regards."

"Why didn't he come himself?"

Jack anticipated his question.

"Len has me handle the final negotiations for every acquisition."

Jack watched Jeremy's expressions.

"Final negotiations, who ever said we were in the final negotiations?"

Jack didn't say anything. He simply let his question hang in the air. Jack knew this was the time he needed to start verbally pushing Jeremy around if this sale was going to happen. He also knew it was time to follow and implement Len's instructions. So, he pressed in.

"What are you waiting for? You know you want and need to sell."

"Excuse me. Where did you get that? Aren't you being a bit presumptuous?"

"Look, let's not play games. Here are a few data points. Correct me if I'm wrong. Your partners have already told you and the media they want nothing more to do with JSL. You don't have the stomach to run this company on your own. Neither you nor your senior leaders can find a suitable person to come in and run the company for you."

Jack stopped in order to give Jeremy a chance to speak. When he kept silent, Jack continued.

"How long before your own employees realize you're too inept to run JSL? The word on the street is the only way to keep JSL from losing market value is to sell it to Universal."

Now Jeremy was livid.

"You've got a lot of nerve to come in here and make your baseless statements about me and my company. I have a good mind to have security throw you out of the building.

Jack waited to hear what he said next. He didn't say anything. He just glared at Jack.

"Look, I don't mean to sound harsh but time is running out. If you drag your feet any longer, we will walk away and the value of JSL will suffer. The market is waiting to see what happens. Virtually, everyone knows our two companies are in discussion on this one. Come on Jeremy, let's get on with it. What the heck are you waiting for?

Another CEO would have cursed Jack and walked out. Jack observed him as he leaned back in his chair, closed his eyes, and started rubbing them with his left hand. There was silence in the room. Jack determined he would not be the next person to speak. If an hour passed, he would wait it out. He never took his eyes off Jeremy. He actually felt sorry for him. He needed an exit strategy and Universal was his way out. Jack didn't keep track of the time. Nonetheless, there was an inordinate amount of time that passed without either of them speaking. Finally, Jeremy said,

"What do you want from me?"

Jack waited to make sure there was nothing else he wanted to add.

"I simply want you to tell me you are ready to move ahead with the sale."

"What if I'm not ready to sell?"

"That's a foolish question because you are ready to sell and you know it."

"What are you a fortune teller, a mind reader? You can tell what I'm thinking?"

"We need to get on with this now! We will set a date and a time to conclude the sale or Universal is prepared to walk away. So, I need your answer right now!"

He watched Jeremy squirm in his chair. He could see he was physically uncomfortable. Finally, he heard him whisper something.

"Okay, I'm ready to move forward with the sale of JSL."

Jack pushed the point.

"What did you say?"

He repeated his words a bit louder,

"I'm ready to move forward with the sale of JSL."

"Great. I will let Len know. Then we'll get the process started."

He made direct eye contact with Jeremy.

"Trust me. You are making the right decision. Later you will thank me for being a little rough on you."

Jeremy didn't say anything. Jack got the impression he was caught between angry, hurt, and relief. Jack got up, walked around the table, and attempted to shake hands with him. Jeremy got up abruptly, brushed past Jack, and walked out of the conference room.

***

"Yes, he begrudgingly decided to move forward with the sale. But I can tell you I will never have a friend in Jeremy Lane. He hates my guts."

Jack was recapping the meeting and going over the next steps with Len.

"Jack, let me remind you, this isn't about making friends. I sent you to do a tough, dirty, nasty job and you did it. Now let's move forward before he has a change of heart."

***

Jeremy sat in his office alone with his thoughts, *I hate that guy. It would be fine with me if he got hit by a bus. But, unfortunately, he was right. I'm not a CEO. I can't run JSL. I don't want any part of it any more. I wish it were different but it's not. Why couldn't this be simple and enjoyable like predictive modeling?*

SIXTEEN

"**S**O, JEREMY HAS AGREED. NOW** what are the steps you're suggesting?

My insider information tells me we could merge the two company's operational areas without a huge expense.""Which ones would be the hardest to merge?"

"The accounting systems would be the hardest. On a scale of one to ten, it would be about a seven. IT, legal, and HR would be much easier."

"Let's talk about HR. What about the people, especially their management team?"

"Great question. When I mentioned HR, I was only talking about their HR systems." Jack observed Len as he made a note on the documents in front of him.

"Okay...but my question still remains."

"How to handle their management would require some thought on our part. I have a few options which could allow us to realize the best outcome," said Jack.

Jack could tell that Len was giving him his full attention.

"I'm listening. So you know, this is one of my key areas of concern." Len leaned back in his chair, put down his pen, never taking his eyes off his vice president.Jack had determined that essentially Universal was buying JSL's customer list, their world class documented process, and the intellectual capital of their people. Jack started slowly.

"Well, first we need to consider giving Edmond a significant role in measuring JSL's employee reaction to the acquisition."

"Okay…what else?"

"We should allow him to immediately notify the employees who will be released. In addition, we need to try to retain the best senior managers and employees. One way to achieve this would be with three or five year stock options. I believe these people represent continuity with the JSL process and client relationships."

Jack was surprised. Len didn't comment. He simply looked off in space with his chin resting between his thumb and forefinger. Over the years, Jack had come to appreciate that look. It told him that Len was pondering what he'd heard. Jack made himself comfortable with the silence.

Finally, Jack heard Len say,

"All three suggestions have merit, but you need to remember part of our ROI, from the purchase comes from letting people in JSL go. Also, their senior management represents the biggest expense. So, we have to be extremely judicious regarding who we keep and who we let go."

Jack realized Len was on board with his assessments. So Jack piped in,

"I agree. Edmond will likely prove invaluable in this element of the process."

Edmond Pearson was the vice president of HR. He had been in his current role for four years and had worked in Universal Systems for ten. He'd come up through the HR ranks. It was clear to everyone on the senior team he valued greatly his current position and he was extremely loyal to Len. Edmond was a short, heavier man about five foot eight, one hundred and ninety pounds. He had a round, pudgy face, thick eyebrows, and brown thinning hair. To his credit, he had a keen understanding of revenue, profit, and business process. As a result, he structured his human resources organization to financially support the overall company. He could be counted on to provide whatever was needed. Len had utilized Edmond for some of his special projects before Jack got promoted to the management team and instantly started demonstrating how effective he was at handling Len's requests. Initially, Edmond disliked Jack because he had been the go-to-guy. Len intuitively saw the potential conflict and had a heart-to-heart conversation with Edmond, gave him a promotional title change to Senior Vice President, and the issue went away. With any impending acquisitions, they didn't have any room for internal infighting. Len needed all hands on deck. This was one of the reasons Jack suggested Edmond. He knew he would do a superior job. After their conversation, Jack sensed Len was ready for his meeting with all of the other senior leaders. As they walked to the conference room, Jack reviewed with Len all of the essential aspects that would be covered during the meeting. He made sure he hadn't missed any details. He knew Len was depending on him.

Jack stepped back to allow Len the opportunity to walk into the conference room first. He heard Len say, in a very collegial fashion,

"Okay, folks, let's settle down. We've got a lot of ground to cover."

Jack noticed by the time Len had made his way to the head of the table, he had already said hello to virtually everyone in the room. He asked about their families or little details he made a habit of remembering. He was definitely a man who cared about his people, and they all appreciated him for it.

"Let's get right to it. What open issues do we have concerning this acquisition?"

***

AT UNIVERSAL SYSTEM'S LEADERSHIP MEETING

Seven people were a part of the senior management team. Each of them was in attendance for the final meeting to decide if Universal was definitely going to acquire JSL Consulting. Some of the members of the team had played a bigger role than others , but they all were required to be a part of this meeting. Jack knew Len was a very collaborative leader and he wanted the benefit of the team's best thinking.

Len asked.

"Who wants to go first?"

There was a brief lull before anyone spoke. It seemed that they were all weighing the potential impact of their comments.Finally, Brian Franks, the Senior Vice President of Sales and Marketing spoke up. He'd been with Universal Systems for nine years.

"Len, I don't think we have a choice. If we're going to continue to be a recognized leader in our market, we need to add JSL to our portfolio."

"Okay."

Because of the brevity of Len's reply, Brian felt obligated to continue. "Consulting is the logical addition. Up until now, clients and prospects haven't seen us as a real consulting force. This acquisition will translate into more business for us overall."

"Brian, I see your point. Thanks for that. So, your vote is a 'Yes', we should move forward?"

"Correct."

"Okay, other comments?"

"I disagree with Brian's very liberal assessment." Toni Lucas, Vice President of finance and operations, in her short three years with the company had transformed the profit picture of Universal. Her investment advice had been sound and when she spoke, Len listened. Her small stature, just over five feet, and her understated attire would cause the casual observer to call her mousey.

Her steel blue eyes and stern face didn't conveyed her to be either mousey or timid.

Jack watched as Len turned to her with a curious look on his face.

"Toni, why are you disagreeing with Brian?"

"Currently, we have the highest profit margin in the industry. When I look at JSL, their profits are significantly lower than ours."

"I see. So, from a financial perspective, should we walk away from the prospect of acquiring them?"

Jack anticipated that Toni's response would be insightful. She looked down at some notes she'd made. Then she said,

"Not necessarily, but we should consider two things. One, work to reduce the purchase price and two, focus on decreasing JSL's expense model so there is less disparity between their profit margins and ours."

"I totally agree we need to drive for the lowest purchase price possible, but have you determined where the expense reductions would come from?"

"I certainly have. People reductions would be the big one. Also, IT systems, HR systems, and legal services would need to be consolidated immediately." Jack could tell from the smirk on Toni's face as she looked in Len's direction that she felt confident with her assessment.

"Wait a minute! You can't consolidate HR systems immediately." This came from Edmond Pearson.

"We don't want to alienate the JSL people. Remember, we are buying their customer lists and their consulting process. The people are directly responsible for their best-in-class documented process."

Now there was some obvious friction in the room. Toni had made a great point regarding the profit picture. Edmond also had a very compelling argument that needed to be considered. If they weren't careful, they could lose the people in JSL who were needed to drive the consulting process.Jack decided to speak up.

"You know what, you both have valid concerns. Toni, what would be the longest possible timeframe we could hold off on any HR system consolidation, given the profit concerns you mentioned?"

Jack knew she wouldn't hesitate with her answer.

"We could reasonably delay it no more than ninety days after acquisition. If we waited any longer, we'd have real financial issues." "Okay, so if we waited no more than ninety days and aggressively moved forward to identify the people we wanted to stay and those we targeted to leave, Edmond, could we then consolidate the HR systems with little or no problems?" Jack watched Edmond as he calculated the impact of the question. He wrote something down in his notebook. Then he spoke up.

"It can't be one day short of ninety days. That would be the only feasible alternative." Jack was waiting until Len chimed in. He didn't disappoint.

"Then it's settled. As a way to maximize our return from the acquisition, we will consolidate systems. IT and Legal will be the first ones, followed by HR three months later. Does anyone have any other thoughts or concerns?" As Jack looked at the team around the table, he sensed that there was still some anxiety. There were other members of the team who were fidgeting with pens and squirming nervously. It seemed that this issue regarding consolidating systems was not the only one. Finally, the real issue came out. "Len, I think we generally agree this acquisition is a good move. The real questions are, where the people at JSL fit in and who is going to own the customer relationship?"

This came from Michele Thompson, Vice President of Client Services. Michele was quite tall for a woman. She stood six feet and had a real athletic build. The story was she missed qualifying for the US Olympic team in the Heptathlon. As a black woman, she'd planned to follow in the footsteps of Jackie Joyner-Kersee and win a gold medal. She pulled a hamstring on the day of the finals. While she willed herself to compete, she missed making the team. She had a reputation for being fearless. So her comment was not uncommon. Jack had alerted Len to the possibility of this concern. So when Len turned and looked at her before answering it was out of great respect. He also knew that there was likely some emotional subtext buried in her question.

"What do you mean 'who will own the customer'?"

"Since we are buying JSL, their process, and their client lists, we should own the customer." Len agreed with her assessment."True, but why is that even a question?""Well, I don't want my client services people fighting in front of the customer with the JSL people."

"I understand your concern but that scenario won't happen."

Jack loved Michele's subtle moves. She turned her head sideways in Len's direction, but her elbows remained on the table with her hands on top of each other."How can we be assured of that?""Our objective is to make sure all JSL personnel we retain understand that they fall under the confines of Universal Systems."

"Okay, how will we make that transition happen?"

Jack thought Len was a master at deflecting questions to the person he wanted to take ownership for an issue. So when he turned to Edmond, Jack wasn't surprised.

"That's a great question for Edmond. He and his HR team would need to put together an orientation series to cover this topic and others. Edmond, what are your thoughts?"Jack was confident Edmond would fire off a quick reply."It is my recommendation we hold those sessions Len mentioned. But I also don't want the JSL people to end up feeling like second-class citizens. We could have some fallout among people we don't want to lose."Up until this point, Tom Wallace, the general counsel, hadn't said anything. Jack had noticed earlier that he sat quietly taking notes. All of a sudden, he found his voice."Lenard, I agree with Edmond. I believe we need to have someone from Universal run JSL Consulting."

Tom was the sharpest dresser on the senior management team. He wore Hickey Freeman and other high-end custom-made suits. He looked like a corporate lawyer, crisp, polished, authoritative, and professional. He always spiced things up with accessories like expensive cufflinks and neckties. He was a bit shorter than six feet in height but he appeared taller. He worked out three or four times a week so he was in great shape. The story was he and Len had worked together at Len's last firm. The two of them developed a very good working relationship. So when Len was recruited to Universal and was later promoted to CEO, he asked Tom to come and be the General Counsel.

"Run JSL Consulting, what do you mean?" Len said.

"It's simple...someone from our team would become President of JSL and would remain on the senior leadership team of Universal."

Jack could tell this was a point he hadn't fully considered. So, Len was quiet for a moment. Then he asked,

"So, in your mind, what would that achieve?"

"Well, it would send a message to JSL that we cared so much we named someone with clout to run the consulting practice."

Jack saw clearly that Len was angling for more from Tom.

"Anything else you can think of?"

"Yes, it would also send a great message to the analysts and shareholders that we intend to fully optimize the best elements of JSL into the overall business process of Universal."

"What about our own employees? What will they think?" The question came from Brian Franks.

Jack realized that when Tom became engaged, he was all in. He rotated in his chair to face Brian.

"They too would believe it to be the right thing because we'll hold town hall meetings to explain our strategy. The question is...if this makes sense, who would be the likely candidate to lead JSL?"

Now there was a definite pregnant pause in the room. Tom

had come up with a brilliant plan. It would be a winning strategy and a great opportunity for whoever became JSL's new president. With the exception of Len and Tom, everyone else on the team would be advancing their career with this assignment. Jack was looking at everyone in the room. Jack could tell from Len's body language that he had something to say. He didn't hesitate."Tom, as always, you have a way of introducing great ideas. Thank you for your contribution."

"No problem...happy to help.

"Okay, so I take it that based on all of the discussion and our collective analysis, we are all in favor of acquiring JSL?" There was a unanimous response.It hadn't been said yet but Jack could tell that the meeting was over.

Then Len made a final statement.

"To the question of who would run the JSL operation, I need to give that some serious consideration. So, for now, our meeting is adjourned."

After they got back to Len's office, Jack spent a few minutes recapping the meeting with Len before he headed back to his own office. He was exhausted. All of the meetings had worn him out. He thought; *I can't wait to walk out of here and get on the road. I need some downtime, Yet, I promised Gloria I would call her.*

"Hey babe, how are you? How did your day go?" Jack waited for an answer which never came. "Babe, what's wrong? Are you okay? What happened?" There was a long pause. Finally, Gloria responded.

"Jack, we got another one of those letters again today."

"What...how could you tell?

"It was the same as all the others; no return address, only one page, and all of the letters were out of a newspaper or a magazine."

"I get it. 'G' what did it say?" Initially, there was no reply. Eventually, she said, the words were "Your wife will suffer!"

"I'm so sorry, babe. I know it must have frightened you. I'm coming home right now. Will you be okay until I get there?"

"It's just a letter. 'J', I'll be fine. It just shook me up a bit."

"I bet it did. I'm on my way home. I'll see you soon, honey. Okay?"

"Yeah, okay. I want to know when this will stop."

"Babe, we'll talk about it as soon as I get home."

SEVENTEEN

HAZELTON FEDERAL CORRECTIONAL INSTITUTION, WEST VIRGINIA

"**A**LL RIGHT, FRAZIER, LET'S MOVE it out. You've had enough sunshine for one day. Let's go!"

Catherine had heard those words all too often over the last six years. As she got off the same bench she'd sat on for more days than she cared to remember, she started to make her way back to her cell. Catherine didn't need to look where she was going. She had walked in the same direction so many times she could do it with her eyes closed. Fifty steps to the front gate and the first guard and then wait thirty seconds until the gate opens. Fifty more steps to the second gate and the second guard and then wait another thirty seconds until the gate opens. Seventy-five more steps included walking up a flight of stairs and then she arrives at her cell. She stood there for forty-five seconds and then her cell door opened. She had to get in her cell within fifteen seconds or she'd cause an alarm to go off.

Once inside, Catherine sat down on the one chair in her tiny 8' x 9' space. The same space she's lived in for the last six miserable years. It was pretty grim; a twin bed, a small desk, a tiny book shelf held about eight books and a small four-by-six inch photo of her husband and two daughters. When Catherine was incarcerated, her daughters, Sara and Rachel were eight and eleven. Now her oldest was eighteen and soon to be a senior in high school.

With their father, they would come and visit Catherine every three or four months. She looked forward to every visit. Little by little, the time between visits lengthened and before long, the visits became only twice a year. Over the last three years, they came only once during their summer vacation. During the latest visit, Catherine asked her husband Frank why the change. His response was,

"The girls are uncomfortable coming here"

"Why?"

"They say it's creepy and the guards keep looking at them in weird ways. The whole time they're here they feel tense and uneasy.""Okay, okay…I get it. Where are they now? Did they go to the bathroom before I got here from my cell?"

"No…they're back at the hotel. Like I told you, they think it's creepy here. They didn't want to come."

"What! They didn't want to see me?"

"That's right."

"But I need to see them. I need to stay connected to them. I'm their mother, for Pete's sake!"

"Catherine, you should tell it to them. Maybe you should write them a letter or call them. Don't tell me."

"You're their father. They'll listen to you."

"They're both teenagers and I'm not sure who they're listening to these days. I struggled to get them here the last time you saw them. I'm not sure what you expect from me""Frank, you know I've tried. You saw how they looked at me and then stared off in space when I talked to them. I'm counting on you because I'm not getting through to them."

"Hey, I get it all the time. Welcome to the club!"

"Okay, I'll call them when my phone privileges come up, but know I need your help with this."

Catherine had been watching Frank's every move. In the past, when he had something uncomfortable to say, his left eye would twitch. She noticed it was twitching. All of a sudden, Frank said,

"Since we're on the subject of coming here, there's another thing you should know. The costs associated with getting here are astronomical. Flying from Atlanta to Charleston, renting a car, driving here, buying food, and staying in a hotel have become enormously outrageous."

"I know it's a real sacrifice. Maybe you could drive."

"Drive! Are you kidding? I can't take all that time to drive here and back. I've got to get them home for school. Plus there's no one to share the burden of driving. I can't afford to put my daughters at risk. That's not an option."

Catherine could tell that Frank wasn't fond of the conversation. He had a frown on his face the entire time they talked and his twitch became more apparent. She decided to change the conversation.

"How are you doing? How are you getting along? Have you heard any more from the attorney about my parole heating?""-Look, Catherine, I need to be honest with you. I'm not doing well and I haven't been for a very long time now. I've tried to mask it whenever I come here or talk to you on the phone. I'm not dealing with this whole thing well at all."

"Well, how do you think I'm doing? I've been sitting in this stinking hellhole for the last six years."

"Catherine, do me a favor. Stop that right now! This is exactly the reason why I never bring this up. I don't want this to turn into your little pity-party."

"But it's true. You get to go home every night, sleep in your own bed, and spend time with our girls, while I'm stuck in *this* place!"

"For Pete's sake, will you quit it? Cut it out."

"Can you deny it? Can you say it's not true?"

"I'll tell you what I can say...I didn't cause this. I didn't defraud the federal government. I didn't get arrested."

"Oh, don't go there! That's not fair." Catherine realized that

Frank was now staring her right in the face. His eyes were bulging out of his head.

"I'll tell you what's not fair. You go and get yourself arrested for some stupid company that turned its back on you. You deplete almost every red cent we had. If my parents hadn't stepped in with more money, your daughters and I would be living on the street. So don't tell me what's *not fair!*"

Catherine stopped looking at him. She averted her eyes to the floor. They started to burn as tears welled up. The only words she could muster up were,

"You're right...I'm sorry, I'm truly sorry."

She could tell from Frank's expression that he wasn't buying her apology. She saw this emotional tidal wave of rage building in him that was about to explode. So, she repeated,

"Honey, I'm so sorry. I realize now how wrong I was. But we can fix it. We can put it all back together." Catherine watched as Frank looked at her, cocked his head, and smiled. She could tell it wasn't a happy smile. It was one with a sinister bent to it. And then he spoke.

"We can fix it? We can fix it...that's a laugh. We couldn't fix this with all the crazy glue in the world. We are so done!" Catherine was determined not to give in to what she was hearing.

"Wait, wait, don't talk like that. There's nothing that can't be overcome. I love you and the girls. I didn't realize how much you meant to me until this all happened. In addition, I'm coming up for parole. I've been a model prisoner. My lawyer told me there's a great chance that I could get an early release, perhaps this year or next."

Catherine looked for the twitch in his left eye. It was gone. She could tell that he was looking right into her eyes without blinking and with no twitching. His next words slugged her even harder. "Look, any real love I had for you was lost during that ugly trial. When I heard all of those vicious things you'd done, at first I couldn't believe it. It was like they were describing another person." She kept her eyes on him, trying to anticipate his next words. She watched him take a deep breath and then he said,

"Catherine, I've filed for divorce. Since you're incarcerated and I had nothing to do with it, I can legally file and take full custody of my daughters. The court will arrange your visitation rights which will likely commence upon your release."

She was about to say something but he beat her to it.

"There's nothing left to rebuild. Any and everything evaporated years ago. You're a convicted felon. Every place we go your record would follow us. I don't want that and I certainly don't want that for my daughters. I've been hanging in there for the last six years. I honestly don't know why. But I've come to realize this is completely hopeless."

When Frank said that, it was like the sound of one of the prison doors slamming in her face.

"No escape, no second chance" was all she could hear. She thought of one more thing that might help to grant her a stay of execution."

"Frank, I know I screwed up. I know I hurt you. But if Jack Alexander hadn't got me arrested, I could have recovered and none of this ugly prison stuff would have ever happened."From the look on his face, Catherine could tell she had said the wrong thing. He screwed up his face and let loose with another tirade.

"Of all the insensitive, inhuman things to say, you have the nerve to accuse that guy for the things you did. All he did was report your wrongdoings to the authorities. You see, you still haven't taken full responsibility for your actions. I'm sick and tired of your mess."

Catherine watched him stand up and move toward the door. He abruptly stopped, turned briefly, and said,

"Live and be well. Stay far away from me."***

After Frank left, Catherine was taken back to her cell. She was a complete wreck. She couldn't believe what she'd heard and what had happened. After all these years, her husband was writing her off, walking out on her, filing for divorce, and taking the kids with him. She wouldn't see her girls anymore while she was locked up in Hazelton. She kept saying,

"How could he do this to me?" She threw herself on her bed and wept for hours. The more she cried, the more she came to realize Frank was right. She had brought all of this on herself. No one forced her to do the things she did. She approved every one of those inflated consulting rates to the D.O.D. She thought she had created a foolproof system. If she had stayed with overcharging regular private sector companies, the system wouldn't have gotten off track. How was she to know Universal Systems would decide to buy DTA Partners? If that hadn't happened, the scheme could have gone on for years. Catherine started to remember the beginning of the end.

"Catherine, you need to keep it up, stay with the original plan. No one will uncover this. Think about it, this makes your profit picture look great!" This came from DTA's CEO, Priscilla Edwards. She had recruited Catherine to be part of the scheme once she got hired. "I'm concerned that people will start digging and this entire plan of ours will get unraveled."

Priscilla waved a hand at Catherine,

"I assure you it won't. No one will be looking that closely." Priscilla went on in an assuring fashion,

"Look, this isn't the first time I've mapped out a plan like this and everyone has always been successful. By the way, I didn't notice you complaining when you received those huge annual bonuses."

"Yeah, I know, but I'm still nervous about the announced merger."

"Look, the board told me I'm going to be a co-CEO with the CEO of Universal. So, I'll be running things. You'll be fine."

"Are you sure?"

"I haven't led you astray yet, have I?"

"No, no you haven't."

"Okay, so are you still on my team? Can I trust and count on you as I have in the past?"

"Uh, yeah...I'm still on your team."

"Great! Keep me posted on any new developments."

As Catherine reflected, she should have backed out right then and there. Maybe if she had resigned, taken her severance, and gotten another job, she could have avoided all this. She could have been a whistleblower on Priscilla. The government would have shown her leniency. Instead, Catherine believed her and the whole scheme blew up in her face. Priscilla ended up turning on her and blaming her for the whole thing. Now Catherine had lost everything, her husband, her family, her reputation, and all her assets. She thought, *if Jack Alexander hadn't been so intent on revenge, I could have avoided all this. It's his fault.*

CHAPTER

EIGHTEEN

FRANK HAD TOLD HIS DAUGHTERS a portion of the conversation with their mother, especially the part about her wanting to see them. He explained the importance of staying in a relationship with their mother.

"As long as you live you will only have one mother. You need to get reconciled with that fact."

Sara told her father she agreed with him.

Rachel had the opposite reaction.

"Mother or not, I don't have any interest in staying in touch with her. If I never saw her again, it would be fine with me."Rachel thought, *why does she want to see me? I told my dad I won't ever go back to that prison again. Why should I go back there? I don't have a relationship with her anymore. She hasn't been a mother to me for all these years. She's a criminal and a convicted felon. She's where convicts are supposed to be, in jail. I'm so done. Why should I ever again leave Atlanta, fly to West Virginia, drive to that miserable town, and stay in a flea-bitten motel overnight to go out to that godforsaken prison? I don't want to have anything to do with her ever again. When I needed her, she wasn't there. This is all her fault.****

As Catherine's older daughter, Rachel had suffered for eight years. Her mother's arrest, trial, conviction, and prison sentence were extremely hard on her. Looking back, as an eleven year old she'd loved her mother and was close to her. She would spend hours sitting in her mother's home office reading books and doing her homework assignments so she could be near her. Sometimes, Rachel would listen curiously to her mother's conversations. She would sit there imagining what these faceless people looked like. She pictured some to be fat. Others she saw as tall and lanky with sweaty palms like her Uncle Ed. She hated shaking his hand whenever he came to visit. His hands were both sweaty and chubby. It felt like rubbing together mashed potatoes. Still others she pictured as handsome and charming with a great smile and bright, shining white teeth.One of her mother's rules was Rachel had to sit quietly, not say a word, or make a sound while she was on the phone.

"Mommy's got to talk to some important people for a while. So you can sit here but you can't talk, okay?"Rachel thought about that the first time her mother explained the rules. Then she asked, "How long will you be talking on the phone?"

"About forty-five minutes."

Rachel pondered that for a moment. Then she asked.

"What if I get hungry or have to go to the bathroom?"

"You can get up quietly, go, and then you can come back."

Again, Rachel thought this over. Then she simply said,

"Okay Mommy."

There were many times when Rachel would sit and look at the clock on her mother's desk. She'd finished all of her homework and she'd get tired of reading her book. So, she'd sit and watch the time go by, counting the minutes until her mother's conversation was over. Regardless of how long the calls took, Rachel was content to sit there next to her mother. She longed for the times when her mother's calls would end and she would decide to take a break. Then the two of them would sit and talk. Rachel would tell her mother about school, her teacher, her little girl friends, what everybody wore to school that day, the boy she had a crush on, and all the other things that happened when she wasn't with her mother. When she had her mother's attention, she felt like the most important person on the planet. Rachel lived for those times when her mother would smile at her based on some story she told. Sometimes,

Rachel would ask her mother about her work.

"Why do you have to talk to so many people on the phone?"

"Well, I have to make sure that they are all doing what they need to be doing."

Rachel turned her mother's answer over in her mind. Then she asked,

"Is it like finishing all of their homework?"

Rachel absorbed the smile from her mother, who said, "Yes... a lot like that."

When her mother said that and gave her a special look, Rachel felt like she had given the right answers and won the National Spelling Bee competition.Rachel was a smart young girl. At eleven years old, she was in the sixth grade. Her results from her standardized tests showed she had the reading ability of a eighth grade student and her math scores were even better. Therefore, she was in accelerated classes and she was doing well. But she simply wanted to be wherever her mother was.

Rachel struggled most whenever her mother had to travel for business. She would leave on a Sunday night and not return home until Thursday. Rachel would mope around the house when she returned from school, longing for her mother's return. The only consolation was her mother would call home every evening at 8:00 p.m. to find out how everything was going. Her Dad would let his daughters talk first and Rachel would let her younger sister, Sara, talk before her because she knew she would be quick. Sara also missed her mother but she was more of Daddy's little girl. She went everywhere and did everything with him. Frank would take the trash out to the curb at night. Sara's voice would echo throughout the house,

"Can I come too?""I'll be right back.""I know but I want to

come with you." As a result, she learned to throw a football, hit a baseball at a very early age. She knew every player's position on the basketball court and would regularly call fouls before the referees would. Frank would have to demand that she go to bed or finish her homework. Of course Sara would whine,

"I know, Daddy. I will go up to bed but I just want to watch 10 more minutes of the game with you." So, she missed her mother but not the same way that Rachel did. Once Rachel got on the phone, her entire demeanor changed. She was happy again. She'd ask her mother endless questions regarding her trip, what city she was in, how her flight had been, the hotel she stayed in, what she had for dinner, and, most importantly, when she would be coming back home. Rachel lived for those brief phone calls. Each one would tide her over until her mother called the following night. Whenever her mother was to return from a trip, she made sure she finished all of her chores and her homework. That way there would be nothing standing in the way of her reveling over the arrival of her mother.

Things took a hard left turn when her mother was arrested. She had gone to Chicago for a trip. Nothing was out of the ordinary. She told Rachel she would be back in two days. When her mother didn't return as planned and didn't call, Rachel started to worry. She asked her father in the car on the way to school the next day,

"Where's Mom? She was supposed to come home last night. What happened? Where is she?" Rachel noticed her dad didn't answer right away. His hesitation bothered her. "What is it, Dad? What aren't you telling me?"

Finally, her father answered,

"Your mother has been detained. She'll be home soon."

"Daddy, what does 'detained' mean? And what day will she be here?" Again, she watched as her father continued to look out of the windshield and hesitate before answering her. In the meantime, her little sister who was sitting in the back seat piped in,

"Mommy has a meeting. Mommy has a meeting"

Irritated by her father's non-response, Rachel lashed out at her sister.

"Shut up Sara, I'm trying to talk to Daddy!"

That caused her father to speak.

"Rachel, don't you tell her to shut up and don't use that tone with her.""Daddy, I'm sorry, I want to know when Mommy's coming home."

"Like I said...she's been detained...delayed. She should be home in another day or two."

"Is she okay? Did you talk to her?"

Again she was bothered that her father didn't respond. He looked straight ahead as he drove. Finally she heard him say,

"Yes, you mother's okay. I haven't talked to her but someone called me and told me she was fine."

"Who was it? Who told you?"

"Her attorney, her lawyer called me."Rachel thought for a moment. Then she asked,

"Is Mom in trouble? What did she do that was wrong?"The car pulled up to a stoplight. Rachel watched as her father turned in her direction and asked,

"What makes you think she's done something wrong?"

"Well, one time when I was sitting in Mommy's office with her, she told me a lawyer is somebody you use when you're in trouble."She experienced her father's silence again. Only this time, it was for a much longer time.Eventually, he said,

"Rachel, you're right. Your mother is in some trouble but she is going to be home in a couple of days and then she'll tell you all about it."As Rachel was about to get out of the car, she turned and said,

"Why can't you tell me?"

Her father looked out of the windshield, tried not to look at Rachel, hid his tears, and said,

"Because I don't know all of the details and it would be best coming from your mother. Plus, we are at school and you have to go in now. I'll pick you up after school. Have a great day."

"All right...I love you, Daddy."

"I love you too."

CHAPTER
NINETEEN

RACHEL WAS SAD FOR THE next two days. She had trouble sleeping. She started daydreaming about what was going on with her mother. Her father kept being evasive, saying he didn't know any of the details.

Three days from the day when she should have arrived originally, her mother came home. Her taxi pulled up at the house in the early evening and her mother got out and came up the walk. Before she could get halfway to the door, Rachel ran out to her and buried her face in her mother's coat. She cried uncontrollably for what must have been five minutes.

Finally, they were all sitting down on the living room couch. Her sister Sara was starting to fall asleep. Her father picked her up and started rocking her. Rachel blurted out,

"Mom, where have you been? What's going on? Why do you need a lawyer? What bad things did you do?" Rachel watched as her mother looked at her father, then down at Rachel, and started talking slowly.

"Rachel, first of all, I'm sorry I've been gone longer than I told you I would be."

"Okay, but what bad things did you do? You told me that you need a lawyer if you've done something bad." Rachel sensed something was wrong because her mother hesitated and then said,

"I haven't done anything bad or wrong. There are some people who said I did. I had to get a lawyer to prove I'm innocent."Rachel thought about that for a moment. Then she said,

"So, the lawyer fixed everything. Now no one is saying you did bad things?"

"Honey, it doesn't work like that. There has to be a trial and a judge listens to everybody talk and then a jury, decides if I did something bad or not."

"What's a trial and who's a jury?"

"Rachel, a trial is a discussion, sort of, where people talk and other people listen. The people listening are the jury."

Rachel pondered her mother's answer and then asked,

"So, do you have to leave again to go to this trial or can you talk on the phone like you normally do?"

"No, I have to go back to Chicago for the trial but it won't be for a while. In the meantime, I'll be here with you, Sara and Daddy. Okay?" "Mommy, I'm glad you will be home with us. But can I ask you one more question?"

"Sure, sweetheart, what is it?"

Rachel took her time forming her question. Then she asked,

"What happens if the jury says you did something bad? What would happen to you?"She felt scared because now her mother stopped talking again. The look on her face was one Rachel hadn't seen before. Her mother looked at her dad and then looked again at Rachel."That won't happen. So we have nothing to worry about." Her mother's words didn't match the look she had on her face.

"But what if they do? What would happen to you?"Now her mother was dumbfounded. She had tried to gloss over it but Rachel would not let her.

"Well, if that happened, I would probably have to pay a fine. But don't you worry. It will all be just fine, Honey."

But it hadn't been fine.

Shortly after Rachel's eleventh birthday, her mother was found guilty, sentenced, and eventually went to prison. This began a downward spiral for Rachel. Kids at school started a barrage of nasty comments and name-calling. Every school day someone would yell,

"Your mother is a jailbird; your mother is a jailbird."

Even her best girlfriend Lucy chimed in and started calling her "convict." No one would talk to her and she felt horribly alone. Before and after school, parents would look at her with disgust. Rachel told her father and he tried to explain it away. But Rachel was scarred and wounded by all of the endless taunting. At the end of the school year, her father took her out of that school and put her in another one at the start of sixth grade. But it didn't take long before everyone found out who she was, and the taunting started all over again. In the midst of all this, she thought she'd found a friend.

One day, a seventh grader walked up to her and said,

"Hello". He talked to her about normal stuff. After school, she told her father and he said it was a good sign of better things to come.

For the next few weeks, her new friend, Thomas, would walk with her in the halls, sit with her at lunch, and show a real interest in being her friend. Then one day after school, as she was waiting for her father to pick her up, Thomas walked up to her with three of his friends.He said, "Hey, Rachel, what's up?"

"Nothing much, waiting for my Dad to pick me up. By the way, I asked him if it would be all right for you to come over to my house one day and he said yes. What do you think?"Thomas looked first at his three friends, smiled, and then said,

"Why would I want to come to a convict's house?" Rachel was shocked and hurt.

She couldn't believe her ears.

"Thomas, that's so hurtful. Why would you say that?"

"'Cause you are the daughter of a convict and the fruit doesn't fall far from the tree. At least that's what our science teacher tells us in class. It won't be long before you're in prison with her." He and his buddies started laughing as they turned and walked off.

Rachel began crying uncontrollably as her father drove up. She got in the car and said,

"Nothing" when her father asked her what was wrong and why she was crying.

Once they got home, she told him and he was furious. He was tempted to go back to the school, find Thomas, and strangle him. Her father did the next best thing. "You should be ashamed of yourself letting a young girl deal with the abuse these students have put on her."

Dwayne Johnson, the school's principal sat behind his desk, looked uninterested in what Frank had to say. "You are supposed to protect your students, not let them fall prey to this disgusting behavior. I'm seriously thinking of writing a scathing email to the superintendent, or better yet, going to her office and telling her what's going on in the school."

Now the principal sat up a little straighter. To begin with, he was a short guy, maybe five foot six. His ergonomically designed chair could be cranked up so he appeared taller when he sat down. It was up so high that his feet were off the floor. He had a big, thick neck; probably from playing football as a lineman in high school and community college. At forty, he was seriously balding. He had a bad comb-over that still exposed his hair loss. The acne on his face was like that of a teenage.

"Mr. Frazier, you are out of line. I've been doing everything I can for all of the school kids here, including your daughter."

"Well, obviously you haven't done enough. My daughter has been traumatized by students in this school. Since you are the principal, it's your job to protect her."

"I can't be with her 100% of the time that she is in this school. I need—"Frank interrupted him.

"No, maybe not, but you need to take action whenever a student is being injured or abused, and my daughter definitely has been."The principal muttered under his breath,

"It's you and your wife's fault."

"What did you say? What did I hear you say about fault?" Frank asked.

"Nothing, nothing…I said the wounds hurt like someone used salt."

"Why, you little coward, are you kidding me right now? You aren't even man enough to repeat that ignorant comment again. I want the transfer papers to move Rachel to another school, and I want them by tomorrow. Hopefully, another school will be more understanding and more protective than this sorry excuse for a grammar school."Dwayne countered,

"Frankly, that's not enough time to get transfer papers together. We'll need more time, maybe a week."

Frank stood up, put his hands on the desk that separated the two of them, leaned over it, and said,

"I'll have those papers tomorrow or my next visit will be to the district superintendent." With that pronouncement, he turned and left the principal's office.

He put their house up for sale, took his two daughters out of school, rented an apartment way across town, and Rachel started going to her third school in two years.

It was fortunate for her no one figured out who she was. As a result, she had a relatively stable school experience through the rest of grammar school. But by then she was deeply scarred. She didn't trust anyone. She didn't want to be with people. She went to school, did what was expected of her, and became a loner.

CHAPTER
TWENTY

BY THE TIME SHE GOT to high school, she started wearing Goth-type clothing. She dyed her hair black, worn black lipstick, dark eyeliner, and dark fingernail polish. She also decided, against her father's wishes, to get a number of tattoos and a series of ear piercings. Everything about her shouted, "Stay away. Don't come near me."

In spite of it, she still managed to be a solid 'B' student. Day after lonely day, she stayed secluded in her room reading supernatural and science fiction novels, listening to punk rock, and drawing weird images.

Her father tried to intervene. He talked with her about life but she wasn't having it. She felt that her mother had abandoned her and did some horrible things that caused their separation. Rachel was so angry. She felt her mother was the cause, the reason for all of the abuse she experienced. She had loved her mother deeply; in truth, she still did. But every time her father told her they would be going to visit, she fought against it. She ranted and raved about not wanting to go. Once she actually ran away from home and stayed in a motel with money she'd saved from her allowance. Her father was distressed and upset.

"Rachel, I get it you're angry and hurt but running away is

not the answer. It doesn't solve anything. I was out of my mind with worry."

Rachel pleaded,

"Dad, I'm sorry. I felt I didn't have a voice and you were going to make me go see her regardless. I didn't see any other option. I still don't."

"Running away is never the option when there's family conflict. I'm your dad. It might not seem like it but you can talk to me. I will always try to understand. I love you, Rachel, always have; always will.""Yeah, well, by giving me an ultimatum sure didn't feel like love."

Her father calmly explained,

"I wasn't giving you an ultimatum. I was trying to work out an acceptable solution.""Really?"

"Really!"

"Look dad, I don't want to go to that prison ever again. And don't try to make me." She waited for her father's next comment. She looked down at her hands. She had balled them up in tight fists. They reflected exactly how she was feeling.Her dad looked at her and calmly said,

"Okay...if you decided not to go anymore, I'm fine with that."

That was the last conversation they had on the topic. Rachel also agreed she wouldn't run away again.

***

Frank had a quiet moment as he sat at the kitchen table looking over his family's finances. He reflected back on all of the years of craziness and upheaval; he had been trying to keep some semblance of a family together for his daughters. He had little or no hope for his marriage to Catherine. He had tried to hang on and pray for a miracle that would get her an early prison release. Nonetheless, the last appeal denial squelched any hope of that happening. Along the way, the appeal had eroded the last of their savings, forced them to take out a second mortgage on their home, and caused him to set up a payment plan with the lawyer for the balance. Their finances had been under water due to the legal tsunami Catherine's stupidity had caused. Frank sat there remembering the set of events that had negatively impacted their finances. During Rachel's sophomore year in high school, Frank realized he would have to re-enter the job market. He needed to provide for his daughters and keep a roof over their heads. It had been many years since he had held a job outside of their home. He had been in Human Resources and had worked his way up to a Senior Director with a major consumer products company. While he still had some friends and contacts, it had been years since he'd conversed with them regarding his profession. Frank decided it would be best to put together his game plan. First on his list was determining what had changed in the HR field. He also decided that he needed to re-establish himself with all of his friends and business relationships. Two other important inclusions were putting together a comprehensive resume and starting to investigate available positions to apply to.

After more than two month passed, he was still on the outside looking in. He'd submitted his resume to several job posting but still hadn't gotten an offer.

"We decided to go with another candidate. You've been successful when you were in the job market. We're not sure you can keep pace after being away for so long. We'll keep your resume on file." He was starting to get desperate. The money he had in reserve had dwindled. If he didn't find a job soon, he'd have to start selling stuff. One night, after his last rejection letter, he said a prayer before he went to sleep.

"God…I don't know if you are even listening or if you're interested but I'm in trouble. I've got these two kids who need me and I need a job to support them. If you even care, help me." He fell asleep.

Frank had previously tried to get in touch with some of his old business associates. They were tough to track down since he had been out of the game for so long. He had talked to one guy who said,

"I understand you need a job, my friend, but I can't risk bringing you here with that criminal conviction hanging over your wife's head. I'd be risking my reputation...sorry."

Frank tried to defend his position. He explained that he and his children were innocent bystanders. He needed to get a job in order to provide for them. Nothing he said made a difference. Frank was crestfallen but didn't stop searching.

A week later, he finally caught a break. He talked to a former boss who was now an executive vice president for Horton Pharma, a pharmaceutical firm headquartered in Atlanta. Bob Foster had always liked Frank and his work ethics.

"Bob, thanks for calling me back. It's been a long time. I wasn't sure you'd remember me."

"Remember you...are you crazy? How could I forget you? You were one of my best guys. I couldn't believe it when you fell off the map."

"Yeah, well, I made the choice to be a stay-at-home dad. I didn't want my daughters to become latch-key kids."

"Hey, I get that...I give you lots of credit. I also had been following the unfortunate circumstances involving your wife, her trial, and conviction. I'm sorry...what a tough deal."

Frank waited a few seconds before he responded. He wanted to choose his words carefully.

"It's been tough on us. That's the reason why I was reaching out to you. Catherine was convicted and she's been serving time in prison. She was the principal breadwinner. Now I've got to find a job in order to keep things together for my children." There was silence on the phone. Frank didn't sense he should add anything else.

Thankfully, Bob spoke up,

"Man, that's got to be hard on you. How can I help?"

"I need a job. We used up all of our savings on the trial and the appeals. Things are super tight right now. I've been on the job hunt for months and I still haven't landed anything"

"I can't imagine the spot you're in.""Honestly, if it takes too much longer, I may have to sell all our possessions...I may have to sell them regardless."Frank waited for Bob to respond. He didn't disappoint.

"Okay, so let me tell you a few things. Not much has changed in HR. It's still the business of providing the best service to the business units; finding and filling open jobs, and insuring that the policies and practices are being followed."Frank decided to interrupt him,

"Yeah, but some terminologies and processes have to have changed in six years."

"Frank, some have but most haven't. A smart guy like you would be able to pick up things in no time."

"I hear you...I've found some of those new terms but I'm not sure I have the right ones"

"Look, I'll send you a few files that will help you get the party started. Give me your email address. I'll send them to you later today."After Frank gave him his contact information, he said,

"Bob, this is great but the problem is I still need to find a job. And I can't start working until I get an interview. And I can't get an interview without a job to apply to."

"Well, problem solved...send me your resume and I'll ask one of my managers to see what might match up with roles we need to fill."

There was silence on the line. Frank was listening, unable to speak. He heard Bob ask,

"Frank what's the problem? Don't you want my help?"Slowly Frank found his voice. He was overcome with emotion and his voice cracked.

"No, no...I appreciate your offer to help. It's that I'm a little overwhelmed right now. This is the first bright sign that I've had in months. I...I don't know what to say..." He stopped for a moment in order to compose himself. Then he started up again.

"It's just that things have been so hard and no one...no one has been willing to help me. Thank you Bob...thank you so much." The tears started to roll down his face. His chest began to heave so much that he had to put down the phone.Frank barely heard Bob's voice.

"Frank...Frank are you there?"He blew his nose and picked up the phone.

"Yes...yes I'm here. Sorry I got so emotional. I just"Bob interrupted him.

"For what it's worth, I understand the crack you're in. As you know, I've got children of my own and I'd be trying to do the same thing. I get it. Know this, most people would applaud you for what you're doing."

"Thanks, those are kind words. They're words I need to hear."

"Hey, Frank, I'm sure you'd do the same for me if the situation were reversed. Remember, I'm pulling for you."

"Thanks...thanks again."

"No worries...so, let's get started. Get your resume over to me this afternoon. I think you told me you need to find work ASAP."

That conversation led to an interview and an offer. Whether or not Bob was instrumental in the speed of the process, Frank would never know. But what he needed was a job and he got one. As a manager of HR sourcing, he was responsible for a small department that filled job orders from different areas in the company. In his last position, six years ago, he had held a similar role. So he was happy. The medical benefits for him and his children gave him the coverage they needed. Based on his start time and the location of his office, he was still able to drop them off at school every day. Since the bus dropped his daughters off two blocks from home, they could manage in the afternoon until he got home.

CHAPTER
TWENTY-ONE

FRANK'S SPIRITS WERE LIFTED. HE would be able to take care of his daughters. Yet, he was troubled. His wife would be incarcerated for a long time. Her original sentence was ten years and she had served only six. He'd fallen out of love with her because of all of her illegal business affairs, all the trouble she had caused, but mostly because of her unwillingness to take responsibility for her actions. After reviewing his financial condition, he realized, even with his new job, he didn't have enough money to afford the rental house they were living in. The more time Frank sat and reflected on things, the angrier he got. When he reflected over the emotional abuse his daughter Rachel had experienced; and was still experiencing, he wanted to curse out Catherine and spit in her face. But he knew he needed to bottle up his anger and get on with the care and feeding of his daughters. His daughter Sarah asked him one day,

"Daddy, why are we moving? You said you liked our house."

Frank picked her up, hugged her, and sat her down in his lap. He felt her head snuggle against his chest as she waited for him to answer.

"Sarah, honey…I do like our house but we don't have enough money to live here anymore. We have to move so you and your sister can still have a nice place to live." Frank had to watch the tears brimming in her big, brown eyes."But, Daddy, this house is a nice house. And I like being here. I don't want to move. Can we just stay here?" Frank loved his young daughter with her long brown hair cascading down her back. She was a pretty little girl and her father's darling. He loved both of his kids, but he had a special place in his heart for Sarah. As Frank looked down at her, he remembered when she had a bad thing happen at just six years old.One of the little boys in the neighborhood dared her to climb a tree.

"You're just chicken. I'm going to build a tree house in this very tree. If you climb the tree with me, I'll let you be in my tree house.""Jimmy, I want to be in your tree house and I'm not afraid to climb the tree with you." She had followed Jimmy up the tree and halfway up she slipped, fell, and broke her leg. When Frank heard her crying for him, he ran outside and found her sprawled on the grass.He called out,

"Jimmy, get down from there and go tell your folks to call 911." He looked down at his daughter and calmly said,

"Sarah, it's okay, it's okay, sweetheart. Daddy's right here." After the ambulance came and loaded her in it, she cried all the way to the hospital.

"Daddy, it hurts so bad, please make it stop, please make it stop."After the doctor finished setting the break, he gave her a mild sedative. Frank held Sarah and comforted her until she calmed down and then fell asleep in his arms. From that day on, Sarah held a very special place in his heart. While he loved Rachel, she was much stronger and had a strong affinity to her mother.

So here he was trying to convey to Sarah why they would have to leave their home and move. It was a hard choice but one that had to be made, without feeling sorry for himself. He took his kids out of school, moved across town and started renting an apartment large enough for the three of them. Once he enrolled them in their new school, things seemed to settle down. Frank had the greatest concern for Rachel since she was the one most affected. She did have one bad situation with a classmate. Overall, things moved to a "new normal."

Frank was amazed at how quickly he was able to get adapted to the workplace and HR management again after being away for so long. He started working hard right from day one. He got to know all of the people on his small team. His peers were very supportive, trying to give advice, suggestions, and recommendations that would help him. The overall HR team was made up of different departments: policy and practices, compliance, training, talent acquisition and retention, succession planning and hi-potential identification, and performance planning and counseling. There were managers over each department. They reported to two directors, and the directors reported to a vice president who was also over Administrative Support. In turn, this VP reported to Executive Vice President, Bob Foster; the same Bob Foster who was Frank's friend, former boss, and had been instrumental in helping Frank get hired. "Hey, Frank, how are you? Are you doing any good out there?" That was Bob's way of relating.

"Bob, you'll never know the difference this job makes in my life and my family's."

"Hey don't worry about it...I was happy to help. As I said before, if the situation had been reversed, you would have done the same for me."

"But it wasn't...I'll be forever indebted to you for what you've done. Thanks again."

"You're welcome...now go out and perform in the superior way that I remember."

"You can count on it."

***

It turned out that Frank's department, Talent Acquisition and Retention, was one of only two departments that had two managers. Frank was the manager responsible for Talent Acquisition and his peer, Laura Hilton, was the manager responsible for Retention. Laura was about five foot five, maybe one hundred and ten pounds. She had one of the brightest smiles Frank had ever seen; very warm and inviting. But it started with her eyes; they were a shimmering brownish color. Frank was struck by how they reminded him of aspects of the glorious rays that would burst through the clouds as the sun would start descending; glowing and vibrant. He felt immediately drawn to her without her saying a word. Laura was in her late thirties, early forties and it was clear she took pride in her attire. Frank was mesmerized when he was introduced to her. He did everything he could to stop from staring at her.Laura was very cordial.

"Hi, my name is Laura…Laura Hilton. Your name's Frank… Frank Frazier?"Frank stumbled over his words.

"Uh, huh, yeah…I'm Frank."

She reached out her hand and Frank stared and looked at it.

Laura chuckled a bit.

"Normally when someone extends their hand like this, it's customary for the other person to shake their hand when being introduced."

Stumbling over his words while trying to recover,

"Oh, oh…sorry, my mind was someplace else. It's good to meet you. I look forward to working with you." He shook her hand but he couldn't take is eyes off her. He followed with,

"How…how long have you been at Horton and in HR."

Laura corrected him.

"Well, first, no one in the company says Horton…it's either 'H' or 'Horton Pharma'. And I've been in the company five years and in this department since I started."

"You came to Hort…I mean H as a manager in HR?"

"No, I was hired as a senior recruiter specialist and after two years they made me one of the managers; fortunate for me…huh?"

"Yeah, that's great. I look forward to working with you."Laura smiled and laughed a bit.

"You already said that."

"Oh...sorry, I'll have to be more careful...huh?" They both laughed. It broke the tension for Frank.

"No worries...look, since we'll be working together, if I can help you with anything in the department, let me know."

And she certainly had helped him. She knew all of the people on the HR team. Plus, she had worked closely with all of Frank's people. So, she was able to give him valuable insights into his direct reports. There were particular processes and tools the company had for acquiring talent, basically to find and hire people. Laura helped Frank understand the use of every tool and the details of the recruiting process. Over time, they held joint team meetings and they collaborated regarding the reports they presented to management.

Time moved by quickly. One month turned into three months and three turned into six. Frank's team's performance was exceptional. His team was finding excellent candidates and filling business unit job orders at an accelerated rate. The hiring managers were so pleased that there was a steady stream of "appreciation" emails to Frank's boss. Between him and Laura, they were making a name for themselves. Personnel acquisition and retention were the two most frequently used terms at virtually every Director's meeting.

"As one of the directors of HR, I get an earful from the business units whenever we screw up," said Mike Thompson, Frank's boss, at a large, internal Directorate HR meeting. "But over the last few months, I've been getting calls and emails telling me how pleased many of them are with the fine efforts of Laura and Frank's teams."

There was applause that interrupted his speech. He waved his hand and beckoned them to come up and stand next to him.

"I could give you all the statistics on their results but I'll simply tell you what one of the business unit VPs said to me in a note I received."

Someone from the audience blurted out,

"Tell us, Mike...tell us." Everyone broke out in laughter.When everybody settled down, Mike read,

"'Your guys in Talent Acquisition have become Best-in-Class by bringing and keeping talented people. Thanks a bunch...and keep it up'."

People started clapping and whooping it up. The applause was genuine. Mike again had to calm the group down.

Then he said,

"So, Laura and Frank, congratulations and continue the great work. It's being noticed and appreciated."

As Frank drove home after that meeting, he reflected over the last few months. He realized he was blessed that things had been working out so well. His wife was still in prison and Rachel was still having a rough time of things. He was now the breadwinner. He could keep a roof over his daughters' heads, buy them clothing, and occasionally take them out to a nice dinner and a movie. As he headed north on the I85 expressway in the Thursday evening traffic jam, he realized that he owed a lot of his success to his hard work and his collaboration with Laura. She had been true to her word regarding her help. She also was one of the smartest people he'd ever worked with. He found out she had both an undergrad degree and a master's in English literature and Spanish. Somehow, she fell into HR and liked it. She decided to stay. The best part was everybody liked her. The word in the office was she'd been married to an abuser, both physically and emotionally. She was wise enough to get out of that situation, and they had no kids.He allowed himself to continue to focus on Laura as he inched his way through the expressway traffic. Out of nowhere, an image of Catherine flashed across his mind. He thought, *In two days, we are driving off to that prison again. Nobody wants to go. I especially am not looking forward to it. There's nothing left between us, and I need to open my heart to the possibility of someone else.*

TWENTY-TWO

IT BECAME CLEAR TO FRANK that Rachel was experiencing abuse from both teachers and classmates at school and in their neighborhood. After watching how this affected her, he was determined to try to shield her from it. He had already moved them to different schools and neighborhoods twice, but she was still suffering. He watched his soft, tenderhearted, loving daughter dramatically change under the weight of the harsh and nasty treatment of those she considered friends. He watched helplessly as she changed right before his eyes. Her manner, clothing, music choices became different and dark. She became a person he hardly recognized. Frank tried talking with her about it. He tried desperately to explain the callousness of people. He told her that she shouldn't let that affect her, all to no avail. He finally took her to a counselor, thinking that might help. The counselor told him she got nowhere with Rachel.

"For the most part, we sit in silence. She has virtually nothing to say." Frank picked her up from one of her sessions. As she got in the car, he made every effort to talk about anything other than what went on in counseling.

Finally, he had to ask,

"Honey, how did it go with the counselor?" Frank looked over at Rachel.

"Fine…it went fine."

"I don't mean to pry but what did you talk about?"

"Not much."

Her dad pressed her for an answer.

"What does that even mean…not much?" Frank saw she was riveted to the window, looking at the landscape and refusing to turn around. The counselor had suggested Frank not push her too hard into talking about her sessions but as he looked over at her, he couldn't help it.

"Rachel, what does 'not much' mean?"

Rachel turned to him with a scowl on her face and shouted,

"It means I don't want to talk about it…okay?" He was flabbergasted. She turned back to looking out the window. Frank realized he had crossed the line but something inside him made him press on. Maybe it was the anger he felt from all the mistreatment Rachel experienced or it could have been the aggressive tone she'd used. But he pulled the car over, threw the car into park, sat there fuming, and looking out the windshield. The only sound they both could hear was the hum of the air conditioner. Rather than yell, he said in a calm but edgy tone,

"Rachel, I know you're angry. I can't say I have a complete appreciation for how you've been feeling but…"

Frank was surprised when she all of a sudden turned toward him and growled,

"Dad, you have no idea how angry I am. Everything is totally screwed up! If that wasn't bad enough, you force me to see some quack doctor. This whole thing sucks, big time!"

Frank now didn't know what to say. He regretted ignoring the counselor's recommendations. He decided to try a different approach. He reached out his hand and lightly touched her shoulder.

Frank jumped back startled when his daughter snapped,

"Don't touch me. I just want to go home!"

That was the last counseling session. He simply stopped taking her. Through it all, there were a couple of bright spots. She still got relatively good grades. He was amazed since she did very little studying at home. The other bright spot was her art. He happened to go into her room one day while she was at the store. He noticed her sketchbook and opened it. He saw a drawing of a woman. She looked hideous and grotesque but the detail was so intricate and well done. As he looked through the sketchbook, he saw other drawings that were both amazing and distorted. To his chagrin, he realized the original drawing was a rendering of her mother. This was the way she had been internalizing her pain and hurt associated with all that had happened. He made the decision, right then, to support her art talent in every way he could. His hope was that it would lead his daughter to a more positive place in her life.

***

Frank couldn't convince Rachel to attend college. She wanted no part of it. To her, it opened up the possibility of more abuse once people figured out who she was. He was now just focused on her getting through high school. With her graduation day fast approaching, Frank made it his business to find out all the things Rachel needed to complete before her important day. So, he took the liberty of contacting her school to obtain a list. Whenever he asked his daughter, she'd simply shrug her shoulders as if to say

"I don't know and I don't care". He knew she needed his help. She wasn't going to ask for it.

***

Rachel loved her father. She believed his efforts were well intended. She didn't want him meddling in her affairs because he couldn't make her struggles go away. Rachel was content to work things out on her own. She didn't want to see a shrink or have long talks about her life. She wanted to be left alone. She didn't want to be bothered with her list of "to dos." Deep inside, she wrestled with her hurts and her feelings of independence. These were in direct conflict with her desire to be needed and appreciated, even loved. She often felt the desire to run up to her father, fall in his arms, and spill out all the emotions that were welled up inside. But she held off from that because her anger and hurts were too strong. She wanted to lash out at anyone in her path, even those who loved her. So, she'd complete her graduation list, but it would be on her own terms.

***

It was now her senior year and soon time to graduate. While she would finish high school with a 'B' average, she sent no college applications. She wanted to get a job, earn some money, and attend art school. Her father didn't object. He could see she had decent art skills.

One spring day she was walking through the mall. She decided to stop at her favorite coffee shop. She didn't actually drink coffee but she loved the taste of chai tea, the opportunity to sit in a quiet spot, and simply watch people. No one ever bothered her and she would spend hours there. She would often bring her sketchpad and doodle. This time, as she was leaving, she noticed a large poster advertising an upcoming art exhibit. She'd seen these before but there was something about it that caught her eye. She saw the word 'avant-garde'. She wasn't totally sure what it meant but she thought it referred to something unusual or out of the ordinary. Whenever she thought about her own artwork, the word *unusual* came to mind. She still wasn't sure she'd actually go but she wrote down the address and the date before she walked out.

On the evening of Thursday, April 20, Rachel was sitting on her bed, in her room, listening to music. Suddenly, it hit her that the art exhibit was the very next day. Right then she decided to attend. The exhibit started at 6:00 p.m. It was being held at a small gallery across town. Since she didn't have a car and her father wouldn't be home soon, she had to take two buses to get there.

As Rachel waited for the second bus, she wondered why Atlanta didn't invest in a better, more complete transit system. Finally, she arrived at the art gallery. All of the unique things on display fascinated her. She spent long periods looking at different pieces of art. Before she realized it, she had been at the gallery for two hours. Rachel was captivated. She'd decided this was the type of art she wanted to learn. As she moved to the last art piece she wanted to view, a guy walked up to her. Normally, she would either turn and walk away or give an icy, cold stare that said, "Do not invade my space or I will rip your face off." Somehow, she didn't feel compelled to do either. She could tell this guy was a little older than she was, taller and thinner than her father. What attracted her was the way he dressed. He had similar Goth-type attire. His black collarless shirt, black straight leg pants, and heavy black boots communicated that he might follow a path similar to her's, tough, hurt, detached, and different. The capstone to everything about him was the nose ring, the earring, and the chain that linked the two. Rachel had only seen that in magazines and movies. Her total assessment took less than a minute. However, she was still guarded about the possibility of meeting this guy as he walked up.She tried to play it cool when he spoke."Excuse me."

"Yes?" she said.

"I'm trying to get around you to see the painting behind you."

"Oh, I'm sorry." Rachel turned slightly and realized that she was in a corner blocking access to two or three paintings. She felt like such a fool. Here she was gearing up for the probability of meeting this guy when he was trying to find a way around her. As she turned to flee, he spoke again.

"Do you come here often to see other kinds of art?"

Rachel jumped slightly as she turned to face him.

"No, no...I've never been here. I only came because I was intrigued by the word 'avant-garde' on their poster."

What shocked her was what he said next.

"That was the same reason I came."

She watched him as he turned from the art piece, looked at her, and asked,

"Well?"

"Well what?"

"Did it live up to your expectations?"

Rachel hesitated.

Before she could answer, he said,

"It exceeded mine. I'm planning to go to art school and I wanted to find out if 'avant-garde' art forms might be what I want to study."

Rachel was ready to leap out of her skin. Here was a guy she didn't know who dressed a lot like her, wanted to study art, was intrigued by the word 'avant-garde,' and she hadn't told him anything about herself or her interest. This was too good to be true.

She still decided to play it safe. She said,

"Where are you planning to attend art school?"

She was surprised but he gave her his full attention.

"I'm moving to Chicago. I found a great school up there and I don't like the scene in Atlanta anymore. What about you?" Still Rachel didn't feel comfortable with divulging anything.

"Well, I'm something of a wannabe artist myself. I do like to draw the more unusual stuff."

"Cool, I'd love to stand and talk some more but I've got to run. I've got to pick up a friend over in Buckhead."

"Okay...no worries...see you around." As Rachel turned around to look at another art piece that caught her eye, she could sense that he was walking away. A few seconds passed and she heard someone behind her say,

"Hey, would you like me to drop you somewhere?" She turned and realized that the same guy had returned.

"My name's Luke, Luke Martin. What's yours?"

Rachel felt put on the spot. She wasn't sure if she should say anything about herself to this guy. She thought, *Who is this guy really? Is he some random guy with issues? He has some similar interests. This is really freaky since I didn't say anything previously. Oh, okay, I'm going to take a chance.*

"My name's Rachel. I appreciate you wanting to give me a ride but I don't know you. I don't ever take rides from strangers."

"Hey, I get that but I'm no stranger. I'm Luke Martin. We just introduced ourselves. But if you're uncomfortable taking a ride from me, okay, no big deal. Have a nice life. I don't want to scare you. I was trying to be friendly." Rachel looked at him and decided maybe it would be okay.

"First, I'm not scared. There are a lot of creeps around. I live very close to Buckhead. Someone was going to pick me up after I got off the bus. So, if you want to give me a ride, I'll text my friend to pick me up earlier."

"Hey, that's fine with me."

"Okay, give me a minute to let them know. By the way, what kind of car do you drive?"

"I drive a dark blue 2000 Subaru. Do you want the license plates too?"

"I Simply want to let my friend know what to look for."

"Great...I'm fine with that." Rachel wanted to give the impression she was sending a text. This little charade made her feel a bit more comfortable with accepting the ride. She also thought it would make him think twice about trying any funny business.

"Okay, I'm ready, I finished. We can go now."

They walked down the street for about a block and Rachel found herself standing in front of a blue Subaru. Luke popped the door lock and they got in the car. Neither of them said anything for the first few minutes of the ride.

Then Rachel asked,

"How long have you lived in Atlanta?"

"About three years. My father was in the military so we moved around a lot."

"Is he still in the service?"

"No, he retired after twenty-five years and moved us here. I guess that's one of the reasons I want to go to art school in Chicago 'cause I'm use to moving." Rachel thought, *well, if he's only been here three years, he doesn't know anything about my mother.*

CHAPTER
TWENTY-THREE

THEY RODE ALONG IN SILENCE for the next ten minutes. Then Rachel heard Luke said, "We're in Buckhead. Where do you want me to drop you off to meet your friend?"

"Drop me off at the Lenox Square. That's the mall where I'm meeting him."

"Which side?"

"It doesn't matter." After some more silence, Rachel determined that, in classic boy-style, Luke was going to ask her for her number or email address.

He didn't disappoint.

"Hey, maybe now that you know I'm not some weird dude we could grab some coffee or tea in the mall. How about giving me your cell number so I can call or text you?" Rachel thought, *bingo…like I thought, nonetheless, I still don't know this guy. I get the feeling he's okay, but I don't know.* Then she said,

"Uh, why don't you give me your number and I'll call you?"

"So, that's your way of blowing me off? You take my number and never call me?"

"No, that's not it. I don't make a habit of passing out my number to strangers." She watched him as he considered her comment. He then replied,

"Okay, fine, here's my number. You ready?"

113

"Yeah, what is it?"

"It's 404-682-1242, got it?"

"Yeah, I've got it. You can let me off right there, in front of that store up ahead."

Luke slowed down and stopped the car.

"Luke, thanks for the ride. Appreciate it and I will call or text you sometime."

"Okay, maybe in the next couple of days?"

"Yeah, maybe…we'll see."

Rachel got out of the car and headed inside the mall without looking back. She wasn't settled about Luke and her thoughts started to focus on how she would get home.

Luke sat there watching Rachel until she disappeared into the mall. He thought, *Boy, she is nice but she probably won't call. Plus, I don't need anything or anybody to keep me tied to this place.* With that, he drove off into the night.

***

Saturday morning found Rachel in bed. Awake, but lingering as she reflected on the events of Friday night at the art gallery. She was glad she'd gone. Based on what she'd seen, she was definitely going to pursue art school. The word 'avant-garde' was stuck in her head. The image of Luke was also stuck in her head. While she still had some major reservation about him, or any other guys, he presented himself as both nice and genuine. In spite of what she told him, she hadn't decided if she was going to call him. Her thoughts took her back to the journey it required for her to get home from the Lenox Square mall. After the expensive taxi ride, she still had a mile to walk home because she didn't have enough money to go any farther. But overall, she had a good time and it helped her to make some decisions about moving on with her life.

CHAPTER
TWENTY-FOUR

CATHERINE HAD A DIFFICULT TIME accepting the fact that her daughters no longer wanted to come and see her, especially Rachel. Frank was crystal clear about divorcing her. He'd had the papers sent to the prison and the process was in motion. Nonetheless, she couldn't imagine not seeing her daughters until she was released. She had devised a plan that included Rachel. So, she needed to figure out a way to get her to come see her at the West Virginia prison. As she sat down at the small desk in her cell, she re-read the letter she was going to send to Rachel.

Dear Rachel,

It has been very hard on me being here and not seeing you and your sister. At times I could scream but nothing good would come from that. I've had lots of time to think and there's so much I want to say to you. First, I love you very much. This fact becomes more of a stark reality the longer I'm in this place. I fully understand now how I sacrificed my time with you for my business career. I worked hard, I traveled so much, and I left you and your sister home far too often. You were so patient with me while I had you sit and be quiet during all of those phone calls I made. I took for granted that you, your sister, and your Dad would always be there. I led myself to believe that everything I did was for your benefit, that you would have a better life. I look back now and realize I was mesmerized by the power I had, and the control I exerted over others, included you and your sister. I liked the titles I had and the fear I could instill in others. I realize now all that was false, simply not real.I admit I also did some things that were wrong. I broke the law. While someone told me to do it, I knew what I was doing wasn't right. I can honestly tell you I had planned to stop but before I did, someone found out and turned me in to the government. Now I am paying the price for my bad choices. I'm so sorry your life has been negatively impacted by all this. You didn't desire any of the bad things you've experienced. I wish I could turn back the clock and re-do everything. I realize I can't but I would like to explain some important things. Please come and see me. I desperately need to talk with you.

Your father tells me you are graduating. Eventually, I'd like you to make arrangements to come and see me after your big day. I have been saving up the monies I've earned here over the last four or five years. I sent some of it to your father and he has agreed to arrange for your travel and motel stay if you can find it in your heart to come. I promise if you will come this last time, I won't ask you to come back again. I sincerely want make everything better for your future.

With all my Love,

Mom

    As Catherine folded up the letter, addressed the envelope, and put on the postage, she hoped her daughter would read it and decide to come. Catherine had had months and years to think about how she would get back at Jack Alexander for all that he did that caused her incarceration. This was an important link in the plan.

CHAPTER

TWENTY-FIVE

THE LETTER FROM CATHERINE ARRIVED about two weeks before Rachel's graduation day. After Frank opened it and read its contents, he decided not to give it to her until after graduation. He determined she didn't need any more distractions. Also, he wasn't totally sure how she would react to it.

Rachel sat on her bed and contemplated all the things were roaming through her mind. Her graduation was fast approaching and she hadn't fully processed what she wanted to do going forward. She had been thinking more and more about Luke. She still had his cell phone number but she hadn't called him. Art school was looming large in her mind. She knew she wanted to go but she didn't know where. In the back of her mind, she allowed herself to think about her mother. She always thought she would be sharing the moment with her mother, but there was no chance that would ever happen.In the quiet of her room, she came to some decisions. She would call Luke. He seemed to be a nice, okay guy. She did want to get to know him. But she also wanted to know the name of the art school he was going to attend in Chicago. She decided she wanted to get as far from Atlanta and the hurts she'd experienced as possible. If Rachel had her way, she would walk across the stage, get her diploma, and run for the airport so she could shake the dust of Atlanta off her feet. On her decision tree was keeping in touch with her father but no one else needed to know, not even her little sister. She figured her father would tell Sara about her decision. There definitely would be no visits to her mother, no cards, no letter, no pictures, no nothing. Even as the image of her mother came up in her mind, she started cursing and swearing. Finally she yelled!

"I'm so done with her."

Rachel got off her bed and moved to her desk. She sat down in front of her computer and starting searching for art schools in Chicago. She found a dozen and quickly realized her next task was to call Luke. She eyed her phone, found his number, punched in his digits, and waited as the phone rang. "Hello."

"Hey...is this Luke?"

"Yeah, who's this?"

"This is Rachel."

"Hey, Rachel, so you decided to call after all?"

Rachel wasn't sure how she felt about his comment. Nonetheless, she replied, "You don't sound too pleased. I could hang up if I'm bothering you."

"No, no...I'm fine. I'm glad you called.

"How about getting together with me sometime?" There was silence for a short time. Rachel didn't want to sound too eager. After an elongated pause,

"Yeah, okay...I'm going to be at the Lenox Square mall again tomorrow. We could hang out for a little while at Starbucks. Actually, I have a few questions to ask you."

Luke was shocked but he kept his tone even, trying not to express his enthusiasm with her reply. "Tomorrow's great, what time works for you?"

"How about around four p.m.?"

"Okay, I'll be there and I can try to answer any questions you have for me."

As Rachel ended the call, she wondered if she had done the right thing.

CHAPTER
TWENTY-SIX

RACHEL'S GRADUATION COMMENCEMENT WENT OFF without a hitch. Rachel sat in a hot auditorium with four hundred of her classmates through some boring speeches that were meant to inspire. She waited in a long line until she walked across the stage and received her diploma. Later, outside, her father took pictures of her and, just like that, the day was a memory. She didn't want to talk to her fellow classmates, say goodbye to her teachers, or go out to eat. She simply wanted to get rid of her cap and gown, go home, and let the day slip away.

When her father pulled the car into the driveway, she hopped out, ran upstairs, changed her clothes, and got on to her computer. For the next hour, she looked at pictures online and listened to music. She looked at her phone and realized that she had a text message from Luke. She and Luke had become fast friends. She's seen him a bunch of times, given him her number, and confided in him that she too wanted to study art in Chicago. While she was clear she wasn't looking for a boyfriend, Luke loved the idea of her being at the same art school. So, he gave her all of the information she needed in order to get registered. While she hadn't been accepted yet, she felt it would be a matter of time.

Rachel moved away from her computer, put her phone down, and noticed the gifts on the other side of her bed. She could tell from the handwriting that one gift was from her father and the other was from Sara. She was about to open them when she saw another envelope. Her curiosity caused her to pick it up. She examined it and saw it only had her name printed in the front of the envelope. She tore it open and saw there was another envelope inside. It was addressed to her from her mother. Once she realized that, she immediately flung it across the room. The shock of receiving a letter from her mother was more than she could handle. She got up, took her phone, and literally ran out of her room.She sent Luke a text message saying, *Meet me at the mall in twenty minutes.*He responded back saying, *Okay, see you at Starbucks.*She bolted down the stairs saying,

"Dad, can I use the car?"

From the back of the house, he called back,

"Where are you going?"

"I'm going to the mall."

"When will you be back?"

"How about in two hour?"

"Fine…be careful."Rachel found a parking spot, hopped out, and went in to the mall looking for Luke. When she got to the coffee shop, she found him sitting down, waiting for her.

"Hey Rachel, how're you doing?"She threw her purse into the chair next to her and fell into her seat.

"Fine…I'm doing fine."

She was angry and she didn't care how she came across to him.

"Wait a minute, something's going on. I've never seen you like this before. What's happening?"Rachel sat there looking off in space, then she looked down at the table, and finally she blurted out,

"I received a letter from my Mother."

She knew her explanation wouldn't be enough. She watched Luke shrug his shoulders and say,

"Okay, you got a letter from your mother. What's the big deal? What did it say?"

Rachel realized she had to provide some response but she didn't want to. She was silent for a moment. Then she said,

"I didn't open it."Rachel watched Luke tilt his head with a quizzical look on his face."Why not? You received a letter from your mother. You don't open the letter but you're upset. That makes no sense. I'm totally confused."

Rachel thought to herself, *I haven't told him about my mother the jailbird. I'm not sure how he's going to react to this new information. But, I might as well get it out, get it over with.*

"My mother's in prison."Now she studied Luke carefully. She waited to see the shocked look on his face. But it never came. He did say,

"Okay, everybody's related to someone or knows someone who's in prison. Why are you stressing?"

"I'm not stressing. I don't want her in my life."

"Really...what's the big deal?"

"She broke the law, got put in jail, and it broke up our family."

"You know, I don't know your mother but I bet she probably regrets whatever she did."

"I don't care. I don't want her in my life ever again."

"Okay, but because you read a letter doesn't mean that are going to see her again or talk to her. What would be the harm in reading her letter?"Rachel looked out the window. She focused on the people who were walking pass the coffee shop. Luke's question continually rattled around in her head, *"what would be the harm with reading her letter?"* The more she thought about it, the more she realized the truth of his question. She thought, *I would simply be reading her stupid letter. It won't change anything, she still in jail. I'm not going to see her and I'm still leaving Atlanta.* She looked over at Luke. Then she studied her fingernails for no particular reason. All of a sudden, she looked up and said,

"How did you get so smart? It's true what you said about the letter...thanks."

"No worries...I'm trying to help you."

"I know, I know…I appreciate it, okay?"
"Did you get your acceptance letter to the art school yet?"
"What? No, I haven't."
"Have you changed your mind about going?"
"Absolutely not…I could leave this afternoon."

CHAPTER
TWENTY-SEVEN

J ACK WAS AMAZED AT HOW well the board presentation went. He had prepared for every possible contingency. He had reviewed the finite details with Len to make sure he didn't get blindsided. In addition, he had taken the time to talk to the key board members well in advance of the actual board meeting. As was his practice, he rehearsed his presentation out loud several times, using his unique skill for essentially memorizing the key elements so he could present without looking at the slides. Others had commented over the years about this obvious talent of his, a combination of nature and nurture. Jack had excelled at public speaking since before high school. He'd joined the debate team in college and before long he was selected to be on the first team. People were amazed at the volume of information and details he could remember and recite at the right time. When he entered the business world, one of his first managers had recognized his talent and had encouraged him. Jack was best during the Q&A portion. Not only could he segment the question, but he would also frame the answers in a manner that caused the person to feel that it was the most important question. At the same time, he was able to draw in his audience in such a way they hung on his every word. Even his naysayers had to agree that Jack was a skillful presenter.After the two-hour board presentation, Jack was exhausted. But he knew Len would want to de-brief. As the meeting broke up, many of the board members told Jack how much they appreciated the clarity of his presentation. Len moved close to Jack and whispered to him,

"Let's walk over to my office as soon as we are done here. I want to spend a few minutes talking over what happened."

"Great, I'm all for it. I've got one call to make and I'll be there in less than ten minutes." The call was to Gloria. She knew he was presenting to the board. She also realized the significance of the meeting. Earlier, her only request was for Jack to call her after it was over.

Gloria answered her phone on the first ring. "Hey, J...how did it go?"

"Babe, it went great! The board was impressed with the stuff we presented to them."

"So, what did they decide about the acquisition?"

"Come on, Babe, you know I can't say anything about that."

Gloria chuckled into the phone.

"Okay, okay, I'm glad it went well. What time will you be home tonight?"

"I should be there by 6:30 pm."

"Okay, see you then, love you."

"I love you too." As Jack hung up, he realized again how important Gloria was to him and how much he loved her. She'd been in the corporate world, rising to the role of group vice president in an international bank before she left it all behind. She now invested all of her efforts in helping other women and spending time with her elderly parents. But she'd been with Jack through thick and thin. There wasn't one thing Jack couldn't talk to her about. He happened to turn and glance out of his ceiling-to-floor windows at Lake Michigan. Among other things, he could make out what looked like a female swimmer making her way south. The swimmer was steady and consistent. Each precise stroke was like a metronome. It reminded him of Gloria, steady and solid. He knew he could always rely on her.

***

When Jack got to Len's office, he was on the phone so Jack took a seat. After about two minutes, Len finished his call. He sat back in his chair and said,

"So Jack, what was your assessment? And what were the highlights?"

Jack didn't hesitate.

"Len, you handled the meeting in superior fashion."

"You think so?"

"Absolutely. For me, there were two distinct highlights. The first one was when they unanimously agreed that we should acquire JSL. And the second was their overall approval of our plan. That was essentially what I got before they asked me to leave the room."

"Jack thanks, but you know that's board protocol for you to leave. As CEO, there are certain things they will convey only to me."

"No, I get that."

"For what it's worth, Jack, they were singing your praises. Nice job."

"Thanks, Len. I promised some time ago to give you my best."

They talked about a few other details. Len asked a couple more questions, and Jack gave him his assessment. Finally, Len stood up, walked to the other side of the desk, and shook Jack's hand.

"Thanks...now get out of here. I've got fifty other things to finish before the end of the day."

After Jack left, Len paced across the floor a few times. Whenever he had something weighing on his mind, this was his practice. He started to ponder his relationship with Jack. Len thought, *Jack's a great guy. Looking back, I'm glad I hired him and promoted him. He's always been exceptionally loyal to me. I have no doubt he'll continue to do well. I wonder…if I give him this role as President of JSL, how long before he'll be after my job? I wonder…should I rethink my decision?*

***

Len's eyes were on the road but his thoughts were on the events of the last week. It had been a whirlwind of activities and they had literally flown by. He was glad that is was Friday. He was looking forward to spending the weekend with his wife and kids at their cottage. There would be no weekend conference calls and he didn't have to go out of town until Tuesday. So he was thrilled that this would be all family time.

But as he drove home, he reflected on the big items that had to be decided. It was basically unanimous. Universal would move forward with the acquisition of JSL Consulting. The presentation he and Jack made to the Board of Directors was brilliant. There were no naysayers and virtually everyone felt it would significantly complement the offerings of Universal. While there had been some questions regarding personnel, what types of people to keep and to let go, Jack had anticipated every question and his presentation addressed every point. The only outstanding questions were when to acquire and who would run the company. The board told Len they would approve whomever he selected. It was a tremendous vote of confidence. The issue for Len was he had a dilemma. Jack was the best candidate for the job. He was heads and shoulders above all the other members of his leadership team. But Len had come to rely on Jack for every special project and assignment that came up. He knew he could trust him, and Jack was very good. His research abilities were superior, he was a great financial businessman, and he gave presentation like no one else he had ever seen. Len realized that for all those reasons, and many others, it was time to allow Jack to spread his wings. Len drove along the Kennedy expressway in the fast lanes. The sun had gone down below the horizon. But he could still see the affects of it. The sky was a combination of azure, pink, indigo, and marigold. He kept his eyes on the road but they were constantly diverted by what he saw in the sky to the left of him. Occasionally, he would see a plane or two preparing to land at the O'Hare airport. As he drove north he thought, *Chicago is a great city and spring is such a special time. It was as if the sun was giving birth to its children, a vast array of colors. They were giving notice that it was their time to burst forth and go out on their own. This is exactly the case for Jack. It's time for him to move up and move on. I don't know how I will fill his current role but I realize it is time to name him President of JSL.*

With the decision finally made, he started to think about other elements that still needed to be worked out. Among others, he would have to talk to Jack, get a read on whether he was interested in the role. Len thought, *this will be a very good weekend.*

CHAPTER

TWENTY-EIGHT

ONE WEEK LATER

J **ACK'S CELL PHONE WENT OFF.** He looked down and saw that it was Len's executive assistant, Sandy.

"Hey, Sandy, how are you, what's up?"

"Hi Jack, Len would like to meet with you at four this afternoon. Your calendar indicated that you had thirty minutes then. Is that still an okay time?"

"Yeah, Sandy, I can meet him then. Is there an agenda for the meeting?"

"Nope, he said he wanted to talk with you. Should I ask him for a topic?"

Jack knew Len often had random things he needed to discuss with Jack. However, he would generally have a pre-planned agenda. If he didn't give one to Sandy, it would be better not to ask for one. He quickly said to Sandy,

"No, no...that's fine. I'll be there at four p.m." Jack hung up the phone still wondering what Len wanted to talk about. In all the years he'd worked with him, there hadn't been an instance where he wanted to meet without telling him what the agenda was. Since he trusted Len, he decided not to worry. It was 11:00 a.m and he had a ton to finish before his meeting. So, he let it go and went to the next thing he needed to address.

A few minutes before four, Jack was standing at Sandy's desk."-

Jack, someone had an emergency that required Len's attention. He should be done in about five minutes."

"No problem, I'm happy to wait. By the way, how've you been?" Sandy had been Len's executive assistant since Jack had come to work at Universal. She was nice enough but clearly a "no nonsense person." Len had told Jack that Sandy was worth her weight in gold. Sandy was in her mid-forties. At about five foot five, she was in decent shape. She rarely smiled but when she did, she communicated warmth. Her pug nose seemed to balance her big eyes. Her jet-black hair was always in place and never showed a sign of greying. This was apparently the result of frequent visit to the beauty shop. She'd been married over twenty years and she simply adored her two college-age twin daughters. One time they came to the office to take their mother to lunch. To see Sandy with her daughters was like watching a totally different person. She was outstanding at her job. Rarely, if ever, was anything out of line or mishandled by Sandy. Also, if she called anyone requesting anything, you simply complied. No one ever wanted to be on Sandy's bad side.

Sandy liked Jack. It was probably because Len made it known that he thought Jack was a great asset to his leadership team. She always communicated with Jack in a respectful manner. She was never rude or abrupt with him.

Sandy hung up the phone and looked over where Jack was sitting. "Jack, Len told me he would be out in two or three more minutes. Can I get you something, coffee, water, or juice?"

"No, I'm fine." He was content to read his emails on his smartphone. The door to Len's office opened and Len and Edmond Pearson walked out. Len said,

"So, Ed thanks for bringing that to my attention. Let me know if there are any new developments."

"No problem, I sure will." Edmond turned and saw Jack.

"Hey, Jack, how are you? I heard that you stole the show at the board meeting."

"I was just trying to put the boss in the best light."

"Well, guys, have a great day. Sandy, thanks for getting me in so quickly."

"Happy to help, no problem,"Len turned to Jack.

"Come on in and sit down." Before he closed the door, he said to his assistant. "Sandy, change my flight to San Fran to later in the day, around one or one-thirty p.m. There's one other thing that's come up. I'll tell you about it when I'm done here."Jack walked in but stood until Len sat down. Since Jack didn't know what the meeting was all about, he decided that a clue might be where Len sat. Len took a seat at the smaller conference table. Jack sensed that it would be more of a relational meeting.Jack didn't say a word, letting Len start."Jack, how are things with you and Gloria?"

Jack thought, *Now that's an odd question. He couldn't have called me over to his office just to ask how Gloria and I are doing. What's going on?*

"We're doing as well as could be expected. You know we keep getting those mysterious letters I told you about. Other than that, we're fine. To take her mind off of it, Gloria's planning our next vacation. If I had to guess, it's probably going to be Maui. She loves that place."

"Those anonymous letters…I thought they had stopped. What did the police do about it?"

"There's nothing they can do about it. They can't figure out where they're coming from."

"Did they have them analyzed?"

Yep, and there is nothing there that points them in the direction of a culprit. Truthfully, Gloria was a little bit spooked. So getting away is a good thing."

"Jack, how many have you gotten since last you told me about them?

"Probably two, maybe three"

"What did the last ones say?"

"That's just the thing…they're a little goofy. It's as if they are being written to somebody else."

"Like what?"

"Well, this last one said, 'You can run but you can't hide'. We aren't running from anything or anyone. The one before that said, 'Your wife is not safe.' "

"How many have you gotten?"

"Len, I think this is the sixth one."

"I didn't realize that. Tell me again, how long has this been happening?

"It has been over five or six years."

"Is there any pattern to the arrival of the letters? Who do the letters come to, you or Gloria?"

"Yeah, they show up every year, at the same time and they always come to me. At first, I told myself I won't show them to Gloria. But when the third one came, I thought she should know." Jack hesitated. Then he added. "I wish I hadn't showed them to her because it really freaked her out."

"When do they show up?

"They always arrive on the anniversary of when I lost my job at DTA?

"What? Are you sure?"

"Yeah, I went back and checked. It's the same day."

"Jack, I hate to bring this up. But do you think this has any thing to do with Catherine Frazier?"

"I thought about that possibility. I've had extensive conversations with the police and the FBI about it. The answer is no. She's in federal prison and all of her correspondence is monitored by prison personnel. She can't send out anything without it being observed."

"I don't want to tell you what to do. But, as I said before, it sounds like it's a stupid, silly prank."

"Yeah, but why on the anniversary of me leaving DTA? If it weren't for that aspect, I'd tend to agree with you. So, I continue to keep the authorities aware. Thanks for listening. So, why did you want to talk to me? I know you had something else on your mind besides my vacation plans. What's up?"

Jack noticed that Len leaned back in his chair as he started."-Yeah, well, as you know, the board has approved me naming a president to run JSL once we acquire it. I want your opinion about who it should be, or whether we should look for an outside candidate. What do you think?"Jack thought, *so this was Len's agenda. I knew he would eventually want to unpack this topic. Who we name as the president for an important acquisition like this one will be huge. I'm way ahead of him on this one. I've got some options for him to consider.*

"Got it. The very first element is to send the right signal to the market and the analysts. If we hire someone, anyone, from the outside, we're saying we don't have the *gravitas* within Universal to handle this move."

Jack focused on Len's manner as he put both elbows on the table and folded his hands together. It told him that Len was in a very serious mood."You think so?"

"Absolutely...it would be the worse move of all worse moves." Jack waited to give Len an opportunity to mull over his comments. It didn't take him long.

"Actually, I agree. So who do you recommend?"

Jack took a deep breath because he knew Len would have his list of candidates as well.

"Two possible candidates come to mind for different reasons, Toni Lucas and Edmond."Jack hesitated to see how Len would respond. Len came right back and said, "Interesting choices. Why those two?"

"Okay, why Toni? She has a strong financial mind, very smart, well respected, and she's run operations in the past. If we want to insure our return on investment, she would be a very good choice."Jack watched his mannerisms. He looked straight at Jack, with one eyebrow lifted above the other, and said,

"How do you balance those attributes against her sometimes

salty disposition? She can turn people off."Jack sat back in his chair.

"That's true…she would need to be counseled on how to be more endearing. Possibly, we could hire a personal coach for her."

"Would you be surprised to know we've done that for the last fourteen months?"

Jack turned his head to one side and narrowed his eyes.

"No, I didn't know that."

"Yes, so based solely on that factor, she might be a bit of a risk."

"I get it."

"So, what were your thoughts about Edmond?"Cautiously, Jack said,

"Edmond is a strong HR guy. We've already talked about his importance in securing the hearts and minds of the right people we want to keep after the acquisition is announced.""I've also thought about that fact, and you're right. His role is an important one."

Given Len's reaction, Jack picked up a head of steam.

"Plus, before I arrived, he had been your go-to guy for special projects. So, he knows his way around."

"Jack, that's also true but he's never run an organization. He doesn't have strong P&L skills. He isn't that great with reading and interpreting a Profit and Loss statement. We could have the right people on board but still lose our shirts."

Jack backed down.

"Great observation…you know him far better than I do. He could come up to speed with some financial counseling, but probably not from Toni." Jack made the last comment with a bit of a smile on his face.

"Frankly, they were the best choices from the leadership team. So, who were the people you considered?"From Len's pensive manner, he knew he had asked the right question. Jack saw him look down, then out the window, and finally looked back at Jack."Jack, in my mind, there is only one choice."

Jack leaned forward and asked,
"Who would that be? Who have I not considered?"Jack watched
as Len took off his glasses, laid them aside, and said,
"You...you are my only choice."

CHAPTER

TWENTY-NINE

HE SAT THERE SPEECHLESS FOR what seemed like several minutes. So many things ran through his head. Jack thought, *Me…he wants me to take the job? Me…he wants me to be the President of JSL? How long has he been considering this? I had actually considered the possibility of me taking the helm but I figured Len would choose someone who had been with him longer. Wow…what would Gloria say?* Finally he spoke."Len, I'm…honored. I'm a little surprised… shocked. Wow, you've obviously given this a lot of thought. How did you come to this conclusion?"

"You've been with me for quite a while. I've tested you in different ways that would have broken the spirit of the average person. In each situation, you've exceeded my expectations. You personally saved Universal hundreds of millions of dollars and a huge embarrassment with the DTA debacle. You're my strongest business executive and the best person to get the post-acquisition stuff done. Plus, above everything else, I trust you."Once again, Jack was speechless. It was true that he worked hard to please Len and become more than proficient in the roles he was asked to fulfill. He thought eventually he would earn the right to run a major portion of universal's business but he didn't fully consider the possibility of being the president of this new acquisition. He believed he could do it. He was surprised Len was thinking of only him to run it. Finally, Jack spoke.

"So what happens now?"

Jack observed Len leaning back in his chair, all the while looking right at Jack.

"I need to know if you want the job. There is no interviewing process. If you want the job, it's yours. I want to be sensitive to the issue about the prank mail you've received. But if you want the job, it's yours"

"Really, just like that?"

"Yeah, just like that."

"Well, from my perspective, the answer is yes. But I need to know how this will alter our relationship."

"Jack, it's time for you to spread your wings. This is your opportunity to do exactly that. I thought about our relationship, the void that would be created, and how things would work out between us."

"Yeah, that's important to me."

Jack realized that this aspect was as important to Len as it was to him. He needed to hear what Len had to say. He wasn't dissatisfied by Len's next comments."It will be fine. You'll still be reporting to me, in a greater capacity. You'll also have dotted line responsibility to the board for updates and financials but all that will only enhance our relationship."

Jack got a curious look on his face and asked,

"You think so?"

"Yes...now what else is bothering you?"

"Nothing...nothing's bothering me. I'll need to talk to Gloria but I know she'll be all for it."

"Great. Nothing will be announced until we have the acquisition approvals from both companies."

"When would you see that happening?"

"You know like I know, we're probably have it all wrapped up in about two weeks. That doesn't give you much time."Jack was starting to feel more comfortable with the whole idea. He offered,

"I'll be fine once I talk to Gloria. Honestly, the biggest concern for me is who will be your new go-to guy for special projects once I've moved on."Jack watched Len get up, walk to his desk, and picked up a document. He said,

"Well, I haven't completely figured it out but I think I'll have two people, Toni and Edmond."Jack put his head in his right hand and smiled as he reflected on Len's comment.

"That's actually not a bad idea. They both need grooming for different reasons. If you need me to help with the transition, let me know."

"You can count on it." Jack realized that Len was starting to stand so Jack stood as well.

"Jack, congratulations, I know you'll do a phenomenal job. So many of the things you and I presented to the board will be your starting point."

With that, Jack reached out, shook Len's hand, and gave him a hug.

He couldn't fight back the tears that started to well up in his eyes. He so appreciated Len and this was one more reason.He wasn't completely ready for Len's next comment.

"You're like a son and a brother to me. I have watched you grow and excel since you've been here and I have the confidence you will continue to do exceptionally well."Jack wiped the tears from his eyes, stood back, and said,

"I am overwhelmed by your faith in me. Thank you. I won't let you down."

"That's the one thing I'm counting on." Len said with a chuckle.

CHAPTER
THIRTY

GLORIA PICKED UP HER PHONE. "Hey, Babe, how are you?"

"How did you know it was me? Are you clairvoyant? Oh, yeah, I forgot about the wonders of caller ID." Jack didn't get a chuckle from his weak attempt at humor. He decided to ask, "How are you?"

"Jack, I'm fine. What's up? I'm trying to finish a few things before you get home."

"Well, I know it is date night tonight but I was wondering if we could sit home this evening."

"Why, what's going on?"

"I've had a busy day today. A few things came up for me and I don't want to talk about them in a noisy restaurant."

Gloria tried not to read too much into his comments.

"Honey, that's fine with me but what's up, what is it? Is something wrong?"

Jack tried to act nonchalant.

"Uh, no...everything's fine. I want to have you all to myself tonight."

"Okay, I'll pull out some leftovers and I'll see you when you get home."

Driving home, Jack was still on an emotional high from his discussion with Len, and he was starting to accept the fact he would soon be named the new president of JSL. He had to monitor his driving speed because he felt like driving at ninety or a hundred miles an hour so he could get home and tell Gloria the terrific news. If he were in *Star Wars*, he could have gone into hyper drive and been home in a matter of seconds. When he finally got out of the car after pulling into the garage, he literally bounded into the house. Gloria was putting the last of the food on the table.

"Oh, hi, hon…wash your hands so we can sit down and eat." As Jack stood in the powder room washing his hands, he thought about how to bring up the conversation. *Should I blurt it all out, or maybe I should slowly ease into it.* He walked into the dining room, took Gloria into his arms, kissed her, and then announced,

"Len wants to promote me to be the new president of the JSL Consulting Division."

"What…what did you say?"

"You heard me. Len wants me to be the president of the newest division of Universal."

"What did you tell him? She looked up at him.

"I told him yes but it would depend on what you said."

***

"Jack, this is wonderful. I'm so proud of you. You've done so well at Universal working for Len."

"Thanks, Babe. I thought you'd be pleased."

"So tell me all the details. When will you be announced as president? Where will your office be? Will you have to travel overseas? If so, can I come with you? Tell me, tell me!"

"Hold it a minute." Jack smiled at her exuberance.

"I'll be named to the role in about two weeks. We still have to work out a ton of the logistics. I'm not sure where my office will be. Yes, I will have to travel overseas a bunch." He hesitated slightly because he knew she wanted to know most about the travel part. "And yes, you will be able to go with me." Gloria started jumping up and down, dancing around the dining room. The excitement flowed from her. She couldn't contain herself.

"Paris, London, Brussels, Rome, Barcelona, Beijing, Tokyo, Berlin, Rio...did I miss any?"

Jack sat there and watched her as she kept smiling and dancing. This went on for a while. When she settled down, she still had this enormous smile on her face and a gleam in her eye. "You tell Len my answer is yes...yes. Should I call him up right now, tonight, and given him my answer? Where's your cell phone?"

Jack smiled. He was excited to see his wife so happy.

"Babe, that won't be necessary. I'll tell him tomorrow morning. It'll be soon enough." Jack said as he took her hand, squeezed, and gave her a kiss.

"Oh my, this is going to be the absolute *bomb*. I can hardly wait."

CHAPTER

THIRTY-ONE
IN CHICAGO - TWO WEEKS LATER

THE ACQUISITION OF JSL CONSULTING by Universal was a big splash in all the papers and other media outlets. The acquisition was viewed the way Len and his leadership team expected. The general opinion in the media was that this consulting model was one of the most important pieces Universal needed in their overall business arsenal. While the SEC needed to approve the deal, the word on the street was this would dramatically drive up both the stock price and the market value of Universal. The announcement also indicated that Jack Alexander would be president of the new JSL Consulting division, reporting to the CEO of Universal and the board of directors during the first year.

Everyone on the leadership team was excited about the way things were progressing except for CFO Toni Lucas. Within an hour of the official announcement, Toni was in Len's office. Len could immediately tell her feathers were ruffled. "Jack is a better candidate than I am? I don't think so. I shouldn't have to bring this up but I've done more to advance the financials of this company than anyone else has." Len simply sat at his desk staring at her as she went on about how she was undervalued and underappreciated. Finally, he held up his hand, waving it at her. "Look, Toni, the board gave me the authority to hire the candidate I thought best fit the JSL presidency role and I chose Jack."

"I can think of at least a dozen reasons why I'd be a far better candidate."

"I'm sure you can but frankly, Toni, I'm not interested. I made my decision." He let his words hang in the air while Toni sat across from him with her arms folded and steam coming out of her ears. He saw the scowl on her face as she looked at him and said,

"You could have at least given me a little advanced warning that this was going to go down. If you can't tell…I'm not happy!" Len leaned back in his chair, looked at Toni for a few seconds, and then got up and walked around his desk. He sat down in the chair next to her. It forced her to turn and face him. Quietly he said, "Look, for what it's worth, I understand your disappointment. Toni, I value your contribution to the leadership team and Universal. You'll have your opportunities here. You have to be patient."

"Patient…just be patient! I've worked my butt off trying to grow the profit picture for this firm, and this is the thanks I get?"

"Hold on a minute. You've done well in your role as CFO but there were never any promises that this new position would be yours." Len observed the scowl on Toni's face was more evident than ever and she was now sitting on the edge of her chair. He thought her head was going to explode. Nonetheless, Len went on,

"Toni, if it's any consolation to you, I thought about your candidacy and if I hadn't had Jack to consider, I very well might have chosen you." Len noticed that her facial expression totally changed. The scowl left, her body language was more at ease. She moved back in her chair and crossed her legs. Her next comment was,

"Really? You would have selected me if Jack hadn't been in the picture?"

"Well, it would have been a strong consideration. But Jack is in the picture and he is our new president of JSL." Len was amazed that Toni didn't say another word but a twinkle appeared in her eye and a smile came on her face. As she got up from the chair, she simply said,

"Len, thanks for telling me that. For what it's worth, I understand. Sorry I was so hostile. Forgive me, I was out of line."

THIRTY-TWO

AFTER RACHEL FINISHED READING THE letter, she decided she would go visit her mother and listen to what she had to say. Rachel decided she wanted Luke to read the letter. "Read this and tell me what you think." Rachel tossed the letter across the table in Luke's direction. "Don't sugar-coat it…I need to know your thoughts." "Would you like me to go with you to see her? See, I think you need to hear her out."

Rachel was a little surprised at how direct he was and at his offer to go with her. She sat there looking at the letter lying on the table, not focused on the words.

Then she looked up at Luke and said,

"You are still somewhat of a stranger to"

She was surprised when Luke interrupted her.

"Look, I know you don't know me real well. You might be thinking I'm either a kidnapper or an ax murderer. At some point, you have to learn "Still wanting to talk, she jumped in and interrupted Luke.

"Well, I wasn't thinking ax murderer but you could be a kidnapper." She smiled a little and added,

"I don't really know a lot about you. Going across state lines…I don't think so." Rachel shook her head and then gave Luke a doubtful glare.Rachel half laughed as he raised his hands in a surrendered posture.

"Hey, it's cool...I don't need to go with you. You're a big girl. I just thought I'd offer."

Rachel replied,

"Don't get your underwear all tied up in a bundle...I didn't say I didn't want you to go. I'm not sure right now."She smiled but kept watching him as he lowered his hands, picked up his coffee stirrer, and started fiddling with it."What would make you more comfortable? What would make you more at ease with my offer?"Rachel thought for a moment. Then she looked off into space as she said in a contemplative manner,

"I don't know...as a rule I don't trust people."She looked at him as he said,

"How about you coming over and meeting my dad and step-mom? You can talk to them and find out if I'm a social deviant or not. How about it?"

She chuckled and said,

"Why do I need to ask? You *are* a social deviant!"

***

The drive from Atlanta to the Hazelton Prison in Charleston, West Virginia was long but enjoyable for Rachel. Luke did all the driving, which allowed her to appreciate the scenery. They had lots of time to talk about a whole host of topics. She had learned a great deal more about Luke than his parents had told her. In the end, Rachel's dad met Luke and eventually approved the trip. Luke provided Frank with his cell phone, parents' contact information, and a commitment to call him twice each day while they were gone. Frank didn't have to bargain with Rachel about the hotel arrangements. She was the first one to have Luke to commit to staying in a separate room for the one overnight stay.Rachel was still looking out the passenger window when she heard Luke announce,

"We'll be there in about an hour and a half. Do you want to check into the motel or go right to the prison?"She thought for a moment and said,

"I need to take a shower. I'm too grungy right now." She looked at herself in the passenger side mirror.

"In fact, why don't we find a restaurant after I'm done? It will be after four p.m. by the time we get there. I'd rather go there in the morning, see her, and then get out of town.""I'm fine with that. I need to rest up and get a good night's sleep before we head back."

The dinner was not memorable. They settled on ordering one large pizza with every possible topping on it. Luke asked Rachel if she had thought about the conversation she would have with her mother the next day.Rachel was quick to answer.

"I'm not sure, and I don't want to talk about it right now."

She took a break from eating her pizza, looked up at Luke, and heard him abruptly change the subject."Hey, I figured it out, if we leave by 12:00 noon from the prison, we could be back in Atlanta by tomorrow night, no problem."

"That suits me fine."

***

It was well over an hour before Rachel was able to get into the prison and to the place where she would see her mother. Luke agreed that it would be best for him to wait outside. It would likely be too much to explain Luke's presence.

Rachel waited another half an hour in a big open area. In some ways, it reminded her of a low-budget Chipotle. All of the tables were round and made of hard plastic. The metal chairs were riveted to the floor and very uncomfortable to sit in.

Her mother came in wearing her orange prison jumpsuit. When she saw her, she instinctively got up to go and hug her. Then she remembered what the guard had told her, *"There can be no touching or hugging of any kind. If that happens, your visit will be over imme-*

146

diately...no exceptions." The guard knew from the paperwork that Rachel was Catherine's daughter. So he added,

"Frazier has been on her best behavior for several months. So, she is allowed to be in the same room with her visitors instead of being behind a Plexiglas separator and talking on a phone." Rachel was thankful for that because she'd found the other arrangement annoying."Rachel, honey...it's good to see you. Thanks for coming."

Rachel wasn't sure exactly what to say.

Finally, she blurted out,

"Yeah, uh huh...good to see you too."Rachel was fine with the silence. Nonetheless, she could tell her mother had an agenda and she didn't waste any time."You've gotten so big and tall...so grown up since I saw you last." There was dead silence. Rachel stared at her mother, drumming her fingers on the plastic table like she was bored. She wasn't going to give her mother even the smallest conversational opening. She could tell her mother was struggling to find anything to talk about.

"How was your graduation? I'm so sorry I couldn't be there. Did you bring any pictures?"Rachel leaned back in her chair, showing real distain and disinterest. Her only comments were,

"Fine...you've missed a bunch of things. And no, I didn't bring any pictures."Her mother's face took on a serious look. Her eyebrows furrowed up and she spit out,

"Look, I know you hate me, and I probably deserve it. I haven't been in your life the way either of us wanted me to be. For whatever its worth, I'm truly sorry."

Rachel sat there with a blank stare, said nothing, but then her facial expression softened a bit. Still, she refused to give her mother an opening for dialog. To her surprise, her mother pressed on."I asked you to come here because I realize you are a young lady now...a young adult with a mind of your own. So, I want to tell you a few things."In spite of the fact that she had willed herself to not show any interest, she asked,

"What is it that you want to tell me?"

"Well. It's basically a story. I need you to promise you will listen to the whole thing before you comment...okay?"Rachel pondered her request. Then she said in a flippant fashion,

"Okay."

For the next forty minutes or so, Catherine explained to her daughter all of the events that led to her being incarcerated. With each detail, she portrayed Jack Alexander as a real monster, the scum of the earth. She wove the tale so Rachel would see her mother as a loving person.Rachel could tell her mother had come to the end of the story."So, you see I was depicted to be someone that I wasn't. For all these years, I've suffered for something I wasn't responsible for. And this Jack Alexander person ruined our lives."

There was a protracted period of silence. Catherine waited to see Rachel's reaction. Rachel wasn't sure what to say or how to feel. All of a sudden, Rachel's eyes clouded over and tears started running down her face. The next thing that happened shocked even Catherine. Rachel started moaning. At first, it was barely audible. Little by little, her moan turned into a scream. She was screaming, crying, and moaning all at the same time. She put her head down on the plastic table and became inconsolable. The guards came over thinking she had suddenly taken ill. But Catherine assured them she'd be fine. One of them brought Rachel some Kleenex and a cup of water. Then he left them alone.

CHAPTER
THIRTY-THREE

LUKE WAS SITTING OUT IN the prison parking lot the whole time Rachel was inside. He was speculating how the conversation was going. He sat in the car with all the windows rolled down since it was a hot day in West Virginia. He held up one arm and could see the perspiration rings right through his shirt. But in order to conserve gasoline, he refused to turn on the car's air conditioner. Finally, out of desperation, he turned on the AC. Instantly, he started to feel cooler and wished he had turned it on much earlier. As he started to feel cooler, he reflected on the past events with Rachel.Luke thought deeply about him having been one of the boys who had laughed and ridiculed Rachel when she was in the seventh grade. Not long after that, his parents moved to the other side of Atlanta since his dad had to report to a different army office and it was too far for him to travel each day. It turned out his new school was the same new school Rachel's dad had moved Rachel and her sister Sara to. Luke saw her from time to time. Later he saw her in high school, but since he was a year ahead of her, they were never in the same classes. He realized his stupidity but he was still too embarrassed to approach her. He reasoned that she wouldn't remember him but he didn't want to take a chance.When he saw her at the art exhibit, he was reluctant to say anything to her. After pushing back his fears, he decided it was time to meet her. He knew most of the story about her mother. It didn't matter to him. At one point, after he met her, he was going tell her who he was; that he knew her mother was in prison. He wanted her to know that he had made up the story about being in Atlanta for only three years, and how horrible he felt about hurting her feelings. After Rachel told him about the letter, he decided he didn't need to reveal himself. It also provided him with a way to make amends by offering to drive her to West Virginia. He had come to the conclusion long before the trip that he really liked Rachel. He liked her smile and how her brown, hazel eyes lit up whenever she talked about her fascination with art or a new song she'd heard. He found himself checking her out whenever he dropped her off at home as she walked away from the car. Even so, he was always respectful to her. He once brushed his hand across hers as they walked from the coffee shop but nothing ever came of it. So, he wasn't sure when he would try to put the moves on her but he determined he'd take a first stab on their drive back to Atlanta.

***

"So...what am I supposed to do with what you've told me?" Rachel tried talking as she finished blowing her nose and wiping the last, few remaining tears from her face. She was a wreck. All of the blubbering had had smeared her heavy, Goth makeup. She looked a little like one of the Alice Cooper band members, maybe Alice Cooper himself.Through her weeping and smeared makeup, she heard her mother respond.

"Right now...I want you to know how that Jack Alexander ruined my life...our lives."

"Okay...I get that. But what I am supposed to do about it? All of that stuff happened, you're in prison, and so, now what?"

There was stillness between them for a lengthy period of time. Rachel saw how her mother was looking around trying to determine who else could possibly hear her. The sound of her mother's voice was reduced to a whisper.

"Look, honey, I'm coming up for parole soon based on my good behavior. I could be out of here in a few months versus a few years. I've had all these years to figure out how best to retaliate, to make him pay for all the pain and hurt he's caused me...us. The first part of this plan was put in place even before the first day of my prison sentence."

"What? What did you do?"

"I can't tell you right now. But you should know I can't stop now. The plan has already been put in motion."

Rachel's eyes started to fill up again with tears. She looked straight into her mother's eyes and spouted out,

"And then you'll find yourself right back here for an even worst crime, and maybe forever. I couldn't handle that. Why don't you drop all this bitterness and resentment?"

"Rachel, that's not ever going to happen." She lowered her voice even more. She looked to be mouthing the words, "I have a foolproof plan, but I'll need your help."Rachel's eyes got big as saucers.

"Mom, I can't...I can't do something illegal. I'm hurt and angry about what this Jack Alexander guy did to us. But I can't knowingly break the law and maybe wind up in jail."Rachel listened as her mother offered,

"So, we let him get away with what he did to us? Was that you crying your eyes out? Was it my imagination or weren't you deeply injured by what he did?"

Rachel sat there looking down at the balled-up tissue paper. She realized for the first time that her reality of what happened and the convincing story her mother told her were very different. This faceless man had wrecked her life. The more she thought about it, the more she realized that her mother had a point. He shouldn't get away with this. She needed to do something, take some action. She looked up and said,

151

"So what do you want me to do?"

***

It was a long ride back to Atlanta. Rachel was thankful that Luke didn't probe for details on how the visit went and all the things they covered.She listened to him ask only once,

"Was it worth it...was the trip worth it?"

As they rode along the interstate, she looked out the window and taking her time before she answered.

Then she turned to face him and answered,

"Yes...yes it was."

THIRTY-FOUR

"**O**KAY, I HEAR YOU LOUD and clear." Len listened intently as he sat waiting for the boarding announcement for his flight. After he heard all that he needed to, he said,

"Marty, I'm with you. For what it's worth, I realize we need to move quickly. I'll talk to Jack and we'll put things in motion." He started writing in his notebook as he continued listening. Then he added,

"Got it…look they called my flight. I've got to go but I'll keep you posted."

***

Jack's executive assistant Beth was working hard at setting up his itinerary. It was going to be extremely rigorous. He was going to be traveling to multiple overseas locations. At each JSL office, he would meet with the country leaders, hold a town meeting with all the employees, and talk to key customers and prospects, and converse with local government officials. In the end, each stop would last a minimum of three or four days. Jack hoped he would finish the entire tour in three months. Len didn't tell him he had to, Jack decided it was the best way.

"So, when are you leaving for the first set of meetings overseas?" Len asked him at the end of one of their briefings. "I'm not pushing you, I need to know in case the board asks me."

Len observed Jack as he waited for his reply. He needed to handle this discussion in the best possible way.

"I'll be leaving in about a week or so. It's a function of how quickly I can get my visa in order."

Len cleared his throat before he spoke next. He sensed this might be a difficult interchange.

"I understand you are planning to take Gloria with you?"Len knew this would cause Jack to react, and it did. He looked up from the papers he was putting back in his briefcase. He stopped and looked at Len in a curious way."Len, that's a strange question. You've known right from the start that Gloria was going to go with me. She's excited about this trip. Have you got a problem with her going now?"Len furrowed his brow, leaned back in his chair for a moment, then got up, and walked from behind his desk.

"Jack, let those papers go for a moment, come over here, and sit down." Len took a seat at the informal side table in his office. Len watched him carefully as he got up and moved to the table.

"What is this all about?"Len didn't say anything for a moment. He crossed his legs.

"Jack, I've always leveled with you. We have had very open, honest conversations right from the start. So, this one will be no different."

"Okay...what gives? What the problem?"

"Jack, I think it's a bad idea for you to take Gloria with you. The more I've thought about it, the more I realize she will likely be a real distraction for you. This role is important to you, to me, to the entire company. You can't afford to have anything, or anyone, that might throw you off your game."Len could tell that Jack was confused. Len noticed that Jack didn't say a word nonetheless he sat there rubbing his forehead with his left hand

and looking down at the table. Also, he made no attempt to hide the frown on his face.

Len continued,

"Look, Jack, I know Gloria's delighted about the possibility of going overseas with you. I'm sure in her mind it's like a second honeymoon. I know if the situation were reversed, my wife would."Len couldn't recall the last time Jack interrupted him in mid-sentence."But it's not your...it's mine. I've been in the role for less than a month and you've already started second guessing me. I realize how important this is. I understand what's at stake. You wouldn't have given me this role if you didn't think I was up to the challenge. Taking Gloria won't be a distraction. I can handle it."Len didn't immediately reply. With his furrowed brows, it was clear to Len that Jack was worked up. Knowing Jack as he did, Len realized Jack was trying to keep his cool. Len was about to give him a response when Jack held up both hands.

"Okay, okay...I realize you are only thinking of my highest good here. Let's back up. What else is going on here that you aren't saying?"Len uncrossed his legs and sat forward in his chair.

"Good question. All right, I'm getting rumblings that there are some overseas customers that are unhappy with the sale and are thinking of finding a different consulting firm. Also, we knew we'd have some employees who would be super nervous about their jobs. However, we're getting reports that resignations are happening at a greater rate than we anticipated."Len observed Jack's manner and posture change as he described the situation at hand. These circumstances were real and had to be dealt with. Len was a bit surprised when Jack took out his smartphone, opened the "Notes app, and said,

"I've got some ideas about how we shore up these issues but I want to hear what you think we should do."For the next thirty minutes, they went back and forth about how best to address the problems. Nothing had changed. It was like they had communicated over concerns in the past. When they finished it was clear that they had a strategy to head off any potential dilemmas, and they were in one accord.Len believed they had made some significant headway. So, he wasn't thrown off when Jack got up to leave, he was the first one to speak."Len, I'm sorry for losing my head earlier. It's just that""No, no. Jack, I was a little out of line. I shouldn't have brought this whole thing up the way I did. You're a grown man. I should have approached it differently. It's me who needs to say I'm sorry."

Neither of them said anything but looked at each other.Len waited until his last words sunk in, all the time observing Jack's manner. Len listened as he said,

"I appreciate our discussion on the topic. I realize now that you were right...taking Gloria would be a distraction. However small, she would still be a potential hindrance. I know I would have to accommodate her needs in every city. She would be expecting me to spend time with her regardless of how much she might deny it."

Len didn't say a word. He simply listened. Jack continued,

"I wanted her to go with me in order to appreciate the experience with me. In hindsight, it would be better for her to go with me once JSL settles down. You hit me with all that and I overreacted."

"Jack, you're a very level-headed guy. It's one of the reasons I decided to make you the president. I like Gloria...always have. She's a neat lady. I want you to come through this initial period with no blemishes." He waited for Jack to comment. When he didn't, Len continued,

"Look, she'll be able to join you on lots of trips once you get fully immersed into the job. Len hesitated for a few seconds before his next remark. Jack, are you concerned about those mysterious letters you've gotten? Are you feeling Gloria may be in danger if you leave her alone for so long?"

Len closely checked Jack's body language to see how he reacted to the question. He watched as Jack ponder the inquiry before he spoke.

"Yes. I thought about the fact that Gloria would be with me overseas and away from any possible harm. I don't think anything will happen but it was my safeguard. Those letters have been pretty creepy."

"So...?"

"I'm going to talk to her tonight. Trust me...I need to know that she will feel safe while I'm gone. Also, she's had her heart set on this. This won't be an easy conversation.

THIRTY-FIVE

PREDICATED ON THE DISCUSSION WITH Len and before the itinerary was finalized, Jack held a series of short videoconferences with both the Americas and the overseas offices. He determined that this would be a good stopgap measure until he could arrive at each location. Some sessions went well and others clearly had issues. One of the purposes of the videoconferences was to determine which locations had the biggest potential issues. He and Beth re- organized his route so he could get to the "hot spots" first. With the travel schedule figured out, he now needed to face Gloria.

***

"Hey, Babe, how is your day?"

"It's going fine…I exchanged that dress I showed you the other night. I decided on a different one to take on the trip. Since tonight is date night, I figured I'd get your opinion before we head out to eat or would you like to stay in tonight?"

"Uh, the more I think about it, let's stay in tonight. It's been a long day and I'm really beat."

"Hey, I'm fine with that. I actually have some other outfits to show you. So, what time will you be home?" Jack thought about how to broach the subject of the trip.

"Babe, I'll be home around seven" Uh, okay.

Hey, no big deal…I'll find something for us to eat tonight. See you at seven.

"Yeah…see you then. Love you, Babe."

***

"Wow…that was fast. I couldn't believe it when I heard the garage door go up. You must have been speeding on your way home."- Jack walked in from the garage trying, in his mind, to put the final changes to the speech he was going to give his wife about her not going on the trip with him."Yep…I was in a hurry to get home to you. Let me wash my hands and I'm ready to eat."It didn't take long before they were sitting at the table, eating, and sharing small talk.

Jack watched Gloria's manner and could tell that she wanted to know what was on his mind. It didn't take her very long.

"Okay…out with it. I can always tell when something's on your mind. What's going on?"

Jack took a deep breath and jumped in.

"Look…it's not going to work out for you to go on the overseas trip. As much as I'd like it to work out, it's not the right time. I'm sorry, Babe, and I hope you'll understand."It was as if time stopped. Jack held his breath and watched Gloria's expression. Initially it was shock, then hurt, and finally sadness. She didn't say anything. She just looked at him. In her eyes, he saw betrayal. He knew she'd been counting on this trip, planning for it, and directing all of her thoughts around it. He waited and didn't say a word. He decided he would allow her the opportunity to process her hurt and then speak whatever was on her mind. Jack could hear the seconds ticking away from the small clock, an heirloom they kept in the dining room where they sat. Normally, Gloria was quick to speak her mind. But as Jack looked her in the eyes, she was fighting back tears. Yet knowing her as he did, he knew she wouldn't cry and would strive for understanding first."Jack what happened?" She hadn't called him Jack in years and only when she was upset or disappointed with him. Jack continued to look her straight in the eyes and said,

"Babe...we are in some deep waters here. There are offices where people are resigning in mass and customers are making noise that they may leave and take their business to another firm. If I can't stabilize the organization, we will have lost before we gt started. After all is said and done, I need every possible moment when I'm in those countries to secure our revenues and keep the employees we need to run each of these operations." Jack stopped because he wanted to give his wife an opportunity to ingest his comments and respond. He noticed her eyes were less watery. That fact alone was a good thing. "You're basically saying my presence would be a distraction?"

Jack knew what he said next would be catastrophic or conciliatory. He took some extra time to weigh his answer. "Babe, first and foremost, I love you. You are my wife and I am totally committed to you. No job on earth is more important to me than you and our marriage. Yet, if we jointly agreed that this new job should be the one I take, then I need to be diligent to perform the role as best I can. If you've changed your mind about me in this role, please tell me and I'll figure out how to change things." Jack sat absolutely still, looked at his wife, and waited. While there had been obvious tension in the room, it was clear that now it had lessened somewhat. He was ready for whatever she said. She had been sitting across from him at the dining table. She proceeded to get up and sit closer to him. His hands were on the table. She reached over, and touched them.

"I get it. It is a big, huge disappointment but I get it. I wouldn't want you to feel obligated to take time away from the primary reason for going overseas to spend time with me." Her voice was soft but she was very resolute. Jack continued looking right in her eyes and softly said,

"Look...Babe, you mean the world to me. This was hard"

She interrupted him.

"I know you. So I know it was hard for you to come home and tell me this. I knew this wouldn't be a cake walk. Honestly, in the back of my mind I was thinking all along that this was too good to be true."

"Well, why didn't you say anything before?"

"I was hoping somehow it would all work out." She stopped and took a long sigh. Then she said,

"Jack, I'm a big girl. I'm not going to crumble over this. You've got to go do what you've got to do. You need my faith in you and your decisions."

"Babe, there is one more thing. He hesitated for a few seconds before he spoke.

"I'm also concerned that you'll be freaked out being here alone for such a long time while I'm traveling. Those anonymous letters have me really nervous about your safety."

There was silence in the room for a long extended period where they both looked at each other. Neither said anything but they both understood the significance of the moment.Finally, Jack broke the silence.

"Babe, I love you. You are the best woman a guy could ever have."

They stood up and hugged each other. Gloria reached over, turned off the lights, and they walked upstairs to bed leaving the food and all the dishes on the table.

THIRTY-SIX

"**S**O WHAT IS IT YOU want us to do exactly?"

"Do I need to spell it out for you? I want you to do what you've done before; nothing more, nothing less."

"Ok...who's the target and when do you want this to go down?"

"All the details are in the package I gave you. Everything you need to know is included."

He looked down at the package in his hands. He fingered it and was about to break the seal.

"Don't open that here. You'll have plenty of time to go through the contents later."

He looked up and asked,

"What about payment?"

"When you open the package later, you'll see that it's all taken care of. Oh, and one more thing. Make sure you contact me using the agreed method once everything's been handled."He waited to see if there were any other instructions.

"Understood?"

He nodded and said, "I completely understand." As Jonah Broderick walked back to his car parked two blocks away, he knew what he needed to do.

THIRTY-SEVEN

BUSINESS CLASS WAS COMFORTABLE ENOUGH. While it didn't have all the perks of first class, it was way above economy class in terms of comfort, food, and service. Certainly, the price difference made up for it. But at the end of the day, business class overseas travel, done right, was largely about comfort in your seat. It's not like sleeping in your own bed but it allowed you to stretch out. Plus, you get blankets, pillows, and ear plugs. Nothing could take away the constant hum of the jet engines but the ear plugs definitely helped. Then there was the jet lag. Jack had been on many overseas flights for both business and pleasure. He'd been to Europe, Africa, the Far East, and the South Pacific. He'd tried several techniques but he couldn't find a way to conquer jet lag. He'd heard it all, don't go to sleep, get off the plane early in the morning, stay awake until night and sleep normally. That didn't work. Then: force yourself to sleep on the plane, have some wine, wake up an hour or two before the plane lands, go to the lavatory, freshen up, you'll function all day and have no jet lag. That hadn't worked either.

So Jack was simply resigned to being jet-lagged when he arrived at the first of his overseas destinations. JSL Consulting had opened its London office as the first overseas location. Since it was the first and the oldest, it had grown to be the largest, the highest revenue producer, and the most profitable. The word inside JSL was, as goes London, so goes the rest of the overseas operation. The one exception was China. Everyone felt that the sky was the limit with the Chinese market. But for now, London was Jack's first stop on the trolley. The three things he had to achieve during this trip were keeping the employees they wanted to retain from leaving, holding on to the largest clients from the existing customer base, and making sure the local government officials knew that Universal Systems was committed to the stability of the London operation.

Jack was scheduled to be in London for two weeks or longer, if need be. Beth had been working nonstop to fill up his itinerary. She was constantly emailing updates and changes right up until his plane landed at Heathrow.

Jack felt remarkably refreshed when he deplaned. As he walked through the airport, his mind was focused on all of the details that were ahead of him. With his phone fully charged, he started ripping through his itinerary. His first to-do was to text Gloria and let her know he had landed safely. He then called Beth to go over the final updates to his schedule. It was 7:00a.m. in London. He realized it would be 1:00a.m. in Chicago. Beth answered on the first ring."Jack Alexander's office, how can I help you?"

"Beth, it's Jack. Didn't my number come up on your caller ID?"

"No. Maybe it's because you're out of the country. But I have been following the flight and I figured you be calling about now."

"No worries. Let's go over the changes."

They spent the next several minutes in discussion. After some time, Jack was finally content with the schedule. They agreed on when they would talk next and then he hung up. He was in baggage claim when he got a new text message.

Jack, welcome to London. Text me back and let me know when you are walking out of the terminal and through which door. I'll pick you up at the curb. Jack knew that the country manager was coming to get him. He had considered a limo to the office but he felt it was important to be relational, so he texted back,

Tom, thanks for the note. I have my bag and I'll be walking out of 3A arrivals. It was a few seconds later that he got a reply, *Great...look for a silver Mercedes, vehicle number BE54PGL.*

Jack spotted the car and Tom Leeks, London's country manager, standing in front of it. Tom was short, stocky, and about five foot seven or eight. From what Jack could see, he was well over two hundred pounds. At fifty-two years old, he was balding on top and his dark brown hair had more gray than brown. He wore stylish glasses that partially hid the dark circles under his eyes. He had what looked like a sports-related scar over the right side of his forehead. He wore a rather expensive, well-tailored, dark blue, pinstripe suit. He also wore a royal blue shirt that, along with his well-polished shoes and striking cufflinks, made him look like the country leader for a prestigious consulting firm. "Welcome to London, Mr. Alexander. It's a pleasure to finally meet you."

"It's great to meet you as well. Call me Jack."

"How was your flight? Uneventful, I hope." Jack tried to make small talk as they drove away from the airport.

"It was fine, thanks. Tom, I appreciate you agreeing to pick me up. It gives us an opportunity to talk before we get to the office. Did you get a copy of my itinerary?" Jack noticed that Tom turned and looked over at Jack as he negotiated the road. "Yes, I did. Very detailed. But I wondered if you wanted to check into your hotel first and drop off your bags?" Jack was quick to respond.

"Tom, I want to be clear. You and I have a few challenges ahead of us and I want to make sure we get right to them. We could go over to the hotel first. Maybe we could sit in the lobby after I check in. You see, I want to go over the things I put in my communique to you." Jack watched him as he pondered that for a moment and then said,

"I agree...there is a lot to cover."

After Jack checked in, they spent more than an hour going over the details along with what Jack needed to be sensitive to regarding the London people and the operation.

"You need to meet with my management team before we have the town hall meeting with all the employees. I sent you all of their bios and pictures. So, what questions do you have?"Jack thought about that for a few seconds, then said,

"Which of your leaders are key stakeholders in your operation? Which of them might leave? Which represent your biggest headache?"Jack saw Tom look away. From his reaction, it was clear that he was weighing his answer. Before he could speak, Jack added,

"Look, Tom, I'm told you are a real 'stand-up guy'. You have been a key ingredient to the success of this operation. You need to make the decision to be absolutely straight with me. Trust me. I won't accept anything less. Honesty and integrity are high on my list. They are quickly followed by loyalty and confidentiality. If I find that you are violating any of these, I'll fire you on the spot. If you determine you can't live up to these, it would be best for you to resign."Jack waited. He wanted to get Tom's reaction.

He looked at Jack without flinching. Then he said,

"Jack, I was told you were a straight shooter. I did some checking on my own and found out you were the one who saved Universal from potential embarrassment with that failed merger. I totally appreciate that you are a principled guy. Honestly, I wouldn't have it any other way. You have my commitment that I will give you as good as I get. I'm excited about working with you."Jack raised one eyebrow and gave Tom a half smile.

"Well, that's great to hear. Oh, one more thing. You can be sure that I will support you and never leave you hanging out to dry."

For the next forty five minutes or more, they discussed Tom's management team in the manner Jack had requested. Jack took copious notes and asked several questions. Tom gave answers in a very direct and straightforward fashion.Once they were finished, the two of them left the hotel on their way to the JSL London office. Jack was quiet and looked out the passenger window. The scenery was quite interesting. It caused him to think about how much Gloria would have enjoyed this trip. Jack saw Tower 42, formerly the NatWest Tower, which was the first skyscraper in the City of London. Not far away, he could see The Gherkin, a unique bullet-shaped tower. He also saw in the distance the Lloyd's of London building, thought to be one of the most iconic buildings in the city. The Bank of England was not far away. He remembered from the travel documents he and Gloria had read that it would be possible inside to touch a real gold bar. A few minutes later, he got a glimpse of St. Helen's Church which apparently had been completely rehabbed after being battered by the 1992 and 1993 bomb attacks to the city.

In addition, his thoughts took him back to his mother's bridal business in the heart of Chicago's downtown Loop area. It was believed that the origin of the term Loop was not used as a proper noun until after the 1897 construction of the elevated railway that went around the downtown area. His mother's business, Vivienne's Designs, was highly successful. Jack learned much about business and dealing with people from watching and observing his mother. She had a vast array of clients. While she continually worked to enhance each customer's experience, she never let them take advantage of her. That was also true for the people who worked for her. She was exceptionally fair and paid a better than average wage, but she wouldn't put up with mediocrity. If an employee gave her substandard work, lied, or tried to cheat a customer, she would fire them on the spot. At the beginning of an employee's tenure, she explained the rules of employment.

"I expect you to be on time, give your very best with every dress, gown, or outfit you work on, never deceive me or any customer, and don't promise something you know we can't deliver. Finally, if I share something with you confidentially, you are never to share it with anyone." He knew these beliefs because his mother sat down and explained them to him and his three sisters. She clearly demonstrated them with the people she employed. At a young age, Jack employed these very important lessons in his own life, first with his friends and then with the people who worked for him. As a new vice president with Universal Systems, Len had communicated some of these same beliefs to Jack when he was promoted to Len's executive leadership team. So, he felt comfortable communicating these same principles with Tom Leeks. As the car moved along, he said to himself, *Tom probably thinks I'm a jerk. But I can't soft sell the importance of all that lies ahead. If I miss here, the acquisition expectations we anticipate could be lost.*

CHAPTER

THIRTY-EIGHT

AFTER RACHEL'S VISIT TO THE Hazelton PrisonCatherine sat alone in her cell and thought, *Well, I have my daughter back. She was emotionally moved in a way far greater than I could ever hoped or imagined. Maybe I shouldn't have made Jack Alexander such a horrible monster. But I couldn't run the risk that she would be calm and unconvinced. I couldn't take the chance she would remain hard, unmoved, and simply get up and walk out on me. The stakes are too high at this point. If I have any chance of pulling this off, I need her. Well, it's pretty clear at this point that she's definitely on board.*

***

Luke dropped Rachel off at home. She promised to call him later. But she realized as she walked to her front door that she needed some significant time alone to think about all that had transpired at the prison with her mother. She was also drained and absolutely exhausted. Luke had tried on the way back to Atlanta to open up about her time with her mother. But after a couple of failed attempts, he gave up. He settled for benign conversations about art school and Chicago. After he'd said all he could about when he'd be leaving and where he'd be staying, he asked her to talk about her plans. All in all, the conversation was mostly one-sided.

As Rachel sat on her bed, in her room, she concluded that she hadn't changed her mind about leaving Atlanta and going to art school in Chicago. She was certain she'd be accepted. She wasn't ready to tell Luke. Her father was encouraging her to go. And the conversation with her mother hadn't done anything to dissuade her. In fact, once her mother realized Rachel's intentions, she encouraged her even more to go.Her mother told her,

"Pursue your dreams. Your father told me you have a great artistic eye and your work is quite good."

Rachel was very surprised by that.

She was even more surprised when her mother added,

"I think Chicago is a great city. It's very cosmopolitan and much safer than living in New York. Once I'm out of this place, I'm thinking of relocating to some place like Chicago." Rachel was speechless. Her mother continued.

"If you're in Chicago, that might help me make up my mind."

The bigger dilemma for Rachel was trying to decide how, or if, she would be a part of her mother's scheme associated with Jack Alexander.

CHAPTER

THIRTY-NINE

JSL CONSULTING OFFICE - LONDON

JACK WATCHED TOM PULL HIS car into the parking garage.
Since Jack was buried in his own thoughts, Tom hadn't said much during the drive.

Jack noticed it when Tom looked over at Jack. With his left eyebrow raised Tom asked,

"Are you ready to face the music? Is there anything else that you want to cover?"

Jack was quick to reply.

"Yes, I'm ready and no, there isn't anything else we need to cover. How much time do we have before the first meeting?"

"About fifteen or twenty minutes."

Jack opened the passenger door.

"Then let's go do this. We've already talked enough about the agenda."

As soon as Jack walked into the conference room everyone stood up. Tom had seven managers. They carried titles of either practice directors or managing practice directors. Some were responsible for multiple practice areas or lines of business, such as finance, marketing, sales, and/or manufacturing. Others were responsible for one area like predictive modeling, which covered multiple lines of business or for a client's entire business. Each of Tom's managers came up to Jack and introduced themselves.

After a few minutes, Jack watched Tom close the conference room door as a signal that the meeting was going to start. Jack had already organized his notes as Tom stood at the front of the room.

"Folks, all of you are aware of both the acquisition by Universal Systems and Jack Alexander being named the new president of JSL. He and I have talked extensively about our operation. He was anxious to make London his first stop on his overseas tour and meet all of you. During my discussions with Jack, I was very impressed with his knowledge of our business as well as our consulting model." He stopped for a few seconds and looked all of his managers in the eye. Then he continued,

"Yet, I know that you have lots of questions. So, with no further ado, I'll turn the rest of the meeting over to Jack."

Jack waited until Tom sat down and then replaced him at the front of the room. He stood absolutely still with his arms hanging loosely at his side. For a few seconds, he didn't say a word. Then like the sun breaking forth over the horizon, he smiled broadly and said,

"I am so excited to be here. It is both an honor and a privilege to have the opportunity to get to know each of you. Tom was correct. I did want to come here first for many reasons. Your operation is one of the largest. Your practice areas are excelling and breaking new ground throughout JSL and the industry. There are more customer testimonials here than any other operation. It's obvious to me that you folks are doing tremendous things." Jack stopped again to let his words seep in to the people in the room. Then he added,

"I want each of you to know I so value your efforts and your contributions both now and in the future. I'll stop right here in case some of you have questions for me." There was stillness and a quiet in the room, like being in the forest before dawn; the anticipation of the sun rising over the horizon. Jack stood still, looked around the room. He was comfortable with the quiet.Finally, one of the managers broke the silence."I have a question." This came from Martin Camus, a slim man with black curly hair and thick wire-rimmed glasses, probably in his late thirties. Tom had told Jack that Martin had been with the firm for seven years. He was a practice manager and was well thought of by his people and his peers. Tom saw him as a keeper.

"We all sat through your teleconference where you attempted to instill confidence in the face of the acquisition. It has been tough for the London employees to believe all will go well through this transition. In addition, our customers, clients, and prospects are asking questions of us that have been difficult to answer."Jack smiled.

"Was there a question in there?" Realizing the truth of Jack's question, Martin and the others laughed, and that took some of the tension out of the room."Just kidding. I think I understand. As you know, I'm going to speak to all of your employees later today at the town hall meeting. I intend to tell them essentially what I'm covering with you. I'll be sharing with them that I'm excited to be here, to be your new president, and to represent JSL consulting. I'll also tell them of my itinerary while I'm here and who I plan to meet with. I don't know if I answered your question but my objective, and Universal System's, is to expand JSL in every way possible." Martin looked down as he finished writing something in his notebook. Then he said,

"All that's great, but isn't it true that you'll need to offload or eliminate expense in order for Universal to start to recoup its return on investment? Also, since headcount is the largest expense, won't you need to send some people home?" Those remarks hung in the air like the smell of bad eggs.Jack didn't duck the question.

"Martin, there is truth to your comment. Employee headcount is the largest expense and Universal continues to look for the greatest ROI possible. But our approach will be simple. We will merge common systems like benefits, IT, HR, and accounting as quickly as possible. This will certainly reduce the cost of business. As it relates to employees, some people will leave in the normal course of attrition. Poor performers will be asked to leave, and some practice areas will be combined and as a result will need less people." Jack didn't want to steamroll through these items, so he paused again to let his words sink in. Then he added,

"Very shortly, Tom will be announcing some additional revenue-generating programs or practice areas. Those areas will require additional people, some from within the company and some from outside. All in all, we will make every effort to retain best-in-class resources, and people are the largest part." Jack waited for Martin or someone else to comment. He watched Martin as he took notes. He looked up and said,

"Jack, I'm satisfied with your answers. They more than addressed my questions, thank you."

As Martin spoke he last words, there was another voice.***
"Well, I have a few comments I'd like to get your reaction to." This came from Srinivas Subramanian. Everyone called him Srini. He was average height, under six feet tall. He had brown eyes that were slightly cross-eyed. When Srini first came to JSL his eye condition was severe. By using prism lenses and getting vision therapy, the problem corrected itself. While he had a slight accent, he was very articulate. His nose was long and curved oddly at the end but not very wide. Of East Indian decent, he was born in Britain and had attended Yale, an Ivy League school in the United States. In his early forties, he had worked for two other consulting firms before coming to JSL. Because of his prior consulting experience, he'd been hired as a practice director and then promoted to the title of managing director. Tom had told Jack that Srini was very headstrong and often went off on his own. His teams were high revenue generators but he wasn't much of a team player with his peers. There had been constant complaints about his unwillingness to share practice materials for the overall good of JSL's clients. Tom told Jack that on several occasions, he had counseled Srini on the merits of sharing and that he would have to reverse the trend if he wanted to stay at the company. All

of those sessions had been clearly and repeatedly documented. Jack asked him,

"What did you want to say?"

"I appreciate all of your remarks concerning the high regard you and everyone at Universal has for JSL, but it seems to me that you simply want our consulting methodology and then our firm will cease to exist. I don't believe for a minute"

Jack interrupted him.

"Srini…just a minute please. What you said is simply not the case. We have—"Jack was surprised when Srini took it upon himself to interrupt him."Wait a minute…you said you wanted to hear my comments and then you cut me off. That's not right." There was obvious tension in the room as the two of them stared at each other.Then Jack smiled and answered,

"Srini, you are right. I'm sorry…you were talking. Please…go right ahead."Jack saw the smirk on Srini's face. It communicated to Jack that he was going to asserted himself."As I was saying… based on the past, in the consulting industry, larger firms come along and buy up the intellectual capital, keep a few necessary people resources, and trash everything else. There are several indications the same thing will happen here. I, for one, don't want to be caught up in Universal's intended invasion strategy."

There was obvious discomfort in the room when Srini finished. The managers on either side of him demonstrated body language that suggested they wanted to find new places in the room to sit.Jack started in a very deliberate fashion as he looked directly at Srini.

"I appreciate your opinion. You are certainly entitled to have one. I can understand your skepticism. If you reversed the situation, I would—"

Now Jack was startled when Srini loudly interrupted him.

"Obviously, we can't reverse the situation now can we? Jack didn't chastise or reprimand him for his interruption, he simply continued. "I'd be nervous. But I can assure you and the rest of the team that we fully regard and appreciate the employees here at JSL. My aim is to determine new and innovative ways to grow the business exponentially. My intent is that no one of value will be left behind. That is my commitment to you all."Jack was now fully aware of Srini's impertinence. For the second time, Srini piped up,

"That's the point; you and your cronies at Universal will be the ones to determine *value*. And anyone who doesn't fit your *value consideration* will not only be left behind but unceremoniously dumped."

Jack was starting to get a little hot under the collar. He thought to himself, *He sure has a lot of gall to talk like that and make these assumptions. Tom was right. He is headstrong and disrespectful.* Jack couldn't tell if Srini had finished. Had the guy stopped briefly so he could build up another head of steam?Jack took the opportunity to interject

"Srini, it's clear you are disenchanted with the condition here and you've already made up a disaster story in your head. My question is…why are you still here if you are so miserable?" Everyone in the room could tell the frankness of the question took Srini by surprise but he wasn't stumped for very long.Jack eyeballed him and waited."I wanted to hear your ridiculous attempts to try to lull us all to sleep while you and Universal used your acquisition *wrecking ball* to demolish one of the best consulting firms in the business. I, for one, don't plan to be here one moment longer than necessary."Jack spoke up before his next tirade.

"That sounds like a resignation and based on your perpetual insolence here in this meeting, in front of your peers, I'm certain Tom would be more than happy to accept it immediately." Jack then turned to Tom and added,

"Please tell the folks in the IT department that they need to immediately cut off Srini's access to every system and let HR know he is no longer employed at JSL."

Tom got up and immediately left the room. The other members

of the team sat there amazed as they watched all that was happening right before their eyes. Srini was tough to deal with but no one thought he would be so brazen.

Jack looked over at Srini again and added,

"Srini, I'm disappointed in you, your abrasive manner, your disrespect, and total disregard for this meeting. What you said here was both wrong and an attempt to sabotage the values of both companies. I would have been happy to talk with you privately on any issue you had. But unfortunately, you felt it necessary to grandstand and showboat in front of your boss and your peers." Jack didn't think he would back down at all. And he didn't disappoint.

"How dare you try to belittle me. I did nothing but tell the truth." He looked around the room at his peers as he collected his notebook and stood up.

"If you folks weren't so blind, you'd see through this imposter's veneer. I can't wait to get out of here before the walls start caving in."

FORTY

TOM, WHO CAME BACK IN the room, stood up and blocked Srini's path to the door. Jack was pleased with his next comments."Srini, as you know, it is our practice, when an employee resigns or is terminated to walk them out of the building the same day. I had security box up your personal items. I will need your building pass, keys to the office, and your company credit card."

Jack saw Tom hesitate slightly. He looked down at his notes and added,

"Security is outside the room. They will be escorting you from the building. Someone from HR will be contacting you regarding your final settlement. Srini, I truly wish you well."

With that, he moved away from the door, opened it, walked out, and signaled for Security to engage. Srini didn't say another word. He walked out between the two security guards and they disappeared. The silence in the room was such that you could hear a pin drop.***

Jack stood up and said,

"Did anyone else want to follow Srini? If so, now would be the time."

Again, there was an extended hush in the room; no one spoke or even moved."I think most of us felt Srini's leaving was way overdue." This came from Shelley Richards. Shelley also a managing practice director. From Tom's detailed description, she was one of the best managers he'd ever had. Tom had told Jack,

"She's smart, adaptive, very collaborative, and has a strong appreciation for both people and process. The consultants and my other managers like her."

Shelley was not very tall and a bit chubby. Her short brown hair reminded Jack of a heavier Dorothy Hamill, the Olympic figure skater from the late '70s. Her red lipstick, properly applied make-up, and a dainty gold chain around her neck gave her a profession-al appearance that complimented her manner. Jack learned that she had been born in England. She had graduated at the top of her class from Imperial College London. Her first job out of college was for a small accounting firm. After three years, she had enough money to attend graduate school. She scored in the 99% percen-tile and was given a scholarship to London Business School. JSL had heavily recruited her and she'd agreed to come and work for them. Clients were fond of her right from the beginning. She rose through the ranks and became a managing practice director faster than anyone else in the firm. When she spoke, people listened.Jack gave her his full attention, she continued.

"He was the epitome of arrogance. Actually, we found a way to be successful as an operation in spite of him."

Shelley went on.

"I, for one, am interested in hearing the balance of the plans for our operation and the rest of JSL." Every other person in the room signaled their concurrence with her remark.

Tom casually gave a note to Jack. He looked at it quickly and then slipped it into his notebook.

He then replied to Shelley,

"Thank you...there's a lot more to cover. Since you're ready, I'll continue."

The rest of the meeting with Tom's managers and at the employ-ee town hall went well. There were several questions but overall there was receptivity. Over the course of his six and a half days

in London, Jack met with a series of clients and government officials. There were definitely some tense moments but he was able
to address every concern that arose.During his stay in London,
he had a few absolutes every day. He got up at 5:30 a.m. to read,
journal, go out running different routes, call Len with updates on
his progress, and meet with Tom to recap the day and plan for the
next day. Tom briefed him on every person, whether customer,
employee, manager, or government official. Jack left nothing to
chance. The other absolute was calling Gloria every night. Since
London was six hours ahead, they agreed that Jack would call her
every night at 10:30 p.m. London time, 4:30 p.m. Chicago time.

***

"Hi, Babe…how is it going?" Gloria wanted to get right to the
heart of his trip and the details.

Jack answered,

"It's going much better. Honestly, it didn't start off so well, but
that's turned around." He gave her a snapshot of the business
events that had taken place. He expected her to ask more questions. But she simply listened without saying anything more than
an occasional,

"Uh-huh."

When Jack finished, he asked her,

"So, how are you doing?" He didn't get an immediate response
which concerned him. Nevertheless, he waited for her to answer.
Finally she said,

"I'm okay." Her reply let Jack know that something wasn't right .

"Hey Babe, what's going on with you? What do you mean,
you're okay?"

It worried Jack even more when Gloria's answer was again
delayed. Finally she spoke.

"Jack, I got another one of those anonymous letters today." Jack
was shocked. He could feel his pulse quickening.

"What? I can't believe it. It hasn't been a year since we got the last one. What did it say?" She took her time responding.

"It said "We've now got you right where we want you. You won't know where it's coming from until it hits you."

"When did you get it?"

"Just today." Jack waited before his next comment. He didn't want to frighten her.

"Okay, nothing has happened with any of the other letters. Nonetheless, here's what I want you to do. Call Clarence Harper and tell him about it. Explain to him that I am out of the country. He will know exactly what to do."

"But Jack, I feel a little foolish."

"Clarence is a friend. He has experience with these things. Trust me. Just call him." Again there was extended silence before he heard,

"Okay. I'll call him and tell him. But don't worry about me. I'm sure everything will be just fine." Jack could tell from the sound of her voice that she was as confident as her words suggested. Nonetheless, he went with it.

"Babe, I tend to agree with you. Let me know what he says. Okay?"

"I will. You probably should hang up now. Your itinerary indicates you have a hefty schedule in front of you."

Jack had learned over the course of their relationship that he didn't need to sugarcoat the condition of things.

"Yep…you're right about that one. I can only imagine what it'll be like in the other countries, in addition to the language and cultural considerations."

"You'll do just fine. Get some rest, remember to eat, and I love you."

"I love you too, Babe." As Jack hung up, he thought, *I should have brought her with me. If she were here with me now, there'd be no concerns about an anonymous letter or Gloria's safety. I'm going to call Clarence myself. Oh, Lord protect her.*

***

"So that's the situation here. Other than the blowup that happened with Srini, everything else was manageable. I should tell you there were some tense moments with two or three clients but, in the end, it all worked out. Oh, one more thing. Every government official let me know we are on solid ground over here." Jack waited for Len's reaction.

It didn't take long."

"Great…I knew you would be able to handle it. Looks like London is fine…for now. But we have bigger issues right now."

Jack was calm but concerned.

"Like what…what's the problem?"

"We're being told Jeremy Lane is starting up another consulting firm—""What…are you kidding me? They signed both a non-compete and a non-solicitation agreement as part of the acquisition. How can he be doing that? "Jack was in a huff and all lathered up over what he'd heard.

He waited for Len to respond."I'm not sure…he may have someone else as the figure head. Regardless, we've got to immediately shore up every aspect within JSL, especially the clients, prospects, and critical employees."

"Isn't that what we are doing? I'm getting to every country office as quickly as possible."Jack was surprised by Len's next remark."That may not be fast enough."Jack thought for a moment and then asked,

"How much time have we got?"

"I don't know."Jack came back with,

"If Jeremy is going through with this, why don't we file a temporary injunction that would keep their consulting company from ever seeing the light of day?"

"We could, and we thought of that…but the board is concerned the whole thing might be a red herring. If it is, we'd be overreacting. If it isn't, we've given them free advertising."Jack was about to suggest an idea. Then he decided to ask a question.

"Okay…so what do you suggest at this point?"He could hear Len take a deep sigh."Given what little we know at this point, I'm not sure. But I've asked the legal team to look into this. I'll have some answers shortly. I wanted you to make sure you were aware of what's been happening.""Thanks for the heads up. Do you need me to do anything differently at this point?

"No…the best thing you can do is to continue on as you have been. Tell me again…which city do you fly to next?"

"I'm going to Paris from here."

"Okay…check in with me early next week."

"Will do…we'll talk soon."

Jack was deep in thought as he punched the End button on his phone. *Why would Jeremy Lane want to sell his company if he still wanted to be in the consulting business? That doesn't make sense. There's got to be some other explanation for it. I didn't tell Len about Gloria and those letters. It's my problem and I've got to figure a way to insure Gloria's safety.*

***

"Clarence, she would be freaking out if she knew I called you. But those letters worry me, especially this last one she received. I need your help."

"Jack, with you out of the country, I can understand your concern. But as I told you before, we checked them out and there're no fingerprints or return addresses anywhere. We have nothing to go on."

"So, what do I do at this point?"

"Well, you can either come back home or let me assign a man to keep tabs on her. Aside from that, there's not much else."

"Alright, I'll leave it to you. I trust you, my friend."

"Jack, call me anytime. I'll see you when you get back, and stop worrying."

FORTY-ONE

CATHERINE HAD METHODICALLY MAPPED OUT her parole strategy. She'd been a model prisoner from the day she walked into the West Virginia federal prison. So when she submitted her application for parole, she'd been following all of the prison's rules and guidelines. During her initial parole hearing, there were several prison personnel who vouched for her conduct and character, including the prison warden.

"I rarely go to bat for an inmate during their hearings, but Catherine Frazier is an exception. Not only has she followed all the rules since she'd been here but she's started classes to help other inmates get their GED and apply to take classes in college. I would definitely vouch for her rehabilitation during her years here."

In spite of the warden's glowing comments, the parole commission still had to meet in order to consider all of the positive and negative factors. In addition, they also did an extensive pre-release record review. Nine months after her initial hearing, she was given a Notice of Action, which approved her parole and indicated her date of release. A couple of months before her official release, she was assigned to a parole officer. Even before that, she was asked which release location she'd prefer. Her options were the judicial district in which she was convicted or the judicial district of her legal residence.

She told them,

"If it pleases the parole commission, I would humbly ask to be released to the judicial district where I was convicted."

The parole commissioner asked,

"Why there?"

"My legal residence is Atlanta, but my husband has filed for divorce. So, I don't think I'd be welcomed back there." Catherine waited pensively to determine how the commissioner would reply.

"Any other reasons?"

"Yes, my daughter recently moved to Chicago to attend art school and I sense that I can make a fresh start there." Catherine watched the parole board commissioner slowly look down at his papers and then he made a notation.

"I can understand your reasoning for wanting to move to Chicago. Does your daughter realize you would be moving there?"

***

After more than sixteen hours, Catherine got off the Amtrak train at Union Station in downtown Chicago. While she'd notified Frank, her daughters, and her mom and dad, there was no one waiting for her when she walked through the prison gates. She had accumulated some money during her years of incarceration. So, she had what she needed for a bus ride to Charleston and a train ride to Chicago.

As she walked out into the Chicago sunlight, she stood for several minutes listening to all of the metropolitan city sounds she hadn't heard in years. She decided to walk east toward Lake Michigan. As she walked, she took in the sound of car horns, buses moving through traffic, and people talking on their cell phones as they passed by. She had to stop and look up when she heard the screeching sound of the "L" train as it moved overhead. She realized that this cacophony of sound had been denied her. They were all welcomed sounds to her ears. But the more they permeated her mind, the more images of Jack Alexander flashed before her eyes. The same images that flooded her mind every day of her incarceration. Her overarching thoughts were, *Mr. Alexander, you have no idea what's coming. You're probably thinking right now that life is an absolute dream. But you'll soon realize that I meant what I said when I last saw you…"This is your fault. I'm going to get you. I don't care how long it takes. You wait and see. Count on it!"*

***

It was weird for Rachel to have her mother living with her. She had been a child the last time she and her mother had lived under the same roof. Her mother had assured her it would be fine. She insisted sleeping on the couch and since she only had a few clothes and not many personal incidentals, she wouldn't take up much space. Her mother had been right; she hadn't been much of a bother. But it was still weird. The first night her mother arrived was strange. Rachel knew that her mother was coming to Chicago because she'd placed a collect call letting her know her release date and her plans for coming and living in Chicago.

From the very moment her mother walked in the front door of her apartment, Rachel felt uneasy. Whether her mother could sense Rachel's uneasy feeling or not, she came right over to her and hugged her. The she started talking.

"Rachel, it's great to see you. I've been rehearsing this moment every hour I spent on the train coming here, and long before that." Rachel kept her eyes on her mother but without staring. She listened as her mother continued.

"How's your day going? Did you go to classes? I certainly don't want you to interrupt your schooling because of me." Her mother smiled at her. Rachel sensed that she was trying to break down any possible walls of resistance that existed. Rachel sat in one of her kitchen chairs looking at her mother, who sat on her small sofa, and was only half listening. Her emotions were all over the place. She was glad to see her mother but she was bothered by the fact that she was invading her space. In many ways, it would have been better if her mother had come to Chicago but lived someplace else. She was happy her mother was out of prison, but she was unsettled about her retaliation plans for this Jack Alexander guy. While her mother hadn't talked any more about the monster he was and how he'd ruined everything, Rachel was nervous as to what her expected role might be in the scheme her mother had hatched.

Finally, she had to say something to her or she was going to explode.

"Look, there's a part of me that's glad you are out of prison. It was a nasty place. Along with that, you are here in Chicago, in my apartment. Mostly, I like the thoughts of those things. But they are countered by having to share my space with you. Most of all, I'm apprehensive, wary, and tentative about our relationship because so much time has passed. And if that weren't enough, I think you are planning something that could land you back in prison, and you want me to help you. So, pardon me if I don't want to pass out horns, paper hats, and have a party." When she finished, her emotions were more intense than they were before her words came out. But she'd said what she felt. Rachel noticed her mother's face softened like she wanted to get up and hug her daughter again. But Rachel could tell she resisted the urge. Instead she said,

"I can only imagine how hard this is for you. I've thought and said this many times…If I could go back and change the past, I would do it in a heartbeat."

Rachel relaxed by leaning back in her chair. She listened as her mother continued,

"You have every right to feel as you do right now. Trust me… I plan to make every effort to have things go as smoothly as possible between us. You see, you are my daughter and you have experienced so much hell already. I plan to rectify all that. I'll share my plans with you but you aren't under any obligation to help me at all."

"Okay…I hear you. So, what is your plan?"

They spent the next few hours talking. They talked about the living arrangement, her mother's parole, Rachel's school schedule, and especially her plans regarding Jack Alexander. It was well into the middle of the night before they decided to stop and go to sleep.

CHAPTER

FORTY-TWO

DAY ONE

LEN HAD BEEN PLEASED WITH the results from the JSL offices Jack had visited. While there was still some unrest in JSL, Jack had done a marvelous job of quelling most of it. Jack had been on the job for two months. In that time, JSL had made all of its financial numbers, any unwanted employee exodus from the company had been minimal, and no substantial client had left the fold. Therefore, Len made the decision to bring Jack back to headquarters.

When they spoke over the phone, he told him as much.

"Listen, Jack, I realize you haven't finished visiting all of the offices. Nonetheless, good news as well as bad travels very fast. The employees in the offices where you have visited spread the word regarding your genuine interest in JSL, its employees, and clients." Len expected to get a reaction from Jack, when none came, he continued.

"I think the rough patch is over. We still have a few things to sort out but I think you'd be more effective here at headquarters." Len heard him breath what seemed like a sigh of relief. "From all I've heard, I would tend to agree with you. I still believe it would be prudent on my part to visit the other offices at some point. For now, I'm content to come home as you suggest. I'll work with Beth to arrange a flight tour to the other offices as soon as possible."

***

Jack had been home for a month. Gloria was ecstatic that he'd come home early. He'd fallen back into his daily patterns, and he was happy to be home.

Jack walked out the front door of his home to go running. The latest developments in JSL consumed him. He was in a quandary regarding what actions he should take. In spite of being preoccupied with business thoughts, he hadn't missed the glorious start to his day. The sky was fast becoming an amazing collection of colors all melting together: brilliant orange, intense purple, bright pink, and a variety of blues all swirling together; and then a yellow, red orange torch appeared signifying a new day. He felt a surge of energy flow through him as he started running on one of his many paths. This one allowed him to watch the sun's ascent as he accelerated along the trail. By the time he reached the turnaround point, the sun was well above the horizon. There was something different about this sunrise. While it was vibrant and strong, there was something about it that felt a bit ominous. The sun was brilliant and inviting but the sky around it was troubling and foreboding. Jack chose to keep his sights on the sun and not the sky around it. Little did he know that it was a foretaste of things to come.

CHAPTER
FORTY-THREE

CATHERINE HAD CONVINCED RACHEL TO be a part of her scheme. She told her to observe Jack Alexander's movements during his working hours, especially when he arrived at his office in the morning. The intent was to determine his daily patterns. If they could figure out his comings and goings, they would be able to plan their strike with precision and accuracy. Catherine called Universal Systems as a phony reporter alleging the desire to do a story on Jack as the new president of JSL. She was able to find out that he was out of the country and when he'd plan to return. Catherine then instructed Rachel to sit in the parking garage of Jack Alexander's building once he returned to the office. As the president of JSL, he had a permanent parking place. After timing his typical arrival, all she had to do was get to the garage early in order to secure a space close enough to his but far enough away to observe him without being noticed.

Jack was definitely a creature of habit. Unless he was traveling, he arrived at work between 6:55am and 7:10am. Once he parked, he would take the same elevator bank up to his office. He could have taken the much closer escalator to the lobby before getting on the elevator, which was actually faster but he never did.

Catherine told her daughter that the plan was to detain Jack when he arrived at work. That was the extent of what Catherine told her. She told her more details would come as time went on and to simply trust her. Catherine saw that Rachel's face frowned up every time they discussed the plan. Yet, Catherine had conveyed the fact that Jack Alexander was a monster and he was responsible for wrecking her family's life. Payback was the only answer.

Catherine listened as her daughter told her that in order to do what she requested, she would have to stop going to art school. It was actually hard for her to learn that Rachel could potentially lose her scholarship. Nonetheless, Catherine told her that everything would work out fine and to trust her.

Catherine walked by her daughter's room late one night and heard her saying to herself,

"How will all this end up?"

***

Catherine, in her own mind, had laid out her elaborate plan that involved kidnapping Jack, terrorizing him, and holding him for random. She realized it required pinpoint timing and accuracy. There were still many elements she needed to work out. She knew she had to first button it all up before moving forward. It was clear that if her plan failed, she could find herself right back in a federal penitentiary. She also made a decision to shield Rachel from the actual details until the time and day to go live. This was all a huge risk but she had decided that allowing Jack Alexander to get away with heaping pain and suffering on her and her family was not an option. He would feel lots of pain before this was all over. It actually took her much longer to research her options and, devise her plans while still complying with the rigor associated with her parole guidelines. She couldn't risk taking on any partner because she wasn't sure who she could trust. From her accumulated prison funds, she paid cash for two pay as you go cell phones. There were some important contacts she needed to make. So a working phone was an essential ingredient. One of the first things was to activate the ongoing caller ID block feature. She wanted to insure no one would be able to track any outgoing calls from her. She also secured a telephone voice changer transformer. While she didn't know exactly how she would use it, she decided it was better to have it, in case.She had started looking through ads to find remote, secluded places in the Chicago area. This was the most important key to pulling the whole thing off.

***

Rachel arrived at the parking lot at a quarter to seven in the morning. It gave her plenty of time to find a spot within viewing distance to observe when Jack Alexander arrived. As she parked and got situated, she thought, *Boy, this is such a waste of time. I've already been here enough times to know exactly when he'll arrive. I should have told my mother that I was done with this worthless exercise. Why did I agree to be a part of this hare-brained scheme anyway? There's his car...like normal. He's been showing up at five minutes to seven every morning I've been here. I'm sick and tired of this...Hey, what's going on?*

Rachel sat straight up as a car pulled up behind Jack Alexander's car and three men in sunglasses got out. They flashed what looked like guns, said a few words, and then hustled Jack into their car. Before she could fully collect her thoughts, they sped off. She sat there stunned. She couldn't believe what had happened. Here she'd been tracking the man's daily movements into work every day and now some men had abducted him. She thought, *What do I do now? Where do I go? Who do I tell?* She looked around the parking lot and didn't see another person anywhere. No one else had witnessed the abduction. She didn't know how long she sat riveted to the seat of her car. She couldn't move, she couldn't look to her left or right. Her mind couldn't process what she'd seen. She realized she'd never seen anything like that before. Then, she had an epiphany, a moment of sudden clarity. There were numbers that came to her mind 651 9479. She thought over them again and then realized they were the license plates of the car with the men in it. After sitting there still in shock, she decided that she should probably write the numbers down before she forgot them. She thought, *Where am I going now? If I drive home and tell my mother, I have no idea what she'll do. But it is clear her plans regarding Jack Alexander have changed. I need to make a decision about all this on my own.*

***

Rachel drove out of the parking garage and headed south on Wabash Avenue. She drove aimlessly, not sure where she was going. The scene in the garage had had a profound affect on her. She'd never seen anyone kidnapped before. She happened to notice a parking spot. She pulled her car into it, got out, and put some money in the meter. Not knowing where she was going, she started walking purposelessly. She found herself in front of Macy's. She decided to walk inside, thinking that it would take her mind off what she'd seen. But the images kept coming back to her. She walked out of the store and realized she was now on State Street. After walking some more, she went into a restaurant, sat down, and ordered coffee. But nothing changed those images stuck in her head. The aroma from the cup of java caused her mind to wander, *I've got to tell somebody what I saw. Jack Alexander may be a creep like my mother says but he's still a human being. He probably has a family. If something bad happens to that man and I kept my mouth shut, I'll feel horrible and I won't be able to live with myself. If I'm going to do something or tell someone, I need to do it now.*

CHAPTER
FORTY-FOUR

"**O**KAY, LADY...I UNDERSTAND WHAT YOU'RE telling me. I need you to give me the facts. So, again, tell me what happened?

"Well, as I told you. I was driving in that parking garage looking for a parking space."

"Uh huh...why were you in that parking garage before seven a.m.?"

"I told you...I've been looking for a job and I found out there were some likely companies I could go to in that building"

"Great...take a seat over there and someone will come out and talk to you."

Rachel walked over to a long bench that could hold ten people and sat down. There wasn't anyone else in the waiting area so she felt a bit forlorn. She went over in her mind exactly what she was going to tell the police when they asked her for more details. Fifteen minutes passed. "Excuse me, miss...are you the one who came in to report that someone had been abducted?"

"Yes...I told that to the policeman over there." She was pointing to the desk sergeant she had originally talked to.

"Okay, I'm Detective William McClain. Get up and follow me." He turned on his heels and started walking away, not even looking to see if she was following him. He led her to a big open room with computers and phone-filled desks. Police and average citizens filled the room. It seemed to Rachel that everyone was talking at the same time.Detective McClain directed her to a chair and told her to sit down. He started by asking,

"

So tell me what you think you saw."

He used his standard routine of disbelief in order to make the witness earn the right to be believed. He watched her carefully to see how she reacted.

"I was driving through the parking lot looking for a spot. When I found one to my liking, I pulled in and turned off the engine. I turned around to get my notebook from the back seat. I happened to notice this man up ahead and on the other side getting out of his car. I could tell he had parked his car in one of those reserved parking places. Then, another automobile pulled up behind his car. Three guys got out of their car, confronted the man, and the next thing I knew they were forcing him into their car."

McClain sat there with his notepad looking curiously at Rachel. He thought, *A kidnapping from a parking garage, should I believe her? She doesn't sound too credible. I guess I need to check it out. There may be something to it.* Nonetheless, he wasn't convinced.

"Okay...you told the desk sergeant this man was abducted. What makes you think so?"

"It was clear that he was startled and surprised by them."

"How could you tell? Could you see his face?"

"I could tell...okay?"

The detective looked up from his notes.

"Okay, okay...then what happened?"

"I was so stunned I sat there freaked out at what I'd seen."

The detective stared at her trying to determine if she was a kook. Finally, he said,

"Miss Frazier, this is one weird story. Why in the world should I believe you?"

He watched as she looked down at her hands.

She thought, *Is he realizing that I made up part of the story? What else can I tell him about what I saw in the parking lot?* Finally, she said,

"I think I got the license plates of the car that the abducted guy was put in."

McClain sat there as she opened her smartphone and read the numbers she'd written previously.

"651 9479."

He wrote them down.

"Were they Illinois plates?"

He noticed that she was in deep thought for a few seconds.

"No...I don't think so. They were from Wisconsin...I think."

After he wrote that down, he said,

"What was the color, make, and model of the car?"

He started to believe that she wasn't making up this kidnapping story. "Uh, I think it was an American car but I'm not sure. But the car was definitely white."

Detective McClain wrote that information down and looked up again from his notes.

"You told me this guy had parked his car in a reserved space. Did the space have the name of the guy or the name of the company on it?"

"Uh...I think it had a company name."

"What was the name of that company?"

"It was Universal Systems."

FORTY-FIVE

"**GOOD AFTERNOON, HOW CAN I** help you?" That comment came from one of the receptionist at Universal Systems. She was addressing Detective McClain.

Showing his detective shield to the receptionist, he said,

"I'm Detective McClain from the Chicago Police Department. I need to talk with your CEO, President, or the highest person in authority here."

"What is this concerning?" The receptionist was one of four that sat behind a wide desk that spanned the entire width of Universal's massive lobby area. The phones were constantly being answered and it was clear that calls were being routed throughout the office. There were several people waiting for appointments. So the dialog between the receptionist and Detective McClain was heard by most of the people in the waiting area.

"Ma'am, it's police business and I'm in a hurry."

The receptionist was clearly intimidated so she answered,

"Okay...I'll get someone out here for you, detective."

Detective McClain took a seat and directed Rachel to do the same. About five minutes passed before a woman came out, talked to the receptionist briefly, and then walked up to McClain.

"Detective, I'm Sandy Brown, executive assistant of Lenard Shapiro. How can I help you?"

"I need a few minutes with him since I have a very urgent situation."

"He is busy right now, in fact all day today. I can't—"

McClain interrupted her.

"Look, this can't wait. I need to talk to him immediately!"

They stood there looking at each other. There was some obvious tension.McClain was great at intimidation. He laid it on pretty thick and Sandy complied.

"I'll see what I can do." With that, she turned and disappeared. Three or four minutes later, she returned.

"Detective McClain, please follow me." As he got up, he motioned to Rachel to follow him as well. He realized that Sandy was looking at Rachel. He read her thoughts and without missing a beat said,

"She's with me." Sandy was about to say something but then decided against it.She took them into a conference room that had a big table and sixteen oversize leather chairs. She told them to take a seat and then she vanished. About the time that McClain and Rachel got comfortable, the door opened. Len and Tom Wallace walked in. After the obligatory introductions, Len asked,

"So, what's the cause for the four-alarm fire? I was in a very important meeting as I'm sure my assistant told you."

"There's a real possibility that one of your employees has been abducted. I'm here to check it out."

McClain saw that Len was shifting in his chair and looking at Tom. Then he heard Len say,

"Who do you think has been abducted and from where?"

McClain turned to Rachel and said,

"Tell them what you told me."

After Rachel recounted the story she looked at McClain.

The detective asked,

"So what floor of the garage did this happen, what kind of car did the man have, and what did he look like?"

Rachel did her best to answer his questions. Once she finished,

Len and Tom looked at each other. Clearly, they were both notice-ably uncomfortable.

"What's the problem with what she told you?" McClain asked.

He recognized that there was a long pause before Len spoke."-Detective, the problem is that one of our senior executives missed two very important meetings this morning. No one has seen or heard from him, including his executive assistant."

McClain looked back at the two men sitting at the table.

"Did you call his cell or his home? Is this unusual, could he be at another location...and oh, what's his name?"

"Yes, yes, yes, and no. He is extremely reliable and exception-ally communicative. This is highly irregular. It's as if he fell off the face of the earth...his name is Jack Alexander."

"Did someone go down and look for his car in the park-ing garage?"

"Yes...and it's where he normally parks it."

McClain wrote some things down and then looked up.

"Okay...look, I need to make some calls. I'd like to use this conference room."

Len looked at Tom and then said,

"Yes, of course."

"Great...can you show Rachel back to the reception area?" Then he turned to her.

"I need you to sit out there until I get some things nailed down. It won't be too long...okay?"

McClain watched her as she shifted in her seat, got up, and finally said,

"All right...but I need to get back home. I still need to get to school today."

"Got it!" He turned away from everyone in the room, stood up, and then punched some numbers in his cell phone. He turned back to them and waved them out of the room.

CHAPTER

FORTY-SIX

CATHERINE SAT AT THE KITCHEN table with a scowl on her face. She had her cell phone in front of her along with all of her concocted plans associated with Jack Alexander's demise. As she looked over her documents, she continually looked at her phone. She thought, *Where is she? Why hasn't she called? This is so not like her. She knows how important today's final update on Jack Alexander's time of arrival is. What could be keeping her? I'm all ready to pull this off. This could screw everything up.*

***

Rachel kept looking at the time on her phone. She realized that she should have been back home hours ago. She also realized that it would be a big mistake for her to call or text her mother the reason for her not being home.

When Rachel saw Jack Alexander being abducted, something broke in her. All the anger, bitterness, and resentment toward this man virtually disappeared. She realized he was a man, a man who was being put in harm's way. She didn't know the depth of her mother's plans but it would be diabolical in some way. As soon as she saw Jack Alexander taken, she knew that she wanted no part of her mother's or anyone else's scheme. She also knew that reporting what had happened to the authorities was exactly what she needed to have done.***

"From everything that I've seen and heard, we have a kidnapping on our hands. And if the car has Wisconsin license plates, this is an interstate offense and a federal crime." He looked down at his notes while he talked to the special project officer back at the police station.

"Do a quick search on this guy Jack Alexander. He works at Universal Systems." McClain kept writing, then he said,

"What...yeah, I'll hold on. In the meantime tell the captain I'll update him on the situation as soon as we're done here." McClain put his phone on speaker and went on recording in his notebook all the information he had gained.

"McClain...?"

He took his phone off speaker and answered,

"Yeah...whatcha' got?"

"The captain wants to talk to you."

"Okay...but what about this Alexander guy?"

"Well, he's a real straight shooter. He's a divisional president at Universal and has been recognized for super contributions."McClain raised one eyebrow and put down his pen.

"Is that it? Come on, tell me something I don't know."

"Bet you don't know this...he was a whistleblower a few years ago. It looks like he saved his firm from acquiring some other company that was bilking the federal government. A few people served time in prison for this one."

McClain took some more notes and then said,

"What happened to the people who served time?"

"Well, the majority of them only served two years or less, one woman committed suicide in her jail cell even before being tried, but there was one person who was sentenced to ten years in a federal penitentiary."

McClain stopped writing and asked,

"Does this Jack Alexander have a record?" There was silence for a minute.

"Nope, nothing...not even a parking ticket."

"Okay...one more thing, who was the federal agent that handled the case?" After a few seconds, McClain got his answer.

"His name is Clarence Harper, Special Agent Clarence Harper. He's actually here in Chicago and a pretty big guy in the FBI, runs a large part of the country."

"Impressive! Okay, thanks...connect me to the captain, and make it quick."***

FBI Special Agent Harper was on his way to a meeting when his assistant told him that he had an urgent phone call. He decided to take it back in his office. Still standing, he picked up the phone.

"This is Special Agent Harper."

"Agent Harper, this is Captain Foster of the Chicago Police department. We have a case I believe you may have a great deal of interest in."

Agent Harper said,

"Okay...what's up?"

"Do you remember a case involving a company that was bilking the federal government, specifically the Department of Defense? It happened more than seven years ago. There was a guy back then who blew the whistle on the perpetrators and they all got sent to prison."

Still standing, Agent Harper answered,

" Uh, yes...I believe I do. What about it?"

"Well, it now seems likely that the whistleblower in that case was kidnapped this morning...a Jack Alexander."

Agent Harper couldn't believe his ears. He literally collapsed in his chair. Without saying a word, he closed his eyes and his head fell back. In a flash, all of his memories of that old case flashed into his brain. Aside from the details of the case, Jack was his long-time friend from college. He'd gotten directly involved with the case because Jack had come to him. They had sort of tag-teamed on the arrests. Jack had provided him with all of the records. Agent Harper found the guilty party inside the DOD. It turned out there had been a person who had collaborated with the company, DTA Partners, who had been grossly overcharging the DOD for consulting services. In the end, several people had been prosecuted and sent to prison. Jack had gotten a big, well-deserved promotion as a result. There were so many moving parts to that case, it was great when it was finished. Agent Harper thought, *Kidnapped...by whom? How could this be? Who would want to kidnap Jack?*

"Agent Harper, are you still there? Are you still on the line?"

Agent Harper recovered.

"Yes, yes...I'm still here. What do you know so far?"

After Captain Foster gave him all the details, Agent Harper told him that he and his federal investigators would meet his police officers at Universal in less than an hour.

***

"Hello?"

"Hi, Gloria...this is Clarence."

"Clarence...I was just thinking about you today. Did you find out any more about that last letter we received when Jack was overseas or are you calling to tell me I should forget about the whole thing?

Clarence cut right to the chase.

"Gloria, unfortunately, this isn't about those letters. I have some bad news for you."

"What...what bad news? What's happened?"

Clarence didn't waste any time.

"Have you talked to Jack today?"

"No...not since he left this morning. Has something happened to him?"

"Well, I'm still collecting the details but someone reported to the police this morning that three men abducted him in the parking lot of Universal's office building."

"What in the world? Who would do such a thing, and why?"

"I have no idea but my team and I will be doing everything we can to find Jack…and get him back home to you."

He could hear Gloria crying but her voice was strong when she replied,

"Clarence, God knows that I need my husband and I have faith he will be found…safe and without harm to him."

"I'll keep you updated when I have more information. So, keep your phone close by."

The official FBI vehicle raced through traffic as he and his team made their way to Universal's corporate offices. Agent Harper reflected over what he knew thus far. *Why would anyone want to kidnap Jack? What could be accomplished by that? Who could possibly gain from this? Jack has a nice lifestyle but he's no multi-millionaire. So, I don't think this is about a ransom, but who knows. Now I have to ask myself if those anonymous letters are somehow connected to this.*

***

"So what was Jack working on?"

Len was sitting in the same conference room with Tom Wallace, and Toni Lucas. Agent Harper had called ahead and asked Detective McClain to get them together for a conversation. They and the two FBI agents he'd brought with him sat across from the senior executives from Universal.

Agent Harper looked at the Universal executives in front of him and waited. He listened as Len spoke up. "He was recently named president of a company we acquired. He had been working on the integration of that firm into Universal."

"Did Jack have any enemies that either of you were aware of?" Agent Harper looking from one of them to the other as the question hung in the air.

He concentrated on Len's next comments."Jack is a very like-able guy here at the firm. We all have a great appreciation for him. Known enemies...I don't think so."

Harper looked over at Toni as she chimed in,

"There is no one here at Universal who would have any reason to be his enemy. He was a very smart and honest person. We all liked him."Once she finished, Agent Harper asked,

"Why did you refer to him in the past tense?"

Agent Harper saw that she was flustered because she quickly looked over at Len for moral support as she attempted to recover,

"Oh no, I'm sorry...I didn't mean to refer to him in that way. I was simply saying he's a super guy and well-liked by everyone."

Tom Wallace, the general counsel, interjected,

"Agent Harper, we're all very shook up right now. We all think the world of the guy. As the legal counsel for the firm, my chief focus is getting him back to us and to his family."

"Agreed," was the unison comment from Len and Toni.

"So what are the next steps? What are you folks going to do to get Jack back?"

"I don't have all the answers at this point. But I would appreciate your total and complete cooperation as we investigate this case."

"Yes, of course...we'll do everything you ask in order to help you locate Jack and get him back."

Agent Harper added,

"Okay...we'll need this conference room as our command center. Instruct your people that no one is to come into this room. It is officially off limits to all personnel except my team." He inserted,

"By the way, I'd like you to have your locksmith come up here. I need to get the door lock changed." He looked at Len for confirmation.

"Yes...that will be fine. Will you need anything else from us?"

Agent Harper said,

"No...that will be all for now. If we need anything else, we'll let you know. By the way...thanks for your cooperation."

"No problem...anything we can do to help." With that remark, Agent Harper and Detective McClain watched the three executives leave the room.

CHAPTER
FORTY-SEVEN

NO ONE SAID ANYTHING. THERE were some stops and starts after they left the parking garage. Jack couldn't determine what was happening. Maybe they had to stop for gasoline. That didn't make sense because they couldn't risk being seen by someone passing by the car. It seemed like people were either getting in or out of the car at different places along the route. The ride was long and after a while, it was clear they were on an expressway. Jack couldn't see anything because from the moment he was put in the back seat of the car, one of the three men put a thick cotton pillowcase over his head and tied his hands behind him with what felt like plastic handcuffs. His legs were tied up as well, near his ankles.Thinking back to his abduction, he'd gotten out of his car in the parking garage as he had done scores of times in the past. He'd barely noticed the car that pulled up and stopped behind him. Two men with sunglasses had walked up to him. The guns in their hands let him know they were serious. Jack never noticed the third man who stepped behind him. Before he realized what had happened, he'd felt a pinprick, much like being bitten by an insect, and had fallen to the floor of the garage. He couldn't move at all. He was unable to raise his voice or even speak. Jack was aware that his pulse had greatly increased and his heart was racing.

Jack realized that two of the guys had picked him up, gotten him to his feet, and walked him between themselves to their car. Jack's feet weren't cooperating so they literally dragged him across the parking garage floor. He could feel himself being laid down in the back seat. It was like he was in a coma but he was still awake. The questions he asked himself now were the same ones he asked when they'd tossed him in the back of the car. *What's the deal? Where are these guys taking me? What do they want from me?*

Jack tried to remain calm; slowing his breathing while keeping his eyes closed was a technique he'd read about in one of his running magazines. He never thought he'd be forced to try to use it in a position like this. He vaguely remembered the article indicated if the steps were followed, it helped to avoid panic attacks. Jack thought, *Who are these guys? What have I done to warrant this? And how long will it be before anyone realizes that I've disappeared?*

Jack went back over what he remembered. He could picture two of the guys but there must have been a third one. He couldn't visualize many details. He did recall they wore suits, had on hats and sunglasses. He could picture the car. It was a white four-door automobile, but he couldn't figure out the make or model. The interior was beige and the seats were cloth, not leather. He thought, *I hope somebody saw what happened in that parking garage and reported it. God help Gloria not to be stressed out by all this and please get me back home.*

***

Catherine was startled when she heard the key in the door and saw Rachel walk in. "Where have you been? I've been sick with worry. You should have been back hours ago."

She watched as Rachel took her key out of the lock, closed the door, walked over to the kitchen table, and sat down. Catherine noticed that Rachel was looking down at her hands seemingly to gather her thoughts before she spoke. She also realized her daughter's hands were shaking but she pressed them down on the table as a way to make them stop. She waited until her daughter finally spoke.

"I'm sorry I worried you by not calling you but for the majority of my time away from here it couldn't be avoided.""'It couldn't be avoided'...what does that even mean?"

Catherine observed Rachel taking a deep breath before saying,

"Jack Alexander was abducted by three men in the parking garage and then drove away. I saw it all from my car. They put him in their car, put a bag over his head, and sped off."

"What! But why didn't you call me and let me know what happened?" Catherine's voice was elevated, her eyebrows were raised.

"I was stunned, shocked...I'd never seen anything like that in my life."

Catherine studied her daughter. She saw that Rachel's hands were still shaking.

"Okay...So what did you decide to do?"

She waited for an answer."I reported what happened to the police."

Catherine screamed at the top of her lungs,

"You did what? Why in the world would you do that?"

"I decided that no one deserves to be kidnapped like that. Regardless of what you said that guy did to us, he shouldn't have to bear up under that. Yes...I went to the police station and reported it."

Catherine was seething. She balled up her fist and banged on the table. She started growling like a wild animal, full of unbridled rage. She had a mind to slap her daughter but resisted the urge. While she hadn't completely calmed down, she finally said,

"You stupid little girl...you have no idea what you've done."

"Why...what's the problem? You had nothing to do with that, did you? Why should you care?"Catherine's rage subsided little.

"I didn't tell you my entire plan, but we would have abducted him and held him for ransom. I had everything worked out. The last piece was the confirmation from you regarding what time he arrived at work today."

Catherine observed her daughter as she sat straight up in her chair and listened to this master plan being explained.

"I thought you were going to detain him for a few hours, make him feel uncomfortable, maybe even scare him, and then let him go. I'm not the smartest person on the planet but that little plan you outlined would have gotten us both thrown in to prison... you for the second time."

"I've been working on this for a long time. I had others involved as well. Now it's all gone up in smoke." Catherine fell back in her chair and looked up at the ceiling.

"Really...are you kidding me right now? I realize now what a big fool I've been...and how blessed I've been. If this little plan of yours had happened, I'd soon be in jail along with you and your cronies.

" Then she added, "You need to know the police have my name and address. It won't take them long to figure out who I am and who you are."

"And why would they be looking for me?"

"They'll probably start checking for anyone who had issues with that Jack Alexander guy. I bet your name will probably be at the top of the list.""But I haven't done anything...you made sure of that!"

"Yeah, but I'm sure you've got some papers and documents of your little scheme. If the authorities show up here, they will see them and likely decide to arrest you for something tied to that kidnapping. Boy...how stupid I was for getting caught up in this."

Catherine carefully observed Rachel. She could tell there was something her daughter was considering that hadn't hit her until now.

Rachel simply blurted it out.

"One more thing...why were you so upset about me going to the police? Since Jack was kidnapped, there's no way your little scheme could possibly work now." She looked intently at her mother.

"Why all the emotion, what am I missing?" Her mother stared at her daughter but didn't say a word.

CHAPTER
FORTY-EIGHT

AGENT HARPER AND DETECTIVE MCCLAIN sat at the conference table going over the facts of the case. The other agents and two police officers were there as well. Finally, Agent Harper stood and addressed the team.

"Okay folks…what do we know so far? Jack Alexander was abducted early this morning as he got out of his car. He hasn't been seen or heard from since. His cell phone has been turned off. The sole witness thought the car was white and was an American made car." He stopped to review his notes and then added…

"The eye witness also gave us the license plate number on the car. We now believe they were Wisconsin plates. What did the Wisconsin state police come up with? Have we checked it out with the DMV? What have we found out?"

One of the agents said,

"The plates were assigned to a Marie Lawrence from Milwaukee who reported a few days ago that they were taken off her car during the night."

"Okay…anything else?"

The same agent replied,

"We've given the plates to every possible state and local agency hoping we'll get a hit someplace."

"Listen up, people…It's clear the abductors have been planning this for some time and the stolen plates were part of their plan. Detective McClain and I need everything you've got on this one. Let's go folks, we need to find this guy...so we need a break in this case. But a guy I worked for years ago used to say, You make your own breaks."

***

Jack's wrists were in pain and his ankles didn't feel much better. In spite of the pain, he was trying to get his bearings. With the pillow case over his head, being pushed down on the seat, and covered up with what felt like a blanket, he couldn't determine if they were going south to Indiana or north to Wisconsin. He further determined that there was also the possibility he was being taken to one of the western suburbs. All he knew was they were on an expressway.He racked his brain trying to figure out who would kidnap him and why. As hard as he tried, nothing came to mind. He estimated that they had been driving for over an hour, maybe two. He wondered how long it would be before they got where they were going, and what he'd face then. He prayed another prayer. *God help the authorities to find me and help me to have the courage to get through this.*

Agent Harper and Det. McClain reviewed their collective notes. All of the other agents and officers had left the room. Det. McClain felt compelled to share some background information on Jack Alexander that happened seven years ago.

Agent Harper looked up.

"Yeah...what about it?"

"Well, apparently you were the federal agent who led the investigation and the arrests."

He still stared at McClain.

"That's right...why'd you bring that up?"

"I don't know...I got to thinking, could this have anything to do with that old case?"

Agent Harper turned his leather chair so he faced McClain directly.

"What would make you think that? It doesn't appear that these two cases have any correlation at all to me."

McClain picked up his note pad and asked,

"What happened to the perpetrators in that old case? I was told that most of them received reduced sentences because they ratted out the person who planned it all."

"Yep, that's about right...but I still don't get a connection."

McClain replied,

"Maybe there isn't one. But what happened to the one who planned it all?"

"She was convicted and given nine or ten years in a federal prison."

"Harper, what was her name? Do you remember?"

"Okay, I'll bite...her name was Catherine Frazier"

"Yeah, well it says here that she was sentenced to ten years and she was paroled about three months ago based on good behavior."

Agent Harper replied,

"I remember that she lived in Atlanta. Where is she now?"

"Well, she isn't in Atlanta anymore. The parole board apparently allowed her to relocate to Chicago to be with her daughter."

As soon as he said that, they both looked like they had been hit by a bolt of lightning. Agent Harper was the first to speak

"What was the name of the eyewitness to the kidnapping?" His mind was turning over at a hundred miles a minute. They both spoke at the same time.

"Rachel Frazier!"

"You've got an address, right?"

Det. McClain nodded.

"Let's go!" They both grabbed their jackets and flew out the door.

***

"FBI, open up!"

Slowly the door opened and Rachel's face appeared.

Agent Harper flashed his badge and said,

"Miss Rachel Frazier, remember, I'm Special Agent Harper for the FBI. We have a warrant to search these premises."

He watched her hesitate for a few seconds and then opened the door and allowed them entrance into her apartment. Harper had been fortunate to get the warrant by having one of his agents set up a video conference with a judge and show cause. Another agent picked up the warrant and met Harper at Rachel Frazier's apartment.

As he presented the warrant to her, Agent Harper said,

"These papers give us the right by law to enter your home and perform a search of these premises." As he moved into the apartment, five other agents moved in behind him. In seconds, they fanned out throughout the apartment. While they went about their search, Agent Harper kept talking to Rachel.

"Have a seat. We need to talk." He observed her closely as she moved to her couch, sat down, and started reading the warrant she'd been handed. "You are free to read it but I promise you that it is all in order."

He and Det. McClain grabbed two kitchen chairs and sat down facing Rachel. Harper had previously alerted Det. McClain as to what he should ask Rachel. On cue, he spoke first.

"Rachel, why didn't you tell me that your mother knew Jack Alexander?"

Harper and McClain studied her reaction to the question. Harper noticed that she looked down at her hands before she answered.

"I didn't think it was relevant."

"So you were aware that your mother knew him?"

"Yes, but as I said, I didn't think it was relevant. She didn't have anything to do with what happened."

Now Agent Harper spoke up.

"How do you know that?"

Harper watched as her eyes got big and she balled up her right hand into a fist.

"I just know."

At that moment, one of the other agents walked into the living room and whispered in Harper's ear,

"We've checked every room. There's nothing here…it's all clear."Agent Harper took in what he'd heard. He turned and looked at Rachel.

"Where's your mother? Why isn't she here?"

"I'm not sure . Maybe she went out for a walk."

"For a walk…where would she go?"

Just then, the door opened and an agent who had been outside walked in with Catherine Frazier.

***

"Hey Lewis, I realize that none of this comes at a good time. I wish it hadn't happened, but it did. We've never had anyone kidnapped before, certainly not a senior executive."

Len was talking with the board chairman of Universal Systems. He wanted to make sure that he gave the board an immediate update on the unfortunate situation.

He sat and waited for a reply. It didn't take long.

"Len, have the authorities come up with any leads yet?"

"Not a single one. Apparently, there was an eyewitness. I get the sense that everything possible is being done. The Chicago police have brought in the FBI. So, I feel confident that they are taking this seriously."

Len figured out what the next question would be.

"Have you talked to Jack's wife? How is she taking all this? She's got to be miserable."

"I did talk to her. She seems to be holding up reasonably well, given the circumstances. I assured her that we were doing everything we could to locate him." Len remained calm as he waited for the board chairman's next comment.

"Len, I'll notify the board, but keep me up-to-date on any and all developments on this."

"I certainly will. I'll talk to you as soon as I get any updates." He was about to hang up,

"Oh, one more thing…I hate to bring this up but who will be handling his JSL responsibilities in the interim?"

"Yeah, good point…I have been thinking about that as well. I have some ideas. I want to wait forty-eight to seventy-two hours with the hope the authorities will have something definitive. If the situation is the same, or worse, I'll put in place an interim strategy."

"Okay…but don't wait too long to decide."

"Trust me, I won't."

Len slowly put the phone down. He leaned back in his chair and put his right hand on his forehead as he closed his eyes. He thought, *God, if you are up there, I pray you will spare this man and get him back to us safe. He's like a son to me and I don't want anything adverse to happen to him. Thanks big guy for hearing me and answering this one.*

CHAPTER

FORTY-NINE

"WELL, WELL, WELL...CATHERINE FRAZIER. COME on in and have a seat. We were just having a delightful conversation about you." Agent Harper's words were dripping with sarcasm.

He watched carefully as Catherine came in and plopped herself down next to her daughter on the couch. Agent Harper pressed on,

"So, last time I saw you, there were handcuffs on your wrists and you were being led away to start a long sentence in a federal penitentiary somewhere in West Virginia."

Harper knew she would have a response and she didn't disappoint. "Yeah, that was a long time ago in a place far, far away. I served my time and paid my debt to society."

"Oh what a cliché...if I've heard that once, I've heard it a thousand times." He paused and stared at her.

"Nonetheless, I heard you were a model prisoner and got paroled for good behavior."

"That's right...and my good behavior continues." Harper saw that she had a frown on her face with her mouth turned down.

"So, why are you guys here? Why are you pestering me and my daughter?"

"We'll ask the questions. What do you know about the abduction of your old pal, Jack Alexander, earlier this morning?"

He observed that the frown on her face remained and now she folded her arms in defiance.

"All I know is what my daughter told me. I can't say that I'm sorry about it. He probably got exactly what he deserved."One of the other agents walked into the room and motioned to Harper and said,

"You need to come and see this."

Harper got up and started to follow the agent into the next room. He turned to Det. McClain before he left.

"Find out when she left and where she went."

"You heard the question. What's the answer?""Who are you?"

"I'm Detective William McClain from the Chicago Police Department. Now answer the question."

"I was right here all day until I decided to take a short walk to the park for about twenty minutes."

Agent Harper came back in the room, sat down, and looked at Catherine with a stern face.

"You told us you knew nothing about Jack Alexander's abduction until your daughter told you. Is that correct?"

"Yes...that's right."

"I don't believe you're telling us everything. We found paper in the bedroom with the words 'Alexander, detain, and lookout'." Now Harper observed the changed body language of Rachel. Previously, all during the questioning, she had sat on the couch with her legs crossed and looking off into space. Agent Harper went on,

"What do those words mean?"

Harper watched her as she calmly took her time before answering him.

"Those are words on a page. They don't mean anything and don't refer to anyone."

"Really...we are going to ask you two to come down to our FBI offices."

"Are we under arrest?"Harper answered,

"No, you are not…we want you to come down to our command center for some additional questions. So let's go."

***

They were now off the expressway and on to a street. Jack could tell because the speed of the car had greatly reduced and the car stopped from time to time. Jack was trying desperately for any sounds that might give him a clue about where they were and where they might be heading. But as hard as he tried, he couldn't figure it out. Eventually, they were on a dirt road. Jack could tell because rocks could be heard as they sprayed away from under the car's tires.

CHAPTER
FIFTY

"C OME ON, RACHEL, TELL US what we want to know about what your mother has been up to." Det. McClain had been peppering Rachel with questions. Nonetheless, the more questions he asked, the more sullen she became. He observed her body language; folded arms, keeping her gaze down at the table in front of her. He couldn't get her to say one word.

Finally she said,

"Look, I don't know anything. If my mother has been involved in something, you should ask her."

Det. McClain started tapping his pen on his notepad. In a room with only one gray table and three chairs, the tapping sound was all that could be heard. Det. McClain stopped tapping and said,

"I hate to tell you this but if you don't start cooperating with us, we'll put you in one of the FBI's holding cells and keep you here for the next seventy-two hours."

Det. McClain noticed a slight change in her body language. He sensed that the idea of being in a cell for three days was worrisome to her. He thought, *She looks calm on the outside. But inside she's probably screaming to herself "how did I let myself get into this mess? Me, stay in a cell for three days? I don't want any part of this." It won't be long before she cracks.* "Can I call somebody? Aside from my mother, no one else even knows where I am." Det. Mc-

Clain kept jotting down notes in his pad and ignoring Rachel. He thought, W*ell, well, well, look who's finally coming around. I'll let her dangle a bit longer and see how much information I can get from her.* He looked up at her and said,

"Tell me again, what you were doing in that parking garage. Why were you there?"

"What…I told you before. I was looking for a parking space so I could go hunting for a job in the building."

"Come on, Rachel, no businesses open their doors until eight or eight-thirty. You were in the garage before seven am in the morning. Why would you have to be there so early? Why were you really there?"

McClain could tell by her mannerisms the fact that she was uncomfortable. He clearly saw that she looked down at the table while her hands shook. "Look, the parking garage gives an early morning discount before seven a.m. Plus, I figured I would go to Starbucks, sit down, and map out my job search strategy." Then she added,

"Detective, I know my rights…you need to let me call somebody so I can let them know where I am."

"Actually, by law, I don't have to give you anything. Nevertheless, I'm going to allow it. All right, get up, let's go." McClain led her to a small conference room that had a phone. He pointed to it and said,

"There's the phone. Go make your call. Make sure it's not long distance."

McClain stood off on one side of the conference room while she dialed. He wanted to hear everything she said during her call. "Hello."

"Hello, Luke…it's Rachel."

"Rachel, where are you? I don't recognize this phone number."

"Luke, I don't have a lot of time. So listen carefully. I'm here at the FBI's field office on Roosevelt road, on the west side of the city. You can Google the actual address but it's around 2100 West on Roosevelt. I need you to call my Dad and let him know that I'm here. Can you do that?"

"What…you're where? What's going on? Were you arrested?"

"I don't have time to talk. So, can you call him?"

"Uh, yeah…sure, I'll call him, but what else should I tell him? You know he'll want to know."

"Tell him that I haven't been arrested…yet. I could be held here for as long as seventy-two hours. And the agent in charge is someone named Harper…Agent Clarence Harper."McClain figured that she had spent enough time on the call.

"Okay Rachel, that's it. I need you to hang up right now."

CHAPTER

FIFTY-ONE

DAY TWO

AFTER HIS CALL WITH LUKE, Frank leaned forward in his chair, slumped down, and covered his face with his hands. He couldn't believe what he'd heard. "The FBI is holding Rachel and her mother for questioning."

He thought, *That's crazy. Why in the world would they be holding my little girl for questioning? What could she have possibly done? I can't imagine her mother getting my daughter into anything stupid. I never thought it was a good idea for her to go live with Rachel in the first place, and now this. I've got to get on the first plane up to Chicago.*

***

"Don't you want me to go with you?" Frank thought about Laura's offer for a second. He knew instantly what his answer had to be.

"I appreciate your offer but I have to say no…absolutely not. I'm not sure what I'm going to face up there or how long I'll have to stay." Frank knew she would be disappointed but he had to stick to his position. He didn't want to introduce Laura to a situation he didn't fully understand. He watched her. He needed to determine if she was really upset. "Okay, I get it…so what would you like me to do to help?"Frank pondered the question and then said,

"Sarah still needs to go to school while I'm away. Since I don't know how long I'll be in Chicago, maybe you could take her to school and arrange to pick her up. There is a couple in my neighborhood she could stay with."

"I'll do better than that! She could stay with me. She's a great kid and I'd enjoy her company. That way I could take her to school, pick her up, and we can hang out together while you're gone."

"Laura, I'd appreciate that."

"Hey, come on…that's the least I could do. You've got a lot on your mind right now. Don't worry about her. I've got this, okay?"

Frank looked at her and realized again how much he had come to appreciate her, love her.***

"Luke, my plane arrives at O'Hare Airport tonight. It's scheduled to touch down at 6:38 p.m. I would normally rent a car but I don't know my way around Chicago. I realize it's asking a lot but could you pick me up?"

"Mr. Frazier, it's no problem. I would be happy to pick you up when you come in tonight. What airline are you coming in on and what's the flight number?"

"It's American…flight number 639."

"Okay…I'll see you then. Oh, make sure you come out upstairs at Departures. For me, it's much easier to pick up someone from there. Also, be sure to call me as soon as you walk off the plane."

"No problem…thanks for your help." Frank switched topics.

"Luke, what did the FBI tell you when you called to inquire about Rachel?"

"They said if I wasn't a relative or an attorney, they couldn't tell me anything. But I know they are still holding her because she said she would call me if they released her."

"Got it…we'll just have to deal with it once I get to Chicago. See you soon, and thanks for all your help."

CHAPTER

FIFTY-TWO

DAY THREE

CATHERINE SAT IN THE FBI holding cell and thought back over the last several days. *This is really crappy. Here I am sitting in this cell and being questioned for something they think I was involved in. Well, they've got to let us go soon since they can only hold us for seventy two hours.*

My daughter's pretty smart, after all. If she hadn't suggested I dispose of all I had written down and had been working on, I'd be looking at potentially serving some more time in a federal prison. Right now, they have nothing on me or Rachel. One good thing…this holding cell is light years better than the stinking hole that I rotted away in for seven years.

CHAPTER
FIFTY-THREE

LEN PICKED UP HIS DESK phone, hit the intercom button and said, "Sandi, ask Toni Lucas to come to my office. And also tell her it's important."

"Okay...I will."

Ten minutes later, Toni was sitting in front of Len. She'd walked in while he was studying some papers on his desk. He signed something, put his pen down, leaned back, and looked at her for the first time since she'd sat down.

"Toni, this business with Jack has me nervous." He rubbed his forehead.

"I don't know what's going to happen. The board is asking questions I can't answer."

"Len, for all that it's worth, I'm concerned about it too. The FBI thought that either we'd get or Jack's wife would get some ransom demands by now. We probably should do something and pretty soon."

"What would you suggest?"

"I don't know...maybe we should name an interim president of JSL until he's rescued or until we know more."

Len thought about that.

"If we do that, who should we choose?

"It probably should be someone on your leadership team,

someone who knows about the consulting and financial models of JSL. What do you think?"Len took a deep breath and then said,

"I agree…I want you to act as the interim president until we sort this all out. Are you up for the challenge?""Uh…yeah, I would agree to do that if it helps us to get over this rough patch." Then she added.

"When would you want me to begin?"

"I'm prepared to make an official announcement tomorrow. In the meantime, let me know what you need from me." He stood up, extended his hand to her.

"Thanks for being a team player during this time of need."

"Len, I'm happy to help. I'll do all I can to get us through it."

***

"We haven't found out very much thus far. We have our best people working on this."

Gloria listened to everything Agent Harper had been telling her but clearly she was upset.

"Clarence, who would have kidnapped my husband? He doesn't have any enemies? What's the deal? Please make sense of this for me. Is there any correlation between those anonymous letters and Jack being kidnapped?"

"Frankly, I don't know. This whole thing has got us stumped right now. We thought we had a lead but that has gone nowhere.""So what's next? What do you do now?"

"Gloria…typically, by now, we would have gotten a ransom note or call, but nothing."

"Why haven't you notified the local and national news agencies letting them know that my husband has been abducted? What are you waiting for?

"In conjunction with the Chicago Police department, we are initiating that action today. Part of my reason for the call was to alert you before you saw it on television."

"Clarence, I trust you. I'm really upset right now. Thank you for all that you're doing. Just get my husband back home to me."

"We're doing everything we can. I've got to go but I'll continue to keep you posted."

"Thank you." As they hung up, Gloria was lost in her thoughts. She had the TV on but she wasn't watching it. She happened to glance at it and saw a picture of Jack on the screen. She immediately turned up the volume.

***

"And this late, breaking news from Chicago, Illinois. A top executive from Universal Systems, Jack Alexander, was kidnapped three days ago from his car on his way to work. Both the Chicago Police Department and the FBI are working together on this case. Universal Systems has put up a one hundred thousand dollar reward for any information leading to the return of Jack Alexander and the capture of those responsible for his abduction. If anyone has any information regarding this case please call the number on the screen, contact the Chicago Police Department or simply call 911. In other news..."

FIFTY-FOUR

"**W**E DON'T HAVE ANYTHING ON them and we can't hold them any longer. We've got to cut them loose."

Agent Harper looked at the agent and simply nodded his head, acknowledging that he was right.

"Okay...let them go but I want you to put a tail on them and report back everywhere they go. If either of them buys so much as a candy cane, I want to know about it. Got it?"

"Sir, it turns out that Rachel Frazier's father has been here for hours. He says he's not leaving until he talks to you." Agent Harper looked perplexed.

"How did he even know I was on this case?"

"I don't know, but he needs to see you."

"Okay...I'll be out in a minute. Where is he?"

"He's in conference room A, out near the"

"Got it, I know where it is."

***

"Mr. Frazier, I'm Senior Special Agent Harper. How can I help you?"

Harper watched Rachel's dad stand up and walk over to where Harper was standing. He could tell from the frown on the man's face that he was not happy as he stuck out his hand to shake Harper's.

"Agent Harper, I remember you from the trial seven years ago against my ex-wife. I realize completely that you have a job to do. But how can you arrest my nineteen year old daughter for something she had nothing to do with?"

Harper motioned for Frank to take a seat.

"Mr. Frazier, first of all, your daughter was never arrested. She was detained for questioning associated with a very serious crime."

"But you've been holding her for the last three or four days. What's up with that?"

"Legally, we can hold a person for seventy-two hours based on suspicion. Based on when she and your ex-wife were brought in and detained, it's been seventy-one hours. You should know that the two of them are being processed for release even as we speak. They'll be cut loose within the hour."

Harper watched the frown on the father's face relax.

Then he said,

"You can keep my ex-wife forever if you want. I never want to see her after this."

"Look, I don't have anything to do with family drama. I have a serious case I'm trying to solve. So, if you will excuse me, I have to go. By the way, I wish you well."

"Agent Harper, one more thing...Catherine may have had something to do with this kidnapping business but I can assure you that Rachel didn't, and couldn't." The comment hung in the air for a few seconds. Then he added,

"Where will I find my daughter after she's processed?"

"Out the door, turn left, and walk to the end of the hall. They will help you there."

CHAPTER
FIFTY-FIVE

"**WHY ARE YOU CALLING ME** on this phone? I told you never to use it unless it was an emergency. Is it done? Did you fulfill our agreement?"

"First of all, it *is* an emergency. Second, the deed is not done. We have some complications."

"What...what complications? You have the instructions we discussed and you received payment. So what *complications* could you have had?"

"First and foremost, we have the package under wraps. But the payment terms have to be altered."

"What...the payment terms have to be altered! What kind of crap is this? We had a deal and we both agreed, just like we've done in the past."

"Yeah...all that's true but we saw the news. This is some big-shot guy, he's president of some hot division. We'll need more cash or we'll have to let him go on the side of the highway with a note in his pocket implicating my little *phone buddy*. Are you ready for that?"

"If you do that, you'll go down right along with me."

"Not a chance...believe me, you'll find yourself left holding the bag on this one. Remember...this is not my first rodeo." His last remarks created a long pregnant pause. There was nothing more for him to say.

Finally he heard,

"What do you want?"

"I need another $200,000 or we let him go."

"What...I can't come up with that kind of money!"

"$200,000 or we let him go." He was calm, not rushing any of his words.

"I'll need the money in three days. I'll let you know when and where we'll meet."

"I can't raise that kind of money...and certainly not in three days."

"That's your problem. We heard the news. That company of his has put up $100,000 reward. So, you'll have to work it out."

"I can maybe come up with $100,000 in three days...no more."

"Look...$200,000 or we let him go. This is non-negotiable. I'll wait forty-eight hours to hear back from you or get use to the idea of wearing orange jumpsuits for the next twenty years." With that, he hung up.

This has gone bad and nasty all at the same time. Where in the world am I going to get that kind of money in three day? This was all going so smoothly with sunny blue skies and happy times ahead. I know one thing for certain; orange is not a color in my wardrobe.

CHAPTER

FIFTY-SIX

DAY FIVE

T HE BASEMENT WAS COLD AND damp. There were only three windows and they were covered and sealed. The daylight was muted but Jack could tell that it was morning. He estimated that it was about six am. He'd been in this basement for four days and he still hadn't heard anything from his captives except that he was told to turn and face the wall whenever they brought food and removed the old trays. The room was super small. There was only enough space for a small cot, a tiny table for his meals, and an old wooden chair. Off to one side of the room was a toilet but there were no walls so it could hardly be called even a powder room. Jack had nothing to do, nothing to read. His only options: sleep on the cot, sit in the chair, or go to the toilet. Jack thought, *What is the deal? I've asked this question a thousand times now...why would anyone want to kidnap me? I'm trying to stay positive. I've sung in my head virtually every song I know. I've recited Marc Anthony's lines at Julius Caesar's funeral two hundred times. I'm running out of mental options. I've got to try to focus on finding a way to get out of here. With all this time on my hands, I still haven't come up with any ideas. Even with this chair, those windows are too high to reach. Wait a minute, how about putting the chair on the cot? That should put me closer to the window. If I could at least tear off the window covering, maybe I could figure out where I am, or maybe I could get one of those windows open. If so, just maybe...*

***

"I don't know why you're yelling and screaming at me. I didn't kidnap anybody. Neither the FBI nor the Chicago police have accused us of anything."

Catherine, Frank, Rachel, and Luke were sitting uncomfortably in Rachel's apartment after the ride from the FBI field office.

"I don't give a damn. You put our daughter's...my daughter's life and safety in jeopardy. The truth is, you should have never come here to Chicago. Bad stuff follows you wherever you go."

"Just a minute...I served my time, got paroled, and wanted to reconnect with my daughter. You dumped me so I only have my two daughters now."

"Hey, look, I don't want to get into all that. I wouldn't be here if you hadn't created some kind of suspicion in the minds of the authorities. The truth is...you need to leave here and let Rachel get on with her life. It's been tough enough already."

Rachel sat there watching her parents yelling at each other. Finally, with tears in her eyes, she screamed,

"Stop, stop it...please just shut up for a minute!" She watched them both turn and look at her.

"This is officially my home and I get to say what will and will not happen here."She heard her father say,

"Honey, I'm concerned about your welfare."

"Please... let me speak." With her hands in the air and out in front of her,

"I agreed to have Mom come and live with me. Honestly, it has been hard...in fact, super difficult. For whatever it's worth, I now don't believe that she had anything to do with that guy's unfortunate abduction,

Before she could finish, she heard her father interrupt her.

"How can you be so confident?"

"I just know, okay? Plus, I was the one who saw him taken. For the record, there were three men who kidnapped him. So stop going on about what she did.

I didn't like being hauled down to the FBI field offices and getting detained for seventy-two hours. But it was clear that if they had something on Mom, she wouldn't be sitting her in my apartment. So, we all need to *chill out*."

***

"McClain, what's happening at the stakeout since we cut them loose? Have there been any unusual movements?"

"There's nothing unusual going on. Honestly, I think we're barking up the wrong tree...just a sixth sense I have."

Agent Harper came right back with,

"Sixth sense or not, we need to stay on them. There are too many coincidences on this one. I definitely remember the old case. The mother goes to jail, Jack Alexander was labeled the whistleblower. The last thing she says is 'I'm going to get you... if it's the last thing I do'."

"Yeah, yeah, yeah...okay, we're in violent agreement."

"The mother happens to recently relocate to Chicago and the daughter is the *only* eyewitness to the abduction."

Harper let that sink in and then added,

"Too many coincidences for my taste."

"Come on, Harper...we've been over this ground before. There's nothing here. We need to move on so we can catch the *real* bad guys. Trust me...something is going to break soon. So tell me, what else is going on?"

"Nothing...we've got the entire country alerted. We're also using the DDACT system. What we need now is some kind of a break"

FIFTY-SEVEN

"I WAS BEGINNING TO WONDER IF you were going to contact me. Have you got the cash?"

"Yeah...it was tough coming up with it. Now I need some assurances that you're going to follow through with your end of the bargain."

"Wait a minute...let's back up. I'm not agreeing to anything until I get the money."

"Okay, okay...I get it. Meet me at our regular spot in the city. I'll have the package with exactly what you asked for. But I need to know when you will complete the deed."

"Uh-uh, I don't feel comfortable with coming back into the city."

"What...why not? Nobody's looking for you. Look, if you want to get the package, meet me at *the spot* at 6:00 p.m. tonight. I need to get this done and over with."

"Fine...I'll see you at 6. But you'd better have the money or you'll end up in deep weeds." Jonah Broderick hung up. He put his elbows on the table and his head in his hands with his eyes closed; he was buried in his thoughts. *We should have finished this contract days ago. The longer this goes on, the more uncomfortable I feel. But I can't walk away from $200,000. I don't want to go back into Illinois, and certainly not back into Chicago. I've kind of painted myself* *into a corner. It's the only way I'm going to get the money, So, I've got to go. But once I get it, we'll take care of Jack Alexander and disappear.*

***

"Dad, I appreciate you coming here to help me. I'm all right now and soon this whole thing will blow over once they catch those guys who did this and get that man back to his family.

Rachel's dad was sitting in the car with her at the O'Hare airport. He was on his way back to Atlanta. He'd been looking at his daughter ever since they'd parked. He said,

"Honey, I want to make sure you're safe. It's my job...my role as your dad to protect you. If it would make any difference, I'd move up here so no bad thing could happen to you."

"I know, Dad...and I'm so thankful for your love, your heart, and your care for me. I've come to depend on that."

Frank kept his gaze on her. It was as if he was trying to memorize every detail on her face. Finally he said,

"You're my girl...I would have gone to Mars if that's where you were.

Frank watched his daughter unbuckled her seatbelt and melted into her father's arms. Softly she said,

"Dad, I love you. Thank you again for coming...and trying to protect me."

He saw the tears rolling down her face while she used the sleeves of her sweater to catch them. He was so moved that he started crying himself.

"Rachel, I love you too." He sat there hugging her when he heard,

"Okay...you've got to move this vehicle or we'll tow it for you. Let's go, let's go! Move it!" The airport traffic cop was on the driver's side of Rachel's car waving them to move along.

"Honey, I've got to go. I'll call you tonight after I land." "Great... Dad, I love you. Thanks again."

"I love you more." Frank got out of the car, stepped onto the curb, and waved as Rachel drove away. He stood there thinking, *I know I can't control her anymore. But I wish I could convince her to come back to Atlanta. At least she would be closer. In the meantime, I pray for her safety.*

He turned and walked inside the terminal.

***

"So there's no other way for you to get the money? I think it's too risky for you to drive back into the city. The Chicago police and the FBI are on high alert. Anything could happen. I wouldn't do it." Jonah watched one of his partners in crime drinking a cup of coffee while fingering his semiautomatic Smith & Wesson. "I say let's pop this guy like we planned and get out of here. We don't need this grief."

"Hey, it'll be fine. I'll be extra careful. You need to do the dirty deed as soon as I pick up the cash, get close to the Wisconsin border, and call you. There won't be much time so keep your phone with you at all times."

"I still don't like it. But I suggest that you take the Jeep. It's clean and you for sure won't have any issues.Jonah thought about that but came back and said,

"No, I'm going to take the Chevy. The plates are legit now. Plus, it will be faster for me to get there and back."

"Uh-huh, I wouldn't do that. The plates are legit but they're in my name. If you get stopped, you'll have to explain too much. Remember, I've got a record that's not too pretty. Don't do it."

Jonah considered his comments and then asked,

"Is the insurance card in the car?"

"Yeah, so what does that mean?"

"It'll be fine. Be ready when I call you."

***

If I had known that all this was going to be so involved, I wouldn't have done it. It was so easy before. This is so much more complicated. I got

what I wanted but the cost is so much higher. I can't believe he wants $200,000. I'm glad I was able to come up with all the cash. This is all so insane, but at this point, I don't have a choice. I guess it's the price of success. I'll meet him at 6p.m. tonight and our project will finally be complete.

The intercom buzzed, interrupting her thoughts.

"Yes, what's up?"

"Sorry to disturb you, Ms. Lucas, but Mr. Shapiro called and he wants you in his office immediately."

"Fine…call him back and let him know that I am on my way." As she got up from her desk, she disconnected the call and thought, *Interim today…full-fledged president of JSL tomorrow.*

***

Jack sat in the only chair in his basement prison, dismayed. Slumped over, his elbows were on his knees, his hands folded together. With his eyes closed, his head rested on his hands. He thought, *I've been here six or seven days. At this point, I'm not even sure. I've tried everything I could think of in order to figure out how to get out of here. I can't get up to the windows and other than this door, there are no other entry or exit points to try to break out. I've tried talking to these guys every time they bring me food. No one says anything except "turn around, face the wall, and don't turn back or you won't like what happens next." I've got a good mind to tackle the next guy who brings my food and simply make a break for it. It can't be worse than sitting here doing nothing— Hey, wait a minute, why didn't I think of this before?*

***

"Thanks Toni, for coming over so quickly." Toni saw him motion for her to sit in one of the chairs in front of his desk.

"Have a seat." She could tell that he had been crying or near tears, as his eyes were red. "I'm worried…and the board is worried. It's been a week since Jack was kidnapped and we haven't heard anything." Toni watched him try to compose himself by clearing his throat and wiping his eyes."I had a long talk with Agent Harper from the FBI. He said that it is highly unusual for it to go this long without hearing from the abductors if they wanted a ransom. I don't know what to think."

She saw his eyes start to tear up again and felt compelled to speak up.

"Len, actually it's still early. The FBI doesn't have a crystal ball. We all have to have faith and patience."

"Yeah…I guess you're right. Jack has become like a son to me. I can only imagine how his wife must be feeling right now."

"Len, trust me…it will all be over soon."

"I hope you're right..

Toni waited a few sentences trying to gauge her next comments. As she was going to speak, Len said,

"Toni, I need you to handle an earnings call late this afternoon. It turns out that I have a conflict."

Toni smiled slightly as she realized that Len was exhibiting more trust and confidence in her.

"No problem…Is there anything special you want me to cover?"

"Yes, aside from the normal updates, you need to give them a progress report on JSL and what you've observed as the interim president."Toni perked up but didn't want to appear too eager.

"Len, you can count on me to handle the call. I'll be extra sensitive to Jack and JSL. Leave it to me."

"Great…that certainly takes a load off my mind."

FIFTY-EIGHT

"LOOK, SOMETHING HAS COME UP. I can't meet at 6 pm tonight. We have to make the handoff tomorrow morning."

"Wait a minute…If this is some kind of a trick, you'll find yourself either dead or in a federal prison."

Toni rushed to attempt to assure Jonah,

"No, hold on! I have a small complication. I've got a thing that came up and I can't get out of it. It's no big deal but I need tomorrow morning to work it out"

Toni could tell that Jonah wasn't happy with the change because he was quiet for a while. She figured it was best to let him work it out in his mind,."Okay…but you'll need to meet me closer to the Wisconsin border."

"The Wisconsin border, that's too far away. Can't we meet some place closer? I've got some other obligations"

"Hey, if you want to change the time, then I'm changing the location. You'll meet me at the Shell gas station on Grand Avenue before the Gurnee Mills Shopping Center. Get there by 9:00 a.m. sharp and, for your sake, don't be late."

Toni slumped down in her chair, her hand over her eyes, and said,

"Fine…I'll be there at 9. Look, I've got to go." As she hung up, she thought, *The sooner this is over, the better. Once I see him tomorrow, everything will hopefully get back to normal…the new normal.*

FIFTY-NINE

"LET'S SYNCHRONIZE OUR WATCHES. IT'S 7:30 a.m. I should be calling you no later than 9:00 a.m., so be ready. When I call, I'll only be thirty five or forty minutes away."

"Great...that will give me enough time to take care of Mr. Alexander, clear everything out, and be all ready to go by the time you get back. I already went over the place for fingerprints. Nonetheless, I'll go over it again to make sure that every print in the home is gone. There will be nothing to connect us.

"Okay...and remember; no loose ends."

"I got it...no worries on my end."

***

Rachel was preparing for school. She took a long time in the shower. It was as if she was trying to let the water wash off the memory of the last few days. She closed her eyes, but she couldn't totally blot out the details of her unfortunate experiences. Abduction, police stations, corporate conference rooms, FBI search warrants, detention, and feeling like a criminal. She so wanted the steam from the hot shower to somehow evaporate all the negatives that had permeated her life.She turned off the water and grabbed her big dark green towel. The remaining steam didn't allow her to see herself in the mirror only a few feet in front of her. She took her hand and rubbed the mirror until she could see her face. Her image wasn't very clear, like the image she had of what it would be like when her mother came to live with her. For some strange reason, her image was recapturing the relationship she'd lost when her mother went off to prison. Little by little, the steam dissipated, and she could see more clearly. It reminded her of the imminent conversation that she was determined to have with her mother before she left for school. The clearer she saw her image in the mirror, the deeper her resolve.

***

"Honestly, I don't totally know why but I sense that he's still alive and that he'll be somehow rescued today." Gloria was talking with her smartphone on speaker. She wasn't looking at it. She gazed out of her dining room window. She was looking up at the blue, cloudless sky.Her good friend Barb replied,

"I agree with you that he'll be rescued. But why are you so sure about today being the day?"

Gloria was quick to reply,

"Today is the seventh day since he was taken. And, as you know, seven is the number of completion. I know it sounds weird but I believe that God is going to provide a breakthrough today."

"Great...let's pray about that." So they spent the next several minutes praying together.

***

Rachel walked out the bathroom and saw her mother at the kitchen table drinking coffee and staring into space.

"Good morning, Mom." Rachel watched as her mother turned her head and looked at her.

"Morning Rachel...how did you sleep last night?"

Rachel didn't immediately answer but walked over to the fridge, pulled out a bottle of orange juice, and sat down.

245

"I didn't sleep very well. I was up half the night. There was a ton on my mind."

"Like what?"

"Well, for starters…you've got to find someplace else to live." She dropped the bomb on her, realizing that there was no gentle way to say it.

"I can't have you here any longer. Mom, you are too big of a liability. Looking back, I shouldn't have allowed you to come here in the first place." Rachel realized that she'd said a lot. So she didn't say any more, opened her bottle, poured out some juice, and waited for her mother to speak.

"Honey, I too have been doing a lot of soul-searching. First, I want you to know that I am sorry that this whole thing got so out of control. I never envisioned things working out like this. I thought"

"How did you think it would work out? Did you think we'd actually abduct him and that there would be no adverse reactions?" She was now staring at her mother with a real grimace on her face.

"You thought that the FBI and the police wouldn't come and cart us off to jail? You had a thought that we wouldn't be tried and prosecuted? What were you thinking?"

"I'm sorry that I put you in harm's way and I guess I wasn't fully thinking about the downside implications. I was consumed with rage, anger, bitterness, and resentment. So, I'm sorry…really sorry." Rachel saw the tears were rolling down her mother's face as they hit the table. She was surprised that her mother made no attempt to wipe them away.

"You're my daughter. You're right…I could have ended up being responsible for putting you in the same place that I got out of. That was totally irresponsible on my part."

Rachel stared at what she was seeing: her mother crying in front of her and wiping her nose with the sleeve of her blouse.

"Mom, okay, okay...thanks for saying that." As she touched her arm

"I see"

Rachel allowed her mother to interrupt her mid-sentence."I need to finish. You see, hate was consuming me and I would have done anything and used anybody, including you, to exact the revenge on Jack Alexander. But I now see that payback doesn't work. I now realize that I needed to look at the wrongs I'd done in the past. I also needed to take responsibility for them."

Rachel allowed her mother to reach out her hand and lay it on her daughter's arm.

"I see that now...more clearly than ever before. Jack Alexander only pointed out those wrong things. I should have never faulted him for that."

Rachel realized that with her last statement, her mother started weeping and crying uncontrollably.

She got up and took a Kleenex box from a table across the room. She pulled out several tissues and handled them to her mother. Minutes went by as she watched her cry and blow her nose. When Rachel thought her mother was done, her tears started all over again.

Rachel didn't make a sound. She was content to wait and watch. She could tell that her mother was coming to the end of her tears. Finally, she heard her mother speak.

"The wake-up call for me was when you came home and told me about seeing that man kidnapped and you deciding to report it to the police. What a noble thing you did."

Rachel watched her sniff and blow her nose again before she spoke next,

"It came to me how responsible you were, not for Jack Alexander but for me as well. You see, if you hadn't come home, told me what you saw, and suggested that I get rid of all those abduction plans, the FBI would still have us in custody. So, thank you for your care and concern. I owe my life, my new life, to you, honey."

Rachel sat in front of her mother, half in shock and half in a spirit of thanksgiving. She had never seen this side of her mother. This was the woman who was so tough, self-secure, and confident. The woman she was seeing now was soft, kind, and humble. Rachel was so moved that she got up and walked to the side of the table where her mother was sitting and reached out and hugged her. Rachel realized that her mother was getting up to hug her as well. Rachel heard her mother crying all over again. She was so moved that she started crying too.She didn't have any idea how long they hugged each other, weeping and crying. But she felt they were able to cross the relational divide that had separated them for so long. With each shed tear, a deeper kindred connection was established, or re-established. Rachel then heard something that deeply moved her.

"You are my precious, precious daughter...I love you."With a compassionate facial expression filled with smiles through her tears, Rachel said,

"I know...I love you too."

CHAPTER
SIXTY

"**O**KAY, YOU KNOW THE DRILL...TURN around and keep your face to the wall."Jack knew in a few seconds, the door would be unlocked and one of his abductors would come in with his breakfast. As he stood off to the right side of the room with the room's only chair within arm's reach, he realized this would probably be his only opportunity to attempt an escape. He thought, *I don't know if this guy has a gun or if he's seven feet tall with a Schwarzenegger build. At this point, I don't care. If I'm going to get out of here, I've got to take a shot.* He called out,

"I can't right now, I'm using the can. I'll be done in a couple seconds."

Kyle Luther, Jonah's partner, stood outside the door and thought, *What difference does it make if he sees my face at this point? This is the last day that he's going to see anybody.*

"Okay...stay where you are. I'm coming in."Jack stood still as he heard the familiar sound of the key opening the lock to his basement prison. His heart was racing. He hadn't fully worked out his plan but that no longer mattered. As soon as the door swung open and his kidnapper took a step inside the room, from behind the door, Jack swung the chair with all of his might into the face of his abductor.

He let out a loud groan and fell back on to the floor. The tray filled with oatmeal and hot coffee spilled all over him. Jack didn't waste any time. He stood over the man and swung the chair again and his abductor passed out. There was a wave of satisfaction that swept over Jack as he looked down at the unconscious person who had been holding him against his will.Jack picked up the smartphone off the floor and tried to get reception to dial out. When he couldn't, he realized he needed to enter a passcode. In addition, the phone was wet because the coffee from his tray had spilled all over it. Looking down at his abductor, he realized that he needed to immediately find a way out of the house. He started moving to the stairs that led up to the first floor. There was no light on the stairway and the stairs were made of wood. So, he had to be extra careful not to make too much noise in case someone was upstairs and happen to come to the stairway door. What a surprise they'd get if they saw him instead of his abductor.

***

The drive north on I94 wasn't as busy as it would have been an hour earlier. Because of the abundance of companies located north of Chicago, thousands of people commuted on this expressway every morning. The sun was now high in the cloudless sky. Based on the weather report on the car radio, it promised to be a very nice day. But in spite of the weatherman's promise, Toni was in turmoil as she drove to the rendezvous with Jonah. She thought, *Why did I agree to drive up here? With all the new computer systems police have, some cop is bound to capture my license. Then I'll have to explain why I'm even on this expressway and where I'm going. Now I have to ask myself if all this is even worth it.*

***

Captain Lou Thompson, Commander of the Wisconsin state patrol officers, stood in front of a room full of officers. Their standard process was to go over all the critical details the troopers needed to know before the beginning of their shift. He'd been talking for the last ten minutes about some new process.

"All right everybody…The state spent a ton of the taxpayers' money on this new technology. The LPR, License Plate Readers, will help us solve crimes. So, make sure you turn them on, troopers." The Commander stopped, looked down at his notes, and then said,

"Last item, and then you'll be free to go. We have some promotions. Patrol troopers Harlan Farwell and Carmen Gonzalez have been promoted to Senior Highway Patrol Specialists…congratulations."

There was a huge round of applause. Some troopers shook their hands or slapped them on the back. There were lots of smiles and well-wishes in the room. Then the Watch Commander interrupted.

"Oh, I forgot to mention this…I know most of you have been asked to work double shifts lately. I appreciate your dedication. We've hired some new troopers so as soon as they're trained, you won't have to put in the double duty. That's all…so let's get out there. Oh, Gonzalez…I need to speak to you in my office."

SIXTY-ONE

THE REST OF THE BASEMENT was also dark and dingy. There was miscellaneous furniture strewn all over. The hallway that led to the stairs was narrow, barely allowing one person to walk through. Jack wanted to turn the lights on but feared that someone else might become suspicious. As he went up the stairs, he hit the third step and it creaked. He hesitated. Jack didn't hear any sounds like oncoming footsteps, so he kept going.

Once he got to the top of the stairs, he gained enough confidence to slowly push the door open. Little by little, he opened it until he could survey the kitchen, living room, and the front door. He saw overflowing ashtrays, paper plates of half-finished food, pizza boxes, containers that looked like Chinese carryout, and near-empty beer bottles. Throughout the place, there was a general state of disarray. There was no one else in the house from what he could see. Then he saw it. There was a phone on the wall in the area between the living room and the kitchen. Slowly he moved toward it. He picked it up and almost shouted out loud when he heard a dial tone. He punched in "9-1-1" and waited. Jack could only hear his heart beating as he pressed the phone to his ear waiting for an operator. He was about to hang up and redial when he heard,

"9-1-1, what is your emergency?"

Jack started to holler into the phone but he forced himself to quietly say,

"Please come and help me. My name is Jack Alex."

A hand disconnected the line while at the same time he felt cold steel against the back of his head.

"Drop the phone now!"Jack was shocked that anyone was there. He hadn't heard anyone come up behind him. Then something struck Jack's head with such force that he fell to the floor with a thud. Before he passed out, the last thing he remembered seeing was a tattoo on his abductor's wrist. He saw a red rose with the words "for always, Lou and Sherry."***

"Gonzalez, I went to bat for you on this promotion thing. I hope you appreciate it."

Trooper Gonzalez squirmed in her chair as she listened to the Commander ramble on about all he'd done for her. After five years as a highway patrol trooper, she had more than earned this promotion. She'd joined the force with a Master's degree in criminal justice. A high school diploma was all that was required. She'd also had two tours in Iraq all before joining up. She'd been cited for bravery, valor, and a host of other things since being with the Wisconsin State troopers. But the Commander was holding her back. He'd said multiple times, and in many ways, her promotions were tied to her providing him with some sexual favors. She resisted and he decided to make her life difficult and promotions a virtual impossibility.

"All you did was to give me what you know I rightfully deserved." She looked him squarely in the face and added, "So what do you want? What's so urgent?"

She watched his face twisted into a gruesome frown. To her, it looked like he was about to spit out an obnoxious reply.

Nonetheless, she heard him calmly say,

"Trooper Gonzalez, I asked you in here to simply say that I am happy for you. I hope there'll be no hard feelings as we move forward."

Neither of them said anything but stared at each other. Finally Gonzalez asked,

"Will there be anything else?"

"No...we're done here." With that, Gonzalez got up, opened the door, made her exit out of the station, and got into her patrol car. As she made her way to I94, she focused her thoughts on the duties of the day.

***

Driving back to Gurnee Miles for the pickup was very straightforward. Jonah thought, *In less than an hour, I'll have the money, we'll put Mr. Alexander out of his misery, and we'll be on our way. It's too bad that the guy has to get bumped off. He didn't do anything wrong. I wish there was some way we could let him go. I'm sure his family will miss him. But I need the pay day. It's all part of the job.*

***

State trooper Gonzalez turned on to I94 going south toward the Illinois state line. The traffic during the early morning was heavier than usual and there were no obvious speeders, especially after her marked vehicle was seen. She drove to her standard stop, about three miles from the Illinois / Wisconsin border. It allowed her to observe the southbound oncoming traffic. She sat there for a few minutes and then remembered to turn on her LPR, referring to the License Plate Reader. Her LPR would pick up and read virtually every plate that passed. The constant *beep* confirmed that the reader was recording each plate.

***

FBI Agent Harper sat at his desk with his elbows on the glass top. His fingers were pushing up his eyebrows as he looked at his computer screen. He was trapped in his thoughts. *It's been a week and we've heard nothing regarding the whereabouts of my friend Jack. I've had agents working on this case literally around the clock.*

254

*What's up? There hasn't been a peep, a sound, a whisper. If this is about a ransom, we should have heard something by now. It's the very thing we tell everybody. At the start, I was convinced that Catherine Frazier had everything to do with this, but now I'm not so sure. The Chicago police have been diligent with their stakeout. Rachel's father leaving town was the only movement. I can't call Gloria again and tell her that we don't have anything at all to report. God in heaven, I need a break here.*His phone started to buzz.

***

Kyle Luther stood over Jack. He was so mad that he wanted to put a bullet in his head right then and there. If Jonah hadn't been so specific with his instructions, this guy would be in another world. Kyle rubbed his forehead. There was a knot starting forming where the chair Jack hit him with had collided with his head. Kyle thought, *If I hadn't recovered when I did, the police would already be breathing down my neck. Where in the world is Jonah? He should have already called me so I can finish the job. We need to get out of here. This job is giving me the creeps.*

***

Toni got to the Shell gas station first, right on the southwest corner of the intersection before the entrance to Gurnee Mills, exactly like Jonah said. She moved her car to the corner, turned right, and drove toward the back of the station at an angle so she could see the cars pulling in.Less than five minutes later, the white Chevy with Jonah in it pulled in. Slowly the car moved up to Toni's car. Toni watched as Jonah rolled down the driver's side window."Have you got the money?"

Toni nodded.

"Great, no need to get out...pass me the bag through the window."

Toni took the black duffel bag from the seat next to her and gave it to Jonah. She observed him as he took it, opened it, and quickly closed it.

Toni said,

"Aren't you going to even count it?"

"Hey, look, I trust you. Plus, you don't want to short-change me. No, I don't need to count it."

She watched him put his car in gear. "Look, I'd love to sit and talk to you all day but I've got to run. Call me if you need me again. Have a nice life."

With that, Toni watched him steer his car back on to Grand Avenue and she knew he was on his way to I94 heading toward Wisconsin.

Toni was looking out her front windshield, yet not looking at anything particularly. She was lost in her thoughts. *Well, that's that. I needed to get this over with and now it's done. Well, at least my part is done. Now I've got to trust that this guy will finish the job. That's the crappy part. If he reneges, I'm basically screwed. So, I have no choice but to assume that it will all get done as planned.* With her last thought, she put her car in gear and headed back to I94. Only she went south, toward Chicago.

SIXTY-TWO

"THIS IS AGENT HARPER." HE sat and waited for a reply.

"This is the dispatcher from Wisconsin. We got a weird 911 call. The person, a male, said...and I repeat, 'Please come and help me. My name is Jack Alex...'"

Harper sat straight up.

"Was there anything else? Did you try and trace the call? Have you been able to determine if it was a landline or a cell phone?"

"Agent Harper, there was nothing else. We traced the call and we found what we believe to be the address in Kenosha since the call was made from a landline."Harper pressed the dispatcher.

"What's happened since receiving the call? Have the local police been notified to go to the scene?"

"Yes...they are on their way."

"Good, can you patch me through to the lead officer?"

"Yes I can."

"Great...do it now!" While he waited, he pressed his intercom.

"Tell Agent Rodgers to get the five-seat turbine fired up. We're heading to Wisconsin and I need to have the helicopter in the air in two minutes."

As soon as he finished, he heard,

"This is Officer Lee."

"Officer Lee, this is FBI Special Agent Clarence Harper. I believe the 911 call you are responding to is part of a kidnapping case. We are on our way by helicopter from Chicago to Kenosha and our ETA is 32 minutes. I need you and your other officers to secure the area. No one goes in or out, understood?"

"Agent Harper, I read you loud and clear."

"Great...get me back to the dispatcher." Harper was saying all this while he got on the elevator and took it to the top floor of the building. As he held on the line, he jumped in the helicopter and it took off. As it lifted off, he heard,

"Agent Harper, this is the dispatcher. What else do you need?"

"We're in our chopper ready to leave. We will need to call in our flight plan and time is of the essence." After he got the location and had the pilot call it in, he started discussing his strategy with the other agents on board.

***

"Trooper Gonzalez, if you're there, pick up on channel four."

Gonzalez heard the call and switched over to channel four.

"This is Trooper Gonzalez."

"You picked up a license on your LPR that is involved in a possible kidnapping. The plates are coming up for a Kyle Luther. His address is showing 11736 K Street, north of Route 50."

"Roger that...I'm heading north on I94, just south of Route 50. Why is this guy a possible suspect?"

"First, his background comes back a bit sketchy and second, we got a 911 emergency dispatch call from a possible hostage at that address."

Gonzalez exited at Route 50 and stopped at the intersection.

"We want you to continue to the address and provide backup at the scene. But make sure you don't come in with any lights or sirens."

"Roger that." The light changed and Gonzalez turned west on to Route 50. She followed the instructions but she drove at a deliberate speed to the address.

***

Jonah was on Route 50, heading west, but still a few miles from B Street that would take him to K Street and back to the house. As he drove, he was puzzled, *Why hasn't Kyle picked up on either his cell or the landline? We kept both for this expressed purpose. I know he won't leave without the money. So, where is he? Could he have had trouble with our hostage? What could have possibly gone wrong? I'll have to sort it out in a few more minutes once I get there.*

***

"How long before we land?"

"Agent Harper, we should be there in five to seven minutes, or sooner. The site is over on the left, just north of Route 50."

"Great, the local police should be there any minute. Connect me to Officer Lee again."

There was silence except for occasional static. Then he heard, "Officer Lee."

"Officer Lee, this is FBI Agent Harper. What's the situation right now?"

"Agent Harper, there's no movement around the house that we can see. There's a Jeep out front but nothing else. Please advise."

Harper thought for a few seconds and then told him,

"Hold your positions. Our ETA is less than five minutes. Do not, I repeat, do not engage."

"Roger that sir. We will not engage."

***

"Central Command, come in. Central Command, come in."

"Gonzalez, this is Central Command. Go ahead."

"I'm on my way to the 911 emergency site and I realized that I am one car behind the LPR license on the white Chevy that you mentioned before. Should I pull him over?"

"Hold your position. I'll check with the Commander."

Gonzalez waited while she kept following the white Chevy at a safe distance.

"Trooper Gonzalez...this is Commander Thompson. I spoke to the FBI. They are on their way to the scene by helicopter. You are to follow but do not...I repeat, do not try to apprehend the suspect."

"Roger that, sir." Gonzalez ended the call as the white Chevy turned on to B Street. Another car turned behind the car she was following. Gonzalez slowed down considerably and then pulled on to B Street as well.

***

Kyle Luther had finished tying Jack to one of the chairs in the kitchen. He found a small, red dish towel and stuffed it in his mouth. With all of the shades drawn, the house was cast in a dark, gloomy hue. Kyle checked the ropes to make sure Jack couldn't untie them. He'd spent the last hour cleaning up the place, putting all of the dishes, boxes, bottles, etc. in big, black garbage bags. Before he got knocked out by Jack, he had spent hours meticulously removing every possible fingerprint. He vacuumed the floors and put every sheet and pillowcase in a garbage bag as well. His fingerprints would be expected but not Josh's. He went back down in the basement to survey the seven or eight foot deep hole that they had dug. It was wide enough and deep enough to bury Jack Alexander. They had created a box to put the body in based on his height and weight. Several boxes, two old tattered couches, some miscellaneous gym equipment, and a dusty old carpet would be stacked over the hole. No one would ever find the body. Since this wasn't Kyle's first rodeo, he knew all the right things to do.

Now he stood over Jack with a menacing look. He spat out,

"I should have put a bullet in your head for that little stunt you pulled. You better hope and pray nobody heard you. If somebody shows up here, you might as well kiss this world goodbye."

Kyle found it interesting that this guy wasn't begging and pleading through the towel stuffed in his mouth. Kyle saw that he was staring up at him with a peaceful, calm look on his face. Kyle decided to walk to the kitchen window, pull back the shades, and look out. Seeing nothing out of the ordinary, he released the shades and looked down at his phone again. The alert on his smartphone indicated it couldn't be used. The he thought, *Jonah's got to get here soon because we need to get down the road.*

CHAPTER

SIXTY-THREE

THE HELICOPTER TOUCHED DOWN ABOUT a quarter of a mile from the house on K Street. Agent Harper and his team quickly exited the helicopter and made their way to the two police cars already in place. An officer approached them and Harper asked over the hum of the helicopter's propellers,

"Are you Officer Lee?"

"Yes sir, I am."

"Has there been any movement since we last spoke? Where are your other officers right now?"

"Sir, there has been no movement at all. We have the perimeter all around the house sealed. We heard on our radio that one of the possible abductors is headed this way. If you want, we can patch you through to the state trooper who is following him."

Harper considered that and then answered,

"Yeah, patch me through to the trooper. In the meantime, tell the other officers to hold their positions and wait for my command."

"Roger that." Officer Lee got on his radio and notified the other officers.

***

Jonah looked in his rearview mirror when he turned from B Street to K Street and noticed a state trooper back on B Street. He slowed down to see if the trooper would turn on to K Street. He breathed a sigh of relief when the state trooper kept going on B Street. Jonah thought, *Not sure what I would do if that trooper followed me. There's basically no real way out of here. I've got a couple more miles before I reach the house. If Kyle's ready to go, we'll split up the cash and disappear.*

***

"Trooper Gonzalez…did he give any indication that he noticed your vehicle on B Street?" Agent Harper tried to remain calm but inside he was super anxious as he talked over the radio.

"No sir…he slowed down a little bit but I followed your advice and kept going north on B Street. What should I do now?"

Harper was very direct,

"Turn around and go back to K Street. Follow him at a safe distance. The local police will approach him from our side, which is in front of him. Once you see them, they'll turn on their lights and sirens. Turn yours on too and we'll sandwich him in since it's a tiny two-lane road. Do you copy?"

"Roger that!"

***

The megaphone was loud enough that Jonah could hear it inside of his car. "This is the FBI. Get out of your car with your hands up."

Jonah could see in front and behind his car, he realized he had no place to go. There were fields on both sides of the road. He knew there was another paved road about a half mile up. But he couldn't reach it from where he was. And there were no other access points.

"This is FBI Special Agent Harper. I need you out of your car with your hands up now!"

Jonah moved slowly out of his car. He raised his hands and stood out in the middle of the road. Officers and agents approached him from the front and back. "Put your hands behind your back and lean on your car." The agents pushed him abruptly down on the hood of his car. After he was handcuffed, Jonah focused on the FBI agent who was talking to him. He noticed that the other agents were searching his car.

"What's your name?""My name is Jonah Broderick. I have a right to know why I'm being stopped. I haven't done anything wrong."

"Where were you headed? And where were you coming from?"

Jonah saw the lead agent motion to one of the agents and say,

"Get his wallet out of his back pocket."

Jonah realized that he couldn't stop the agents from their procedures, which included the lead agent looking at his driver's license.

"Jonah Broderick, what are you doing here in Wisconsin and who is Kyle Luther?"

"I'm going to visit a friend...Kyle Luther."

Jonah watched one of the agents walk over to the lead agent, Harper.

"Sir, you need to see this!"Jonah's eyes followed Harper as he walked to the other side of the car out of his sight. Jonah had an idea of what Harper had found Nonetheless he waited for him to speak.

"So, Kyle Luther is just a friend and you're out driving his car with about $200,000 under the front seat, and a gun in the glove compartment." Jonah figured he would ask about the gun and the money. He decided not to answer. He knew Harper wouldn't be content with his silence."So, do you have a license to carry a concealed weapon and what's with the $200,000 in a duffel bag?"

Jonah took his time answering. Finally he said,

"I want a lawyer before I answer anything else."

"Look, Jonah...we believe you and who's ever in that house down the road abducted Jack Alexander from a parking garage in Chicago and have been holding him here against his will. We already received a 911 emergency call from that house. I believe someone paid you that money that's in the bag to kidnap him and do far worse. That means you brought this man, against his will, across state lines…a federal offense. Your best bet is to cooperate with us so we can get Jack Alexander out of that house safe and sound."Jonah weighed his options. Nonetheless, he said again,

"I want a lawyer before I answer anything."

"So you know, if this guy dies, you'll be up for first degree murder, which probably means a death penalty conviction. So, do you want it to all play out or do you want to help us?"

He didn't take long to respond.

"What do you want me to do?"

Jonah figured what would be asked of him, and he wasn't surprised by Harper's questions.

"Is Jack Alexander in that house? And how many others are in there with him?

Slowly Jonah answered,

"Yes…he's in there. There's only one other person in there."

Jonah waited. He decided that he wouldn't offer any more than was asked of him."Who is it…Kyle Luther? And tell me, what was the plan?"

Jonah looked at Harper sheepishly.

"He's my partner in all this. We were going to split the money and then take off."

"And what was going to happen to Jack Alexander?"

"I have no more to say."

Then he heard Harper say,

"Okay, here's how we're going to do this. And if you're smart, you'll do exactly as I say."

***

"I wasn't sure I would ever see the light of day outside of that house. You are a sight for sore eyes, my friend." Jack Alexander sat in one of the FBI conference rooms debriefing with Harper and a room full of FBI personnel. Jack had seven days of growth on his face from not having shaved. He clothes were filthy and he had an obvious odor from being held in a musty, dank basement for a week. But there was a huge smile on his face that translated into exuberance. He was holding Gloria tightly, and tears were running down their faces, and everyone else's in the room."Clarence... Agent Harper, thank you and everyone else involved for never giving up on me." He started crying all over again. He was crying and sobbing so hard this time that his shoulders heaved. He experienced a slow, but erratic inhalation, holding his breath, and continuing to sob deeply. Gloria tried to console him but finally realized that his tears needed to run their course.

***

"Mr. Shapiro, I didn't want to disrupt your schedule today but we need to talk to you in private." Harper waited before he proceeded.

"Is this about Jack? Is he all right? What's happening...please tell me that you have some good news?"

Harper watched as Len leaned across the small table that separated them.Harper answered,

"Yes...this is about Jack. We found him yesterday in Wisconsin. He was"

"Is he safe? Is he okay? Has he been hurt or harmed?"

"He's a little weak and shaken up but otherwise he's fine."

"Oh, thank God. I'm so relieved."

Harper watched as Len tumbled back in his chair. He could see the man's eyes well up with tears, and he couldn't speak for a few minutes.

Finally he heard Len say,

"When can I talk to him, or better yet, when can I see him?"

Harper responded,

"I understand...but we have a few things we need to resolve first."

"What things?"

"Let me explain because I'll need your help."

CHAPTER
SIXTY-FOUR

GLORIA SAT ON THE KING size-bed as she waited for Jack to finish showering. Based on all of the unresolved issues with Jack's case, the FBI had put the two of them in a hotel at an undisclosed location. No one from the press was notified that Jack had even been rescued. They were escorted into the hotel from the rear and up a service elevator. Until Gloria noticed the room phone, she didn't realize they had put them in a suite at the Peninsula Hotel. She did remember Clarence telling Jack he wanted to try to erase some of the wretched memories from the last seven days. There were FBI agents at their hotel door around the clock. They didn't want to risk something unforeseen happening to him.

As Jack walked out of the bathroom in a huge white hotel bathrobe, Gloria looked at how her husband had been transformed back to the man she recognized. She stood up, walked over to where he was standing, and allowed him to tightly put his arms around her. "I'm so glad you're safe, J. I was worried about you being rescued but I tried to transfer my worries into worship. I told myself that God would bring you back to me." Jack held on to her, closed his eyes, and tried to shut out the world, only thinking of his wife. They held each other for a long time without either of them speaking. Jack opened his eyes and looked around the suite again. A king-size bed, flat screen, wall-mounted television, a sitting room with a relaxing couch, a love seat, and two recliners. In spite of their partial southwestern exposure, they could see the sun going down at night and watch the boats cruise along Lake Michigan down to Soldier Field, the Planetarium, and beyond. But right now, he just wanted to hold his wife and shut out the world. Tomorrow or the next day would be a day for taking in the sights.

***

Toni got to the office earlier than usual, before most of the others in the office arrived. Regularly, she made a practice of starting her work day before the sun came up. This habit allowed her to think clearly about her priorities for the day. Two days had passed since she'd delivered the money to Jonah. She was starting to relax, sensing that all was now in order. As she sat at her desk, leaning back in her oversized chair, looking out into the early morning, and taking occasional sips from her grande latte from Starbucks. She thought, *I finally pulled it off. I got exactly what I wanted. Len should have given me the Divisional President's job right from the beginning. He knew down deep that I was the better candidate for the role. But once he told me in in his office that he would have named me if Jack hadn't been in the picture, I knew what I needed to do. If he had simply named me from the start, Jack Alexander would still be among the living. So, I blame Len for causing me to take the actions I did. Clearly, I was a much better choice anyway. It won't be long before he sees it and thanks me for my superior leadership. I may have taken a non-traditional route to getting here but in the end, it was worth it.*She saw her cell phone light up with a text message that said, *Toni, something's come up and I need you to come to a special emergency meeting in my office this morning at 8:00 a.m., Thanks Len.*

Toni read over the text a second time. She smiled to herself, put the meeting on her electronic calendar with a fifteen-minute reminder, and then moved around two other meetings that would likely create a conflict with Len's request. Then she sat back with a proud, confident look on her face.

***

Sandy, Len's assistant, was at her desk when she arrived.

Toni stopped.

"Hi Sandy, how are you on this fine morning? I love the outfit you have on. Did you get your hair cut? It looks great."

Toni watched Sandy look up at her with a slight smile on her face.

"Thanks...Len's waiting. You can go right in."

Toni gave her a big smile and as she went in she said,

"Appreciate all you do Sandy. Have a great day."

Toni was caught off guard when she saw Len sitting at his three-chair side table. FBI Agent Harper was sitting at the table with him. Det. McClain was sitting in a chair in front of Len's desk. She tried to read something from their facial expressions but she couldn't. Len was looking over some papers and his head popped up as she entered. The two law enforcement people sat pokerfaced. Len said evenly,

"Oh...Toni, come on in and sit down.

The only chair available was the one that allowed all three of them to look directly at her. As she sat down, she said,

"Hey, I came as you asked. What's up?"

She noticed that Len didn't waste any time with his reply. "They found Jack."

Inside, Toni felt like an IED had exploded in front of her. She thought, *Found Jack...how in the world could that have happened? Jonah assured me that everything would be taken care of. How could he have messed up? This is the absolute worst scenario! But they can't tie anything to me. I've got to make sure my reply is even and measured.*

"Oh my goodness...They've found Jack? That is amazing!" She looked from Len to the agents and back again.

"Is he all right? Was he harmed? Where is he now? Oh my God, he's safe!"

She waited to see which one of them spoke. She heard Len say,

"He's fine...he's weak and badly shaken up, as you might imagine."

"Oh...Thank God, so he wasn't harmed?"

She was startled when Agent Harper interjected,

"Why do you ask?"

Toni did all she could to look emotionally moved by the news. In her attempt to recover, she said,

"I've been really worried about him...we all have been."

She could feel Agent Harper's eyes on her. She heard him say,

"Worried...really?"

Toni had no idea where he was going but tried to illicit the support of Len.

"Yes, of course...Len and I were talking about the whole thing earlier this week."

She looked back and forth between Agent Harper and Len. Finally, she blurted out,

"What's going on here? What is it that no one is telling me?"

She waited for an answer. She didn't know what was coming but she sensed that it wasn't good. She heard Harper say,

"We were hoping that you could tell us."

Now Toni was totally uncomfortable. She thought, *Oh my God, what do they know? Have I been implicated? Jonah wouldn't do that. I gave him the money. I've got to be in the clear.* So she played it straight as if she knew nothing.

"I'm sorry, tell you what? What am I supposed to know? I'm totally confused here."

She waited with baited breath. She could see Agent Harper frown as he said,

"Come on Toni...we know everything! We know that you hired Jonah Broderick to kidnap and murder Jack Alexander. We know you paid him $50,000 to do the job. We also know that he extorted another $200,000 from you as well. The most recent details had you driving up to Gurnee Mills to give him the additional monies with the understanding that he would finish the job."

She could see that he was glaring at her and his voice was raised. Her resolve was starting to wane.

"How dare you accuse me of such a heinous act? I had nothing at all to do with any of this business. I like Jack…I've been a fan of his ever since I came here. I don't know where you're getting your information but you're dead wrong…and totally out of line."

She watched Harper sit back, smile broadly, and wave Det. McClain over to the table from the chair where he'd been sitting quietly the entire time. Toni observed McClain get up, walk over to where they were sitting, and place a small recording device on the table. He said nothing, turned around, and went back to his chair and sat down. She had no idea what was next.

But now she heard Harper say,

"We figured you'd deny everything. You know, Jonah Broderick is a pretty smart character. He determined that he wasn't going to take the hit for this all alone."

Toni raised one eye brow above the other and said,

"What is that supposed to mean? Who is this Jonah character anyway?"

She saw this big smile emerge on to Harper's face.

"Oh that's good…that's really good."

Harper hit the Play button. The voices from the recorder filled the room.

"So, what exactly is it you want us to do."

"Do I have to spell it out for you? I want you to do what you've done before, nothing more nothing less."

"Okay…who's the target and when do you want this to go down?"

"All of the details are in the package I gave you. Everything you need to know is included."

"What about payment?"

"The arrangements are exactly as we discussed. You need to follow the instructions with no deviations."

"Yeah, okay…but what about payment?"

"Open the package. It's all taken care of. Oh, one more thing…make sure you tell me when he's been taken down. Understood?"

"Understood…"

Toni was like a wet rag. She sat emotionally wilted as she watched Harper shut off the recorder, fold his arms in front of him, and look directly at Toni. Toni decided it was time t go on the defense.

"I want to talk to my lawyer."

Harper replied,

"And you'll need a good one. You are under arrest. You have the right to remain silent. Anything you say can and will be used against you in a court of law. You have the right to speak to an attorney. If you can't afford an attorney…"

Toni sat in shock as Harper read her rights to her. She was only half listening when Harper said,

"Ms. Lucas, you need to accompany us down to our FBI office right now."

Toni struggled to take in all that was happening. She heard Len's voice. She turned to face him. "Toni, if any of this is true, I am totally shocked that you would have stooped to do something so unthinkable.

Toni looked back at him but said nothing as she was escorted out of his office.

***

Toni had been taken from the Universal Systems headquarters offices and driven by federal agents to the Chicago FBI offices. Since she requested to speak with her attorney, she was given the opportunity to call him before Harper and the other federal agents questioned her any further. Toni's lawyer came immediately.

"Toni Lucas, you are being charged with kidnapping, conspiracy to commit murder, and attempted murder." Harper looked at both of them. When he was satisfied that they understood, he said,

"Your arraignment will be three days from today. At that time, bail will be determined."

"So when can I leave here?"

"I don't know. It's up to the judge during your arraignment."

"You mean to tell me that I've got to stay here for three days?"

"I'm afraid so."

Toni looked over at her attorney.

"Isn't there anything you can do?" "Toni, unfortunately, we have to wait for the arraignment."

"Well, that's just lovely!"

SIXTY-FIVE

TWO WEEKS LATER

JACK SAT IN HIS STUDY at home. He'd closed himself off so he could simply reflect on all that had happened to him during that hellish week. He glanced around the room and tried to take in his surroundings. His home and his study were the same but his view was totally different. The lamp Gloria had given him to adorn his desk still sat in the same place. His computer hadn't been used; it was still in Sleep mode. The printer on the small table to the right of his desk was quiet. There were no printed pages pouring out of the front of it. But all was different for him. Every picture on the wall was in exactly the same place where he and Gloria had hung them, but that was all different as well.

For Jack, his life was now segmented. It wasn't segmented by life before and after his college graduation. It wasn't segmented by life before and after meeting Gloria or by life before and after marrying her. No, Jack sat there engulfed by his life before and after being kidnapped. Before being kidnapped, he was basically trusting and confident of virtually everything within his environment. He'd go places, do things, and not be overly concerned about his safety. While he hadn't been in a fight in several years, he felt assured he could handle himself just fine in a struggle with another guy, maybe even two. Before being kidnapped, he hadn't felt afraid. He didn't look over his shoulder to see if someone was coming from behind to do him harm. There had never been a time when he felt he was in harm's way, controlled by others, or threatened to have his life taken from him.

Since being kidnapped, everything was now upside-down. He didn't feel safe. Even in the company of others or with the FBI, he questioned his safety. He was thankful for being rescued, but the dread and discomfort were very apparent in his mind. As he sat in his study, he knew he was in a safe environment, but there was a part of his brain that still questioned the reality of it. Based on the way he'd been abducted, he now realized his security could be dramatically disrupted at any time, and under the most normal circumstances.

As he sat there, he realized that he had a decision to make. He could continue to dwell on the past and all of the ugliness associated with being kidnapped. He could let the wretched experience define him and change his personality and his view of the world. If he did, his abductors, unknowingly, would have won. Yes, he'd been saved, but they would have branded an inerasable blemish on him and in his mind. He would walk through life distrusting and looking for the loathsome parts of every person.

The other alternative was not to dwell on the past and to move forward. He knew that some people were flawed and would do crazy, stupid things to advance their cause and their own agenda. In those moments, he determined that he would refuse to live life looking for evil lurking in the shadows. He would be more aware of his environment in the future, for sure. But he won't let his abductors win; he would have the last word. He wouldn't let them take up space in his brain. He wouldn't back up, and he wouldn't give in to the fear and unnecessary anxiety. Jack had a life to live with Gloria and he planned to live it to the fullest. Sure, people would ask him about his horrific experience. He purposed in his mind that he would give a fulsome answer. But every time he shared the story in the future of the ordeal and his rescue, his spoken words would provide him with power, power to rise and be strong, even stronger than he'd been before the incident. As Jack processed all this in his mind, he started to feel stronger, a real overcomer. In those moments, he remembered one of his mother's constant reminders. *"The question is not whether trials, ugliness, and difficulties will come in to your life; the question is how you respond to it."* Jack knew what his response would be.

***

With all of the commotion, Rachel and Luke hadn't has a free moment to sit and talk to each other. He had been helpful in shuttling Rachel's dad around and calling people while she'd been detained by the FBI for questioning.They had developed a romantic relationship since she had come to Chicago. They'd spent lots of time together since they were both attending the Art Institute. Their skills had grown during the time spent there. But Luke had realized that he didn't have the same motivation for the kind of art that they were learning. Rachel was extremely talented in body, gender, site, and landscape. She had found her niche and was making real progress.

Luke had realized that he didn't have the same motivation. He was drawn more to advertising, interactive arts, and media. He was strongly considering leaving the School of the Art Institute and enrolling in Columbia College. The school was world renowned for breaking new ground in arts and media education. The true hands-on experience he sought could be obtained at Columbia College. The only reason he hadn't already left was Rachel. All of the kidnapping and arrest drama started when Luke had planned to tell her. Now with her father back in Atlanta and her mother in her own apartment, Luke felt the time to talk to her about it had arrived. Luke didn't feel that his leaving the Institute would be a huge deal since Columbia was within walking distance of the Art Institute. But clearly the issue would be that they wouldn't see each other as often.There was also the long-standing issue he had never told her. It kept nagging him that he had been one of the boys who had ridiculed her about her jailbait mother when they were in grammar school. Back when they first met at the art gallery in Atlanta, she hadn't recognized him, but he clearly remembered her.

As he now sat on her couch in her apartment looking at her, he regretted never telling her. He'd certainly had enough chances but he'd chickened out every time. For some reason, he felt like this would be his last opportunity to come clean.

It was late afternoon and the sun was falling fast, getting ever so close to the horizon. As he looked over at her, he could see the last vestiges of the sun out of the window directly behind her. She was a strong, beautiful woman. While she'd experienced tremendous hurts, she was very resilient. He loved her and he wanted to continue to invest in her and their relationship. Whatever happened over the next few minutes would pretty much determine how, and if, they would move forward in the relationship. Luke spoke first.

"How are you feeling now that most of this drama has blown over?"

"Honestly, I'm feeling a little raw. So much has gone on. I'm not sure how to move forward."

Luke hesitated at her comment. If he told her his one deep dark secret, it might only put more of a burden on her already raw condition. He was in a quandary. If he told her, it could mean the end of their relationship. If he didn't, he'd continue to hold on to this ugly element from their past. He closed his eyes briefly and decided to go for it. "I...I've got something I need to tell you. Well, actually I've got two things I need to talk to you about."

He watched Rachel sit upright, steadying herself.

"Okay...what is it?"

"Well, first I need to tell you that I'm going to likely drop out of school." He looked at her and waited to see how she reacted or if she'd say anything. When she didn't, he kept going.

"I'm not motivated to approach art in the way the Art Institute's curriculum wants to lead me. I realize that I have a passion for creative work in performing media and communication arts."

He noticed she still hadn't moved and her eyes were locked onto his. So, he proceeded.

"So, next term I'll be leaving the Institute and attending Columbia College."

"Have you already enrolled?" "Yes…I have."

"So, it's done? You've already decided? Why didn't you tell me before?"

It was a fair question and Luke had an answer for her.

"I should have told you before and I tried to bring it up. And then your mother moved in and I didn't feel like the right time ever presented itself." He stopped talking and looked at her even more intently. Then he added,

"I'm sorry for keeping this from you and not telling you sooner…Forgive me."

He observed Rachel's every move. He saw her close her eyes and put her left hand on her neck and tried to rub an apparent knots out. He watched her start moving her head in a circular motion, first clockwise and then counter clockwise. He was a little surprised when she suddenly stopped and looked back at him.

"Luke, I understand and forgive you. What was the other thing you wanted to tell me?"

***

Now Luke was in a pickle. He couldn't avoid telling her. She'd asked him directly. So, he had to get it out.

"Rachel, this one is hard for me to tell you. It's actually harder than anything I've ever told you in the past." He paused, leaned back on the couch, looked up at the ceiling, took a deep breath, and turned toward Rachel.

"I'm sure you remember all those horrific things you told me you experienced in grammar school, all that taunting and teasing about your mother." He hesitated to determine if she had a response. Once he realized that she wasn't going to reply, he kept going.

"I actually went to one of the grammar schools you attended. One day, this boy you thought was your friend started saying mean things to you about your mother while you were waiting for your dad to pick you up." He noticed that now Rachel was sitting completely still, looking at Luke, and listening without even blinking. He was too far along to change course.

"There were three other boys with him who started saying some of those same hurtful things." Luke felt he was about to be sick to his stomach. He knew that he couldn't stop but he had this feeling he was about to witness the end of his relationship with Rachel. Yet, there was something inside him that was pushing him, beckoning him to tell the truth. So, in spite of his fears, he blurted out,

"I was one of those boys! I was one of those boys that made fun of your mother's situation. Later that day, I felt horrible about what I had done. I wanted to go up to you the next day and apologize, but I didn't. I actually went to the same high school you attended. But the school was so big that I was sure you never saw me or even remembered me. Later, when I saw you at the art gallery, I knew exactly who you were. I've wanted to tell you this a million times, I just couldn't get the nerve to admit it. Later, I was afraid, as I am now, of losing you. I am deeply sorry. And if you never want to see me again, I understand. I had to take the risk and tell you."

With that, he leaned back on the couch. He turned away from Rachel and stared up at the ceiling. He wasn't sure what Rachel was doing and he was too afraid to look at her. A long, protracted period of time went by. Luke was feeling uncomfortable and thinking the end of their relationship was imminent. All of a sudden, he heard a tiny whisper that was almost inaudible.

"I already knew."

"What…what did you say?""I said that I already knew…most of what you told me, I already knew."

"If you knew already, why didn't you loathe me, hate my guts, and spit in my face? I certainly had it coming."

"I wanted to wait and see if you would ever apologize on your own. I almost told you three or four times that I knew who you were. But each time, I decided to give you the chance to confess in your own way."

Looking down at his hands, "I'm so sorry that it took me so long. You've become a super special person to me and I didn't want to lose you, but I finally decided that I needed to tell you. I'm really sorry. I hope you can find a way to forgive me."

Luke sat there in a daze. He had no idea that he would hear what he heard from Rachel. Luke noticed that she was moving toward him. He was surprised when she took his hand in hers. He felt her other hand touch his face. He realized that she was turning his face toward her.

"I forgive you."

CHAPTER
SIXTY-SIX

AS JACK FINISHED SORTING OUT his thoughts and feelings regarding the kidnapping, his doorbell rang. Gloria was in another part of the house and yelled to Jack,

"I'll see who it is."

Jack didn't answer. But then he heard voices coming from the foyer. He decided to get up from his desk in the study and see who it was. To his surprise, he opened his study door and saw Len Shapiro standing a few feet from him still hugging Gloria. Jack stood there momentarily and then walked toward Len. Jack watched Len release Gloria and he saw the two of them looking at Jack as he walked out of his story. Jack stopped in front of Len. He looked at him without saying a word. Then he hugged Len and then felt Len doing the same. Jack stood there while tears welled up and started running down his face. He never opened his eyes but he could hear Gloria's footsteps as she walked back to the kitchen.

It was the first time they had seen each other since the unfortunate abduction. Jack released Len and stood back from him. He could see the tears in Len's eyes as well. He could tell that Len had something to say.

"This is a $500.00 jacket that I now have to get dry cleaned. It's got snot all over it. I'm sure that some of these snots will never come out."

They both started laughing through their tears. After their emotions settled down, Jack asked,

"Why don't you come into the den? Let's sit for a while."

"Sounds like a great idea to me."

As they made their way into the den, both of them had huge grins on their faces.

They sat down on the comfortable sectional.

"Jack, it's great to see you, to have you back safe and sound. I could hardly contain myself when Agent Harper told me the terrific news."

"Words don't adequately describe how ecstatic I am to be back safely. There was certainly the possibility of so many other unfortunate scenarios."

Jack could see that Len got choked up as he tried to talk.

"I'd been so worried about you. During that period, I realized how special you are to me. There were moments when my mind would run away with me and I'd think I'd never see you again... Jack, I'm so happy to see you."

Jack reached for the Kleenex box that was on the coffee table.

"Len, it means a lot to hear you say that. When I was being held hostage, you and Gloria were the people that I thought about most often. You two kept me going. I refused to give up or give in."

They sat and talked for a long time. Virtually all of the conversation was about relationships and the importance of people. In all that time, they didn't mention work or business issues once. Finally, Jack realized that their time together was coming to an end.

"Jack, I promised myself on the way over here that I wouldn't talk about any business issues. I'm going to slightly deviate from my promise. I want you to know that there is no rush for you to get back to work. Believe me, it will all be there when you decide to come back."

Jack totally appreciated Len's comments. As he walked him to the front door, he said,

"I appreciate it. I've been sorting out my thoughts and I probably have some more processing to do. Trust me, you'll be the first person I call when I'm ready to return. Thanks for your understanding."

"Certainly…let me know if I can do anything for you."

They hugged again as they stood at the door. Jack called out,

"Honey, Len's about to leave. You should come and say goodbye."

CHAPTER
SIXTY-SEVEN

HARPER AND MCCLAIN SAT IN a booth at Merriam's Wine Bar on the north side of Chicago. After all the time they'd spent together on the Alexander kidnapping case, neither of them knew that they both had a propensity for drinking full-bodied red wine. It turned out that neither of them had any interest in beer or hard liquor. Harper had a supervisor when he first joined the FBI, among other things, who had schooled him on all types of wine, so much so that Harper could look and smell a glass of wine and tell so many things about it. McClain's father had owned a high end wine bar when McClain was as growing up. His father had explained the ills associated with drinking. But he also schooled him on the differences in wine.

At the end of their efforts on the Alexander case, when the bad guys were in jail and Jack was back at home, they decided to go out and have a drink together, the two of them. After looking through the wine list, they sat there rotating between bottles of cabernet sauvignon and malbec. They discussed the fact that full-body red wine had more tannin, higher levels of alcohol, and dark fruit flavors. Since they'd taken a taxi to the wine bar, they were content to drink as much as they wanted. "When did you know that Catherine wasn't involved in the kidnapping?" McClain figured that Harper had a solid answer.

"Until I got the 911 dispatcher's call, I still believed that Catherine Frazier was involved. It was too coincidental, too many circumstances pointed to her."

McClain poured himself another glass of wine and took a drink.

"This case was totally weird for so many reasons. If Catherine's daughter hadn't been in that parking garage and reported what she'd seen, we won't have known about Jack Alexander until it was too late, and maybe never."

McClain watched Harper as he leaned across the table.

"Is Toni a grisly piece of work or what? I've been in this line of work for a long time but I've never come across a hard case like Toni Lucas. I think she would bump off one of her relatives if it would advance her career. If Jonah Broderick hadn't agreed to a plea bargain, we wouldn't have gotten the details on the other kidnapping crime. I didn't tell you, but it turns out she had hired that Jonah guy once before. We dispatched a team to uncover the buried body. We talked to the other company's officials and they confirmed that about four or five years ago a guy on their management team had been promoted over Toni and then he suddenly disappeared. After I looked up the case, I vaguely remembered it. One day he disappeared and his coworkers, family, and friends never heard from him again. There was no trace of foul play. He up and vanished into thin air."

McClain asked.

"She hired Broderick back then? How did she even find him?"

"That's the weird part. She put an ad in one of those Deep Web or Soldier of Fortune type sites. Broderick saw it, responded, and the rest is history. Oh yeah...when the guy never showed up again, she was given his position and no one was the wiser."

"So you're saying that when Jack Alexander was promoted to president of that acquired company over her, she figured it was time to have lightning strike twice?" McClain sat back.

"Well, Toni, Jonah, and his little buddy Kyle are going to be away in the Big House for a very long time." He enunciated each of the last four words slowly. Then he sat up straight when it hit him.

"Wait a minute, if they're up for murder one for that crime four years ago. I'm starting to see a real hot seat in their future."

"That's exactly the way I see it. There might be a slight reprieve for Broderick but Toni is definitely going down for the count."

With Harper's last words, they sat quietly, drank more wine, and took in the atmosphere of the wine bar. It was late. And for a weeknight, the place was pretty full. There was the classic wine bar chatter. Most of the patrons looked like they'd come right from work and never left. Women were in heels, skirts, and semi-revealing blouses. The guys mostly had suits on or at least sports jackets and nice slacks. Harper and McClain could sense that their wine bar experience for the night was winding down. They both needed to get home. If they stayed any longer, they'd run the risk of being there, like the old Lionel Richie tune, *All Night Long*. As if they were reading each other's mind, simultaneously they looked at the tab, put money on the table, took a last drink, stood up, and started moving toward the door.

CHAPTER
SIXTY-EIGHT

AN ENTIRE MONTH HAD PASSED since Jack had been rescued from his abductors. The case had received national attention. There had been regular calls and visits from the media. Somehow they had found both Gloria and Jack's cell phone numbers. There were so many calls they stopped answering their phones, unless it was a number they recognized. If that weren't bad enough, they started getting regular visits by the media at their doorstep. Every call, every visit was for an interview or a story regarding the details of what happened. Eventually, they started getting large, competing offers for Jack's story. Gloria suggested, and Jack agreed, that they wouldn't allow the media into their lives regardless.

As every day passed, Jack felt stronger and ready to go back to work. He and Gloria spent time each day processing how he was feeling. He shared different elements associated with the trauma and they would talk it out. Jack always felt better afterwards and looked forward to the next conversation. He could have gone and talked to a counselor. But Gloria was the person who knew him best and always knew the right questions to ask. Correspondingly, Jack listened to Gloria share her feelings. While Gloria told him she was blessed to be able to open up to him, Jack didn't sense he was helping her much at all.

When he picked up the phone to tell Len that he was ready to return, it was a very bright day for Jack. In some ways, he knew that he would probably never fully recover. There would always be that part of him that would remember. But he wouldn't let it define him, and hopefully the pain wouldn't be there.Len was excited to hear Jack's voice and was ecstatic to learn that he was ready to return. Len arranged Jack's first day back to be on a day when the full Executive Board met.

So when Jack walked into the building and took the elevator up to Universal's main floor, he was greeted warmly by everyone who saw him. Len was already in the lobby waiting for him and ushered him into the company's large auditorium. Inside, the room was packed with people from Universal and all of the board members. As soon as he walked in, everyone gave him a standing ovation that lasted for a very long time. Jack was surprised and totally overwhelmed. He pulled out a handkerchief from his back pocket in order to catch the tears rolling down his face. Eventually, the applause subsided. Jack watched as Len began to speak into a microphone that was handed to him on cue.

"Jack, you probably couldn't tell from the applause but two or three people in the room are glad you're back." There was sustained laughter from his comment. Jack even laughed which helped him recover from crying.

"Honestly, we're all so pleased that you are back with us. The place hasn't been the same without you. Since there are so many well-wishers here to see you, I figured you might want to say something to them."

With that remark, Jack hesitantly took the microphone from Len and the applause started all over again. As he looked around the room, he saw a sea of faces. There were many people that he knew and recognized, but there were so many that he didn't. But the thing that was common was their love and appreciation for him. He stood there and basked in the ovation. Finally, the clapping stopped. Jack cleared his throat and said.

"First of all, thank you for all of your thoughts and prayers. The entire ordeal has been extremely challenging. As you would imagine, the recovery has been very taxing on me and my wife. I can say that every day, as I process everything, I continue to get stronger. I'm now to the point where I'm ready to come back and help Universal continue to be the Best-in-Class company we all know that it is." Then he closed with, "Again, thank you for all of your support and prayers. I look forward to getting back in the saddle."

During the final ovation, Jack was shocked when he saw Gloria walking up to him. They embraced while the applause went on. Once it died down, Jack added,

"One last thing…I'm certain that I wouldn't have recovered mentally, emotionally, and psychologically if it hadn't been for this lady, my loving wife Gloria."

This was certainly a day for applause. There was no one in the auditorium sitting on their hands. Again, when it stopped, Jack simply said, "Thank you all."

***

The leadership team and the board of directors met in their largest conference room. There was no official meeting. Len simply arranged an opportunity for all of them to see Jack up close and personal. There were some light snacks and beverages served. For the next hour or so, people came up to him and exchanged private words or simply hugged him and whispered pleasantries in his ear. Jack noticed that Gloria and Len stood back and allowed Jack to be the center of attention. It was good for him, his peers, and the board. Finally, Jack looked over at Len and Gloria with a knowing smile, winked as if to say…*Jack is back.*

***

Jack had been back to work for a month. Clarence Harper decided that it was time to visit to his friend. All throughout the investigation, he had tried to keep the personal element out of it. After the initial shock that Jack had been abducted, he worked the case like any other one. But as it wore on, he found it increasingly difficult to separate his friendship with Jack from the other elements of the case. He had been taught from the very beginning of his training at the bureau *not* to allow his judgment to be clouded by any personal considerations. In fact, the bureau's standard training was that if a case involved a friend or loved one, the agent should recuse himself from it, rather than potentially place the investigation in jeopardy. Clarence hadn't followed the training standard. If he stepped away and something bad happened to Jack, he would never be able to live with himself. Well, it all worked out, the good guy was saved, and the bad guys were locked up.

All these thoughts marched through Clarence's mind as he stood at Jack's front door. He pushed the doorbell and waited. He and Jack had agreed to get together a few days earlier. So, Jack knew Clarence was coming.

The door opened.

"Hey, Jack great to see you man."

"I know right...Thanks for coming over. Come on in."

"Thanks...I feel like I haven't been here in forever."

Jack led the way into the den.

"Gloria's out with some of her girlfriends or she'd be here to give you a big hug again for everything. But since she knew you were coming over, she put out these snacks and something to drink."

Jack observed his long-time friend who picked up a glass of juice before he sat down.

"Hey...no worries, I've seen her a few times since this whole thing came to an end. So, how are you doing at this point?"

Jack leaned forward as he placed his elbows on his knees, folded his hands together.

"A lot better these days. Thanks, man, for asking." He stopped but it was clear that he had more to say.

"I know that I've told you this already but I owe my life to you Clarence. One of the reasons I'm here today is that you refused to give up on me."

"Hey, I didn't have anything else to do so I thought I'd work on finding you." Then he smiled.

"Oh...I also needed to collect the twenty bucks you owed me from the bet you lost back in college."

They both smiled and then they started laughing out loud. After they settled down, Jack asked,

"Hey, I know you can't talk about an ongoing investigation, but what will happen to Toni Lucas?"

"Uh-huh, you're right I can't talk about an open investigation. But I want to tell you a story. It's a fable about some people who got on the wrong side of the law. This person did two things that were very bad. In fact, one was really, really bad. Somehow the authorities caught up with them, put them in jail, and they will probably not live as long as they might have planned." Jack watched as Clarence looked over at him.

"Now since this is only a story, a fable, there's nothing substantial in this tale, it's all made up."

Jack took it all in and then said,

"I would have never guessed that the people in the story would have ever done such a thing. I guess you could work with someone or be a friend and never know them."

CHAPTER
SIXTY-NINE

SHARON WAGNER WOKE UP, SHOWERED, dressed, and sat down to her normal breakfast of scrambled eggs, toast, and coffee. She lived alone, so it was her daily ritual. She looked absentmindedly out her kitchen window at an absolutely gorgeous sunny morning. As she finished breakfast, put her dishes in the sink, she noticed the time on her smartphone. She wanted to be on time for her appointment today. Actually, Sharon hadn't always lived alone. Up until five years ago, she had lived with her husband Thomas. Both of them were from Wicker Park on the north side of Chicago. They had dated throughout college. When Thomas decided to back to get an MBA, Sharon chose to work and wait until he graduated before getting married. When he graduated from Northwestern with honors, he was recruited by BTM, a leading electronics firm in downtown Chicago. He was hired as the assistant CFO. The salary and the signing bonus allowed Thomas and Sharon the opportunity to get married. For two years, he worked hard and was highly regarded by senior management. When the CFO decided to leave for a better position with another company, the management team considered other viable candidates but decided on Thomas. He became the youngest CFO in their history.

Less than a year later, Thomas suddenly disappeared on his way to work. No one saw him after that day and he was never heard from again. The Chicago police and the FBI were brought into the case. And for three years, no progress was ever made. Sharon was heartbroken. She never remarried; she always believed that her husband would somehow return.Over the years, nothing changed for her as she waited, hoped, and believed. Life was pretty mundane until she got a call three days ago from an anonymous source. It sounded like one of the Chicago police department officers that she talked to a lot during the investigation. She asked who she was talking to. The caller never identified himself."Mrs. Wagner, I have some news about your husband's case."

She listened intently.

"It isn't good news but I thought you should know.""I understand but I need to know what happened to him."

She heard the caller say,

"Okay…so listen. Have you been following the Jack Alexander kidnapping?"

"Uh…yes, I've seen some of it on TV."

"Well, it turns out that one of the kidnappers confessed to an earlier abduction done about five years ago right here in Chicago."

"What…what are you telling me? Did you find my husband? Do you know where he is?"

Sharon felt the tears welling up in her eyes. She waited with bated breath for the caller to answer.

"I don't know anything more than what I've told you except this…the person responsible for what happened to your husband is being arraigned in three days at the Dirksen Federal building downtown in Courtroom Two. That's all I can tell you."

"Wait a minute, wait a minute, where is this arraignment?"

"At the Dirksen Federal Building downtown on Dearborn between Adams Street and Jackson Boulevard, again in Courtroom Two. Sorry, I've got to go. I've probably told you more than I should have."

"Wait, hold on. Please just one more question." It seemed that the line had gone dead. "Are you still there? Are you still there? Please don't hang up."

She could hear the caller still breathing on the other end of the line. Sharon pleaded,

"Please answer one more question."

"Okay, what's your question? Make it quick."

Sharon blurted out her question.

"Who is the person responsible? What is their name?"

Now she felt all of the anxiety build from years of not knowing anything. She waited and listened for what she hoped would provide an answer to her question. Then Sharon heard two words that pierced her heart.

"Toni Lucas." Then the line went dead.

***

The bailiff's voice rose over the chatter in the courtroom. "All rise. The United States District Court is now in session. The Honorable Judge Robert Kendall presiding."

Judge Kendall entered the courtroom in his black robe and sat down.

The bailiff then said,

"Be seated. The case of The United States vs. Toni Lucas is now in session."

For the next few minutes, the judge and the two opposing attorneys covered the arraignment topics, advised Toni Lucas of her rights, read the charges against her and insured that her lawyer had a copy of them. Before they covered the bail amount, the judge called the two lead attorneys up to the bench. So there was an apparent break in the courtroom proceedings.

Sharon Wagner got up from her seat in the very back and started walking to the front of the courtroom. She was slow and deliberate. Since there was a lull in the proceedings, no one thought to stop her. She strolled to the front as if she was looking for someone in the first row, behind the defendant's table. As she got closer, she pulled something out of her purse. Then she softly called Toni Lucas' name.

"Hi, Toni...this is for Thomas."

She raised the gun she held in her left hand. It was a Beretta Nano. It felt cold and a little uncomfortable in her hand. She dropped her purse and with both hands, she aimed the gun at Toni's head. She saw the realization in Toni's eyes that told her what was about to happen. Sharon pulled the trigger. She felt the recoil as the bullet exploded from the gun's chamber. She had never fired a gun before; nonetheless, she knew that the bullet would be traveling fast. She knew that Toni would have no time to duck. Sharon saw blood appear at the entry point in Toni's forehead. There was a great splattering of a crimson substance spilling out from the exit wound in the back of her head. Her hair and blouse had blood all over them. Within seconds, she aimed and fired a second bullet that hit another spot in Toni's forehead. She could see that Toni's eyes stared but did not really see anything. It was then that Sharon knew that Toni was dead.

There were screams from people all over the courtroom. Sharon could hear the sound of people running toward her. She never turned around to look. But once they tackled her to the floor, she realized that they were the deputy sheriffs. She could see from her vantage point that the judge took some time to realize what had happened. He pounded his gavel.

"Clear the courtroom! I want this courtroom cleared immediately! Deputies get all of these people out of here right now! Get the EMTs in here! Arrest that woman and get her in lockup."

***

There was an inquiry regarding how Sharon Wagner had been able to get a concealed weapon past security and into a courtroom. When the security tapes were reviewed, they showed that she had clearly gone through security. There was no chance she could have brought the gun into the building. Upon further review, it was determined that she went into the women's restroom before entering the courtroom. As the tapes were closely reviewed, it was clear that she clutched her handbag more closely. Thus, it was determined that the gun was planted long before she arrived. Also, the plant could have only been done by an officer of the law.

Later, federal prosecutors did determine that Toni Lucas had paid Josh Broderick to kidnap Thomas Wagner, kill him, and dispose of his body. Since Wagner was never found, Toni was promoted and given his position. While Sharon Wagner was prosecuted for taking the life of Toni Lucas, the prosecution took into account her grief and heartache associated with what had happened to her husband. No one ever discovered how she came to know any information that was part of the active investigation.

EPILOGUE

CATHERINE SAT CROSS-LEGGED ON THE floor of her new apartment. It wasn't much. In fact, it was pretty bad. There was a tiny living area, big enough for a couch, a coffee table, and a side table. There was a bedroom big enough for a twin bed, a side table, and a lamp. The kitchen was super small. The refrigerator was so small that it sat on the kitchen counter. The official stove was a hotplate. Catherine had the kitchen sink to brush her teeth and wash her face, but she didn't have an actual bathroom. She had to go down the hall whenever she needed to use the toilet or take a shower. Since she didn't have a job secured yet, this was all she could afford from the money Frank gave her as a result of the sale of her possessions and her portion of the proceeds from the sale of their house while she was in prison.She had moved from Rachel's apartment and while it was hard on her, she complied with her daughter's wishes. She sat on the floor and she started thinking, *I almost pulled it off. What a great scheme. I had everybody fooled. I told Jack Alexander that I would get him if it was the last thing I did. I had seven years to think about it, to plan it. I put fear in Jack's mind and terrorize his wife every year. He never knew where those anonymous letters were coming from. I had the foresight to set that up before I went to prison with the woman whose child's medical bills I paid for when he needed a heart transplant. I also formed some interesting* *relationships in prison. Not only did I make some interesting connections, but I also got leads for people on the outside, people who could help me pull off my plan. It required a lot of work but I'm used to hard work. Night after night, I sat in that cell working on all the little details of my plan. I needed a cover for going to Chicago after I got released. When Frank told me that Rachel planned to go to art school in Chicago after high school, I decided to include her in my plan. Writing her and asking her to visit me in prison was a bit of a risk. She could have rejected my request. But I had a suspicion that she would be curious to hear what I had to say. Well, her reaction exceeded my expectation. After her outburst at the prison, I knew she was hooked.*

The parole review board was a gamble. I wasn't sure if they would grant me early release. But I had the warden totally on my side. I knew that I'd score high marks for all the work I'd done helping those other dumb inmates. When I found out my parole was approved, I knew that I had to reach out to my acquired contacts on the outside. Who knew that I would find guys who were professional kidnappers? But I really hit the jackpot when I discovered that they'd already gotten a contract to abduct and bump off Mr. Alexander for somebody else. So I decided to throw in with them. Turns out they were looking for a third person to be involved in the actual abduction. They told me that I would be the one to inject a neuromuscular blocking drug. The drug would paralyze his body but not render him unconscious. Of course I agreed. I told them that I had lots of expertise when, in reality, I didn't know a thing about the drug or injecting it. I figured that I had lots of time to study up on the process. I learned everything I needed to know on YouTube. So I had to dress up in men's clothing, big deal. If anyone saw us when we kidnapped him, they would be looking for three men, not two men and a woman.

After we abducted him, they dropped me off within walking distance of Rachel's apartment. I retrieved my bag that had all my clothes in it. I stopped at a McDonald's, changed, and put the men's clothing in a big garbage can behind another restaurant.Rachel never knew that she was set up. It was intended to have her witness the abduction of Jack

Alexander. I was counting on her having a change of heart, going to the police, and reporting what she'd seen. I figured that the authorities would make the connection to Rachel's last name and mine. It didn't take them long to connect what happened to Jack Alexander and me recently being released from prison. I calculated that the FBI and the Chicago police would want to hold us for questioning based on that piece of paper that I planted in her bedroom.There is honor among thieves and criminals. Once the FBI found Jonah and Luther, I knew they wouldn't turn me in since I was a minor player and I refused to take any money for my role. I told them I just wanted revenge.Probably, my biggest academy award performance was when I cried and got reconciled with Rachel. She believed every word. That girl is so gullible, but it was a great performance. So I'm free and clear. No one is the wiser. But I'm not done with Mr. Alexander. He thinks it's all over but I'll be back! He hasn't seen or heard the last of me.

The End

ACKNOWLEDGEMENTS

TO MY LOVING WIFE GRACE who continues to be my greatest fan. Her love, support, prayers, and encouragement have been what I needed. Time after time, she saw things that I couldn't see. She has loved me through this entire process. Thanks Babe for all your words inspired by God and your deep love for me.

To my multi-talented sister Judi who continued to read multiple edits, give constructive criticism, and constant recommendation that kept me going.

To my niece Vivian who continued to ask me about the books' progress and provided me with a great resource in Tracy McGhee.

To Tracy Chiles McGhee who provided significant insights regarding her Book review process. She opened my eyes to some things that truly helped to make a difference for me.

To Monika Suteski, a truly talented designer, who worked diligently to create a compelling book cover in spite of multiple revisions and changes.

To both Burt and Barb who have been my perpetual cheerleaders.

To Mary Harris who patiently worked with me to see things that needed to be edited, changed, and deleted throughout the manuscript. Her help was immeasurable. She is the consummate editing profession. I truly appreciated her efforts.

To Orvetta Holloway, who read the manuscript and offered an honest assessment.

To my sister Michele who told everybody who would listen about this labor of love,

To my sister Janet who always provides me with helpful items that added to this process.

To Derrick Dunn who suggested that I talk to his wife about important police details.

To Aricel Dunn who offered her police advice that added authenticity to critical parts of the story.

To my friend and brother Lonnie Black who asked me about the status of the book virtually every time we talked and provided me with reassurance that I was on the right track.

To my daughter Tressey who offered to read the very first draft.

To Donnie Chambers who invested time reading the manuscript and providing worthwhile recommendations. ,

To Neal Siegel who said, "Just complete a little bit at a time. Before you know it, you will be finished."

To Jim Teague who always allowed me to rely on his technical skills; along with his verbal and non-verbal affirmations.

To both of my sons, Brian and Marc, who believed in me and expressed faith in my storytelling abilities.

To Dave and Neta Jackson who continue to inspire me with their encouragement and their commitment to writing.

To Pat Maddox who followed virtually every post regarding my new novel, read every posted update, and continued to encourage me.

To God for giving me the original (and continual) inspiration to write.

Jack Alexander will be back in another story
filled with suspense and intrigue.

BE ON THE "LOOK OUT" FOR

John Wendell Adams' new book in 2019
In the meantime, please visit us at
Our Website: http://johnwendelladams.com/
Facebook: johnwendelladams@facebook.com
Twitter: http:twitter.com/johnW_Adams@JohnW_Adams
Thank you for buying *Payback*. Enjoy it!!!

PLEASE GIVE A REVIEW OF THE BOOK ON AMAZON

Go to www.johnwendelladams.com
From the home page, click on the Amazon icon
Scroll down to "Customer Reviews"
Move your cursor over the "5 stars"
Choose and click on the one you want
If you choose to, also write a review
Thank you so much – John Wendell Adams